Deadly Crimes

ALSO BY MICHAEL HAMBLING

Michael Hambling

DEADLY CRIMES

Detective Sophie Allen Book 2

Revised edition 2024
Joffe Books, London
www.joffebooks.com

First published by Joffe Books in 2016
First published in Great Britain in 2013 as *The Two Daughters*

Cover art by Nick Castle

ISBN: 978-1-83526-854-4

PROLOGUE

Gloucester: December 1969

A few days before Christmas, in the cold, dead hours of the night, the city centre streets were bleak and deserted. The rain was falling in torrents. At least the young man had an umbrella which kept his head and shoulders dry, but his trousers were soaked and water trickled down his legs into his shoes.

He held the umbrella lowered to protect his face from the driving rain. He could hardly see where he was going. He raised it a little and saw the sign for Northgate Street. So he was still heading the right way. He continued on and collided with someone coming towards him. He raised the umbrella again and started to laugh, ready to apologise for his carelessness, but then stopped. The other man's eyes were jumping with tension, his expression vicious. He glanced sideways, looking for an escape route. He saw a jewellery shop with its door open. A van. Several men dressed in black, balaclavas pulled down over their faces.

The figure in front of him was now holding a small, black, metal object. He looked at the eyes. They held no pity.

1

He looked up at the sky and found nothing there. Instead of a prayer, he whispered a single name: Susan.

* * *

Poole Harbour, January 2012

The small cruise launch finally came to rest and dropped anchor. It was night and the mist was down over Poole Harbour. A dark figure waited on the rickety jetty that jutted out across the mudflats. A crewman threw a line across and the boat was made secure. The figure stepped carefully onto the slippery deck.

'Quick,' he said.

He kept watch on deck as the two crewmen went below. The younger of them returned almost at once. He led a group of six young women, their faces sickly in the dull light. They shuffled forward one by one across the gangway onto the slimy planking of the jetty. They made their way to the shore where a fourth man was waiting beside an old van. The two crewmen peered into the gloom, but nothing stirred.

The last young woman to reach the shore gasped when she saw the figure waiting at the van.

'Stefan,' she whispered.

She was bundled into the van with the others. One of the women complained when she was pushed too hard. The man who'd hurried them from the boat grabbed her shoulder, spun her around and punched her hard in the face. Then he shoved her through the doors, where she sprawled face down on the floor, weeping. The elder of the two shore-men took a wad of money out of his pocket and handed it across to the crewmen. They returned to their boat, untied the line and disappeared into the misty darkness. On shore, the van began to make its way westwards, along a boggy track.

Seated beside the driver, Stefan chewed at his finger nails. His own cousin. He'd had no idea she would end up being caught in their elaborate snare. What could be done?

He would have to speak to Barbu and then one of the bosses. The thought made him nervous. He knew how cruel they could be. He had seen what they did to some of the young women. He had even been involved himself. But he couldn't just leave Nadia here with these men.

They pushed the girls in through the farmhouse door and herded them upstairs. Then Stefan went to see Barbu.

'That girl, the one called Nadia. She is my cousin, Barbu. We must get her out of here,' he said in Romanian.

Barbu laughed. He spat on the floor.

'You think we will change the plans just for that? After all the money, and the danger of bringing them across? You are mad. Forget it, Stefan. Put her out of your mind. Just get on with your job. And make some food, quick. We've had nothing since we left France.'

Stefan was dismayed. He went into the kitchen and started to prepare a stew out of tinned meat and vegetables. He opened a fresh loaf of bread and set plates and cutlery out on the worktop. He placed a helping of food on each of the eleven dishes and called to Barbu that the meal was ready. Barbu and one of the other men took plates upstairs for the young women.

Some time later, three of the men pushed the girls into the large downstairs room. The young women looked exhausted and panic-stricken. Barbu had poured glasses of fruit juice for them. He added the drug Rohypnol to each glass. Nadia refused to drink. She looked at Stefan, but he would not meet her eye. One of the other men tried to force her to drink, but she spat it out. Barbu stalked across the room and slapped her face, hard. She shrank back away from him. Stefan came forward and pushed Barbu away from his cousin.

'What are you doing?' said one of the men in English. 'Fuck off, you dickhead!'

Barbu pushed Stefan out of the room and closed the door behind him. Stefan stalked down the corridor to the kitchen, where he began to kick the wall in frustration. This was becoming a nightmare. He could hear the girls screaming as the men pushed them back up the stairs. He knew exactly what was going to happen now. He had often taken part himself. What could he do? He sat in the kitchen with his head in his hands and the minutes ticked by. Then the gang leader walked in and Stefan looked up at him. Maybe he would understand.

CHAPTER 1: MOTHER, FATHER, DAUGHTER

Monday and Tuesday, Week 1

Susan Carswell had just finished eating and was stacking the dishwasher when her doorbell rang. She looked out of the kitchen window of her flat but could see nothing. Her street in the upmarket Bristol suburb of Clifton was its usual quiet self. It was a Monday evening in January, and most people were at home indoors, insulated from the chill January air. She walked through to the small hallway, smoothing down her pale grey shift dress, and looked through the peephole. A smartly dressed young man was standing, waiting. He looked as if he was an official of some sort. She engaged the security chain, as her daughter had instructed her, and opened the door an inch or two.

'Yes?'

'Ms Susan Carswell?'

'That's right.'

'I'm Detective Constable Peter Spence from Gloucestershire police. Here's my warrant card.' He held his wallet open close to the gap so that Susan could clearly see the identification. 'I'm from the cold-case unit, investigating the death of a young man some years ago. I think that you may be able to help us. May I come in?'

'Of course. I'd be glad to help. My daughter's a detective chief inspector.'

She closed the door, released the chain and reopened it. She beckoned the man to follow her through to the lounge.

'Would you like some tea or coffee? I've just made a pot of coffee and was about to pour myself a cup. It's a new blend and tastes lovely.'

'That would be fine, Ms Carswell. It would go down a treat on a chilly evening like this. It is Ms Carswell, isn't it? Not Mrs?'

'Yes. I'm not married. I never have been, despite having fifty-nine years on my clock. Excuse me while I fetch the coffee. Please sit down.'

Her voice was cheerful, matter-of-fact. It masked the tension that was beginning to gather in the pit of her stomach. She went through to the kitchen, poured two coffees, spread some biscuits out on a plate and carried it all back to the sitting room on a tray.

'It's ready to drink. It's had its five minutes in the cafetière. Now, please tell me how I can help you.'

'It's a complicated story. Recently, a major crime gang from the West Midlands was infiltrated and broken up and a number of arrests were made. The Thompson brothers? You may have read about it in the papers.'

'Yes, I do remember. And Sophie — she's my daughter — has talked about it. She worked in the West Midlands crime squad some years ago.'

Did he look at her more carefully? Susan wondered if he'd guessed who her daughter was.

'Well, this gang has been operating for decades. One of the brothers is dying of cancer and has been talking to the local police. The gang started operating almost fifty years ago, so you can imagine how much work there is, clearing it all up.' He took a sip from his cup. 'Apparently one of their first serious crimes was a late-night break-in at a jeweller's shop in Gloucester. It's been preying on the mind of Billy Thompson ever since. A young man happened to walk by and witness the break-in. Someone in the gang panicked and shot him. They shoved the body into their van as they made their getaway, and dropped it down the vent of a disused mine shaft. It lay there until two weeks ago. When Billy finally talked about it, the West Midlands force contacted us and we retrieved the remains.'

Susan's cup was raised midway to her lips. She put it slowly down again.

'How long ago did this take place?' she whispered.

'In 1968. Forty-three years ago.'

'Was it Graham?' she asked.

'Yes, you have the right name. We've traced one of his friends who was at university with him here in Bristol. He remembered your name.'

Susan got to her feet and walked unsteadily through to her bedroom. She came back a minute or so later with a small, old and rather blurred snapshot of a young couple at a party. She handed the photo over.

'Yes, that's the young man. We've got a successful DNA match with his parents and they've given us a photo. His name was Graham Howard. Is that right?'

Susan managed a slight nod. 'So his parents are still alive? Both of them?'

'They're in their late eighties. The father is still alert and very active for his age. I think he's eighty-six. His wife is two years older. She's not so fit, but is still mentally very bright.'

'Did they have any other children? I don't remember Graham talking of any siblings.'

'No. He was an only child.'

All those years of not knowing what had happened to their only child. What must their lives have been like? So she wasn't the only one who'd been through hell, thought Susan.

'Would I be able to meet them sometime?' she asked.

7

'I'm sure they'd like that. They don't know about you yet. As I said, I only found out this afternoon from one of his old student friends. The parents told me they'd be happy to have visits from anyone who was a close friend at university. I think they are relieved that the uncertainty is finally over, after more than forty years of not knowing what happened to him. They are understandably upset but are showing a lot of courage.' He took another look at the photo. 'Are you the young woman?'

'Yes. I was only sixteen at the time, but he didn't know that. He thought I was eighteen and that I'd left school. I have a daughter by him. He never knew I was pregnant. He just vanished and it broke my heart.' She paused and drew a breath. 'So his parents don't know that they have a grand-daughter. And two great-granddaughters.'

Middle-aged and smartly dressed, her dark hair show-ing flecks of grey, Susan looked composed but the news this man had just delivered had struck her like a bomb exploding. Underneath her well-groomed, ordinary appearance a mael-strom of emotions swirled.

They talked for a while longer. After the police officer left, Susan sat weeping. She had been strong for so many years. Now she felt fragile, vulnerable and alone. Finally she phoned her daughter.

* * *

DC Spence arrived at the cold-case unit premises at Gloucester police headquarters at eight thirty the following morning. As he passed the reception desk, someone stood up from the row of seats along the wall and followed him to the door leading through to the offices. He turned and saw a fair-haired woman in her forties.

'I'm Sophie Allen,' she said.

'I didn't expect you so soon, ma'am.' He looked past her at Susan Carswell. She looked tired. 'I was really impressed by your mother, ma'am. She must have been almost overwhelmed by my news, but she held herself together. She doesn't look as though she's slept much since I saw her.'

'No. Nor have I. And there's no need for the ma'am. I'm not here in an official capacity. Do you think it might be possible for us to see my grandparents? I've been waiting forty-two years.'

* * *

Not long afterwards, Spence was in a quiet area of Gloucester, ringing the doorbell of a detached house. Sophie and her mother stood back while he spoke to the elderly man who answered the door.

'Good morning, Mr Howard. I won't stay, if you don't mind. I've brought Detective Chief Inspector Sophie Allen, and Ms Susan Carswell to see you. They have personal information about Graham that is not really within my remit. All I will say is that I am satisfied that everything they will tell you is true. It will all be confirmed by DNA tests, but that will only be in a few days' time.'

He turned to Sophie. 'I'm going back to the office. Please contact me if you need anything. It's been a pleasure to meet you, ma'am, even in such difficult circumstances.'

Sophie nodded to Spence. She felt as though she was ready to collapse into a heap on the ground. But her protective shell remained in place.

The man at the door smiled apprehensively and asked them in. He had a slight stoop and a thin face. He showed them into a neat sitting room.

'I'm James Howard. My wife Florence is in the kitchen, so I'll just get her if you don't mind waiting. Please have a seat.'

Sophie looked around her. Hanging in a prominent position and turning sepia with age, was a photo of a young man. He had an open, smiling face and long hair. Sophie took out her purse and extracted the photo that her mother had given

9

her that morning. It showed a teenage Susan Carswell and the same fair-haired young man.

'Mum, I feel as if I'm about to fly apart. It's like when I gave birth to Jade, and took too much gas and air. Everything just feels weird.'

'I can hardly speak myself. I'm too choked. Please, you do this. They're your grandparents. I just . . .' She didn't finish.

Just then a woman entered the room slowly, followed by James Howard. Sophie replaced the photo in her bag and stood up.

'This is my wife, Florence. Now, who are you again?' He looked anxiously at Sophie. 'I hope it's nothing bad.'

'I'm Sophie Allen, from Dorset police. But I'm not here on official business. This is my mother, Susan Carswell. I have something so wonderful to tell you that I really don't know how to start. So I'm going to blunder straight into it. You may need to hold on to your hats.'

She approached the elderly lady and took her hand.

'I'm your granddaughter. My mother, Susan here, became pregnant by Graham shortly before he vanished and I'm the result.'

The elderly couple stood immobile.

'Even better, I have two daughters. So you have two great-granddaughters, Hannah and Jade.'

Sophie showed her the photo of her mother and father at the student party.

'This is the only photo we have. It was taken soon after they met. Isn't that right, Mum?'

Susan nodded. Sophie put her arm around Florence and took hold of James's hand.

'My grandparents. We've found you after all these years.'

* * *

They were sipping tea, seated around a pine table in the conservatory. Apart from the occasional tear, the crying had largely stopped. Sophie sat silently next to Florence, gently squeezing her hand.

'We've always wondered who Susan was. Your name appears in the last few entries of his diary. So Graham never knew about you being pregnant?' asked Sophie's grandfather.

'No. How could he?' Susan whispered. Her voice trembled. 'We only became lovers a week or two before he disappeared. The last time was in his room at the halls. I can still remember the music that was playing on his stereo set. It was at the very end of the autumn term, and he was planning to catch the last train home to Gloucester. We left together and parted on the street corner. I went home and he turned towards the city centre to get a bus to the station. I never saw him again. I nearly died of a broken heart.'

She started sobbing again. Sophie had never seen her mother so emotional. She had always been so cool and controlled, almost distant in her manner. But now more than forty years of self-restraint was dissolving away in front of her daughter's eyes.

'And how did your parents react when they found out?'

'They threw me out,' she answered. Tears rolled down her cheeks.

'What?' The elderly couple looked utterly shocked.

'Just when I needed them most. I was confused and terrified and felt so alone. And so vulnerable. I was only sixteen, and they threw me out onto the streets. I've never forgiven them. I never will.'

'Oh, my dear,' said Florence. She went to Susan and embraced her as tightly as her tiny form would permit.

'Graham didn't know I was only sixteen. I lied to him about my age. I pretended that I was older and working in one of the local banks, but I was still at school. I loved him so much. I wanted to kill myself when he didn't come back. So many times I felt like killing myself.' Her words emerged in a mixture of whispers and choking sobs. 'I went from a schoolgirl's dream of heaven to a hellish reality in a couple of weeks. That Christmas was wonderful. We were apart, but the feeling of being so totally in love was overpowering. I really was walking on air. And then he didn't come back. I called at his halls on the day we'd arranged and he wasn't there. I asked some of the other students, but they didn't know anything. They were all busy catching up with their own gossip. I thought that he'd just been delayed or was ill, so I kept going back. And, of course, he was never there. I panicked. I cried all the time. And the students in the rooms around his didn't seem concerned. Then one of their girlfriends said that he'd probably switched to a different university. London, maybe. And I cried even more. I felt humiliated because they began to guess that I was much younger than them. So I stayed away for a while and just wrote, but never got an answer. Weeks went by, and I missed a period. I was frantic with worry. I couldn't talk to my parents about it, so I confided in my Auntie Olive. She was a nurse and arranged for me to get a check-up. When I knew I was pregnant, the first thing I did was go back to his room, but it was still empty. I was still in my school uniform. I saw the students whispering to each other. I felt so empty. I left and never went back. I told my parents about the pregnancy soon afterwards.'

'How did you survive?' Florence asked.

'My aunt took me in. She was wonderful. She looked after me during the pregnancy, and then found me a job as a cleaner at the local doctors' surgery after Sophie was born. Once Sophie was old enough, I got a job on the reception desk. For the last twenty-five years I've been the practice manager.'

'And have you ever married?' said Florence.

'No. I had several serious relationships. One came very close to marriage, but there always seemed to be that little something missing. I couldn't go through with it. I have a man-friend at the moment, but I can't say where it's heading.' She paused. 'Looking back on it all now, it seems as though it happened to another person. A few short weeks that shaped my life. All those years ago, but sometimes it's as clear as yesterday. I watched and worried when Sophie became a teenager, and now I worry about her daughters. Sometimes I can't believe that it all happened. But then I look at Sophie and I know that it was all real, it really did happen. And he really did exist.'

There was a silence. Finally Florence turned to her granddaughter.

'And you, Sophie?'

Sophie spoke as calmly as she could, but it wasn't easy. 'I owe everything to my mother. My whole life. There's nothing in my life that isn't down to her in one way or another. She loved and cherished me throughout my childhood. She got me through my difficult years as a teenager. She made me work at my studies. She encouraged me never to give up. I went to Oxford and studied for a law degree. And here I am, a detective chief inspector. I have a husband who I love dearly and two daughters, Hannah and Jade. And now I have found my grandparents. I am filled with so much mixed-up emotion that I can't speak properly.'

'Oh my goodness,' Florence said. 'Our granddaughter. For forty-three years I've been eaten away by bitterness. I've hidden it from everybody, even James. And now it's gone — you've lifted it. It's almost too much for my old body and mind to take.' She looked at Sophie shyly. 'Can I meet them soon? Hannah and Jade?'

'Of course, Gran. I'm not one to hang about, you know.'

Sophie's mobile phone started ringing. She glanced at the caller display.

'Sorry, everyone, I have to take this.' She walked out to the hallway, and tried to compose herself. 'Hello, Barry. I didn't expect to hear from you again so soon.'

* * *

The call had come into the Swanage police station at nine twenty-seven precisely. The receptionist who took the call was very clear on this point. She had just made herself a coffee to wash down her painkillers. Her younger sister's hen party had been rather too raucous for a Monday evening. She'd drunk too much, had mixed her drinks and was now suffering the consequences. She had glanced at the clock as she swallowed the first tablet and realised she had another eight hours to get through. The ringing of the telephone jarred. She listened to the caller with increasing disbelief.

'And where exactly are you, sir?' She waited. 'I'm sorry. It sounded as if you said you are calling from the top of Ballard Down. Oh, you did say that. But how can you possibly see the top surface of the Agglestone?'

She listened again. 'Are you sure it's a body, and not just a bit of tarpaulin or an old coat that's caught and flapping in the wind?'

She waited for the response. 'Okay. I'll pass it on and get someone to check it out. Can you stay where you are until someone reaches you?'

She listened again. 'Sorry, sir. I forgot that the weather can get a bit blowy up there. Give me your details, please, and your home address, and we'll be in touch as soon as we can.'

She replaced the phone.

'Oh, God,' she groaned to nobody in particular. 'Why couldn't it have been a normal, quiet day?'

* * *

Half an hour later, DS Barry Marsh took the call from the officers in the squad car. He drove out to Studland village with his young assistant, DC Jimmy Melsom.

Melsom looked puzzled. 'Sorry, sir. I didn't catch all the details. What's going on?'

'Apparently there's a man's body lying on the top of the Agglestone. And it doesn't look as though the death was natural. Someone out walking on the top of Ballard Down spotted it through his binoculars and phoned in. A squad car unit went out to investigate. We need to go and assess whether it is suspicious and whether forensics are needed.'

'Sounds weird to me. Why would anyone put a body up there? Surely, if you'd killed someone, you'd dump the body in a pond, or down a pit? There are enough of those around here. Why drag it to the top of a huge rock? Are you sure someone isn't just taking the mickey?'

'Ours is not to reason why, Jimmy. Let's just do what we're told, eh?'

CHAPTER 2: THE AGGLESTONE

Tuesday, Week 1

The Agglestone lies about a mile inland from the small, coastal village of Studland. It is a huge anvil-shaped lump of sandstone perched on a mound rising from the grim sparseness of Black Heath. In winter its brooding presence dominates the heath.

Marsh left the car in a narrow lane. A crime scene tape was already stretched across the footpath leading to the rock, with a squad car parked close by. A uniformed officer came across to greet them.

'Can't we get any closer in the car?' asked Melsom.

Marsh gave him a withering look. 'And churn up the surface of the track? Come on, Jimmy, you're a detective now. The first thing I did was to order the area to be sealed off. The paths around here are all sandy. Even just a couple of vehicles will wipe out any tracks. I just hope the squad that got here first haven't ruined the surface.'

Melsom looked crestfallen. 'Sorry.'

'Morning, sir,' said the uniformed constable. 'We have two men at the rock itself, and the other car is at the north end of the path. The trouble is that there are so many paths all over the heath. We haven't been able to close them all yet. Once we get another couple of squad cars here, we can seal the whole area.'

'Any medical people or forensics here yet?' asked Marsh.

'No. But they're due any time now. We've marked out another path so that the main track isn't disturbed. Just look for the blue markers.'

The two detectives started the ten minute walk towards the huge rock. A chill breeze was blowing in from the sea.

'Will we have to call in the DCI?' asked Melsom.

'Only if I think it might be murder. If it's just a natural death, then we'll deal with it locally. Disappointed?' Marsh said.

'Kind of. It opened my eyes a bit, being involved in a murder case. And she took the time to explain things to me. She made me feel important.'

'You got carried away by her looks and brains, didn't you?' Marsh laughed.

'All I can say is that life at the station hasn't been the same since that case closed and she went back to HQ. Even you have to admit that. It's all a bit boring, isn't it?'

'But that's routine police work, Jimmy. In our patch a murder comes along once in a blue moon. You got hooked, didn't you?'

Melsom shrugged. 'I quite fancy being in charge of a murder squad.'

'Get real, Jimmy. She's got a law degree and a master's in criminal psychology. What have you got? A handful of GCSEs?'

'But I could work at it. You know, get the force to sponsor me with the Open University or something. Think of McGreedie, that DI at Bournemouth. He didn't come up by the fast track. She thinks a lot of him too. He's really good.'

'Do you realise the pressure they're under? Do you want all that strain and anxiety? I always thought you were an easy-come, easy-go sort of person,' said Marsh.

17

'Yeah, but I may not always be like that. Anyway, all I was saying is that they've both had an effect on the way I think about things.'

'Well, that's a good thing. Let's face it, you weren't exactly the world's most thoughtful detective, Jimmy. So if working for her has made you see things differently, it's all to the good.'

They approached the Agglestone mound from the east. Two uniformed officers were standing guard, and had marked out a narrow path across the mound's surface to the base of the huge rock above it. A ladder stood propped against the side.

'We kept our approach to that line you can see,' said the taller constable. 'Just to warn you, it isn't a pretty sight up there. We didn't go too close.'

Marsh told Melsom to remain below, and started to climb up. The ladder didn't take him all the way to the top. He scrambled the rest of the way along a protruding shelf of rock.

At the summit, in the exact centre of the rock, a man's body lay spread-eagled. The lower part of the body was still clothed in a ragged pair of jeans but the upper torso was bare. Marsh started by the feet, forcing himself to look at one section of the body at a time, trying to distance himself from the horror in front of him. The throat had been cut, leaving a gaping wound open to the elements. Streaks of dried blood had coagulated around the body's open mouth. The eyes had been pecked out. Crows probably, thought Marsh. He looked away and took several deep breaths before bending down to look at that curiously gaping mouth. There was something odd about it. He took a pen from his pocket and gently inserted it. The tongue had been cut out. Marsh backed away and sat on the rock edge, looking out to sea.

A minute or two later, Melsom's head appeared above the edge of the rock. 'Are you alright, boss?'

'Don't come up any further, Jimmy,' said Marsh. 'We need to get a forensic cover over the body as quickly as possible in case it starts to rain. Can you phone in to county HQ and arrange it? And you may get that wish of yours sooner than you expected. It's a murder alright. I'm going to take some quick photos up here, then come down and wait. I want you to do the same around the base. Stay on the marked path as much as you can, but get photos of the ground. I know the forensic photographer will do a far better job than us, but we can make a start in case the rain comes on before they get here.'

Within another hour the forensic team had arrived and a cover was fixed over the body. SOCO officers were inspecting the surface of the rock and all of the climbable routes to the summit.

Melsom sipped a coffee provided by one of the support staff.

'So will the chief be coming?' he asked.

'She's on leave for a couple of days. She's in Gloucester for some reason but she'll try to get here by evening. I've been on the phone to her and I've spoken to the superintendent at HQ. What we have to do now is visit this chap, Kirby, who spotted the body this morning. We'd better get going. You can finish that coffee in the car. Give me the keys. I'll drive.'

* * *

David Kirby was a retired civil servant. He lived in a bungalow in a quiet suburb of North Swanage.

'I was expecting you hours ago,' he said.

'Well, sir, our first priority was to secure the area, check the body and get forensics in,' Marsh replied. 'You were next on the list. We need to hear your account in detail, if you don't mind. May we come in?'

'Of course.'

He showed them through into a neat sitting room. A stout, grey-haired woman put her head round the door and asked them if they'd like coffee. Kirby didn't introduce them. Marsh heard the sound of clattering cups.

19

'So, Mr Kirby. Tell us how you came to be out on Ballard Down, and how you spotted the body.'

'It is a body then, is it? I had trouble convincing the woman I spoke to on the phone,' said Kirby.

'Well, I'm sure you can understand that it isn't every day our receptionist gets a call about a body being discovered like that. Most people phone 999 in an emergency. Why did you choose to phone the station?' Marsh asked.

'I wasn't absolutely sure about it. It certainly looked like a body, but I thought that perhaps it was a trick caused by the wind or something. I didn't want to drag the whole of the emergency services out for no good reason.'

Marsh nodded. 'Fair enough.'

'I take the dog out for a walk most mornings. That walk is a favourite of mine when the weather's good enough. I left the house at about eight thirty, after breakfast, and walked up through the houses here to the path that leads up the slope. It was a bit blowy up there, but visibility was good. Once I reached the top I turned inland along the ridge path. The dog chased around looking for rabbits and I wandered slowly west. I always have my binoculars with me because we do get some overwintering birds.'

'So you're a keen birdwatcher?' Marsh said.

'Yes. I took it up before I retired, and it's become a bit of an obsession in the last couple of years.'

'What binoculars do you have, sir?'

'A new set of Bushnells that Marjorie bought me for Christmas.'

'Can I see them, please?' Marsh said.

Kirby left the room and returned with the binoculars.

'These are beauties,' said the detective. 'Your wife must know a bit about these things. Or did you tell her what you wanted?'

Kirby shook his head. 'She's a better birdwatcher than me. Anyway, I was a couple of hundred yards short of the obelisk. You get a clear view of the Agglestone from there and I often look at it. I could see a shape that looked like a body, but I thought it was just an optical trick. I walked on towards the obelisk and had another look. After that, there wasn't much doubt in my mind. So I phoned the police.'

'Was anybody else around, Mr Kirby? Up on that path? Maybe even looking northwards like you?' Marsh said.

'No. It's usually busier at weekends or in summer, but midweek, at that time in the morning, I often have the place to myself. The wind was picking up, so when your woman asked me to stay where I was I lost my rag a bit. I was dressed warmly enough for walking, but not for hanging around for hours.'

'How often do you go up there for a walk?'

Kirby shrugged. 'Maybe two or three times week. It really depends on the weather.'

'When was the last time?'

'Sunday. Three days ago. The mist has been down since then. Today was the first clear day.'

'Could you see the Agglestone then?'

'I can't be sure. If I did, there was nothing unusual about it. But I may not have looked across there. There are only a couple of places where you can see it, and I only bother when the dog's busy sniffing around. If she runs on ahead, I follow without stopping,' said Kirby.

'We'd like you to take us up there, if you don't mind, sir. But don't worry. We'll collect our Land Rover from the station and drive up. It will save us a lot of time.'

* * *

Ballard Down forms the easternmost part of the Purbeck Hills. This chalk ridge stretches from Lulworth in the west to Handfast Point at the eastern end, just north of Swanage. Later that morning, the three men were standing on a path that ran along the top of the ridge. Kirby showed the two detectives the three positions from which the top of the Agglestone could be seen. Looking through Kirby's powerful binoculars, Marsh was able to watch the activity on and around the rock. The top was now under the shelter of a tent-like structure, but there was no doubt that a body stretched out on the surface would have been visible from this position. Melsom took some photos to give an idea of the view. They walked back to the Land Rover and returned to Swanage just as a misty drizzle started to move in from the sea. The top of Ballard Down was now hidden under a blanket of grey murk.

Marsh phoned through to county HQ and spoke to Matt Silver, the detective superintendent responsible for East Dorset, Poole and Bournemouth.

* * *

In the early afternoon they were back at the rock, talking to David Nash, the forensic chief.

'Any clues as to how long the body's been here?' asked Marsh.

'Too early to be certain, but a couple of days at least. It's stone cold, with no residual heat at all. We've just about finished, so we'll move it off the rock soon. It'll go to the lab at Dorchester. I've been on the phone to Doctor Goodall and done everything he asked,' said Nash.

'I'm a bit surprised he's not here.'

'Hurt his hip playing rugby at the weekend, so he can't climb. Don't worry, we've collected all the information we can, and we've been filming everything live. He's been watching from his base.'

Marsh was worried. Neither the DCI nor the senior pathologist had actually been to the scene. It left him with all the responsibility.

'Jimmy, we need to get a house-to-house organised. We'll have to check every home in the village in case anybody's seen anything unusual or suspicious. Let's get back to base and speak to Tom Rose about it. The sooner we get started the better.'

* * *

Inspector Tom Rose was the senior uniformed officer in charge of Swanage and the surrounding district.

'Okay, Barry,' he said. 'We'll pull every man back from anything that isn't absolutely vital and send them all over to Studland. I just hope it's worth it.'

'We all agree, sir. The DCI has been on the phone, and she says we have to get this done as quickly as possible. The body might have been there for days, and people will start to forget. We also need a press release. The super thinks you're the best person for that. Sorry.'

'He's already been on to me about it.' Rose sighed. 'I thought things would quieten down after that business before Christmas. I should have known better. Okay, let's get on with it. By the way, it's good to see you in charge, Barry, even if it is only temporary. I've always had faith in you.'

Marsh was taken aback. 'Thanks, sir. That means a lot coming from you.'

* * *

Sophie Allen arrived late in the afternoon. The incident room was set up and already a hive of activity. She slipped unnoticed into the back of the room and listened as Tom Rose and Barry Marsh addressed the assembled police officers about the house-to-house enquiries. Marsh's ginger hair made him stand out from the group of people surrounding him. Marsh was doing a good job, she thought. His slight shyness masked a shrewd brain and his careful approach had impressed her during their last case together. He finished his instructions and the officers left the room. As he passed, Marsh didn't recognise the trim figure in the tan, leather bomber jacket and tight-fitting cord trousers.

'Hi, Barry. I see you've got everything under control.'

He blushed. 'Sorry, ma'am. I didn't realise you'd arrived. I wasn't expecting you for another couple of hours.'

'Quiet roads. I was going to suggest that we get a coffee so you could fill me in, but I guess you'll probably be heading off with the troops.'

'Yes, that was the idea,' he said.

'Would you mind if I tagged along? I know it's too dark to visit the rock now, but I'd like to have a look at the village. You know, get a feel for the place. I'll go in my car though, so I can head straight back to Wareham when we've finished. I've had a bit of a fraught day.' In fact, Sophie was exhausted.

'We'll be parking in the NT car park, ma'am. Just beside the pub. We've got permission to use it over the next few days,' Marsh said.

'Fine, Barry. I'll let you get on with it. I'll be there about ten minutes after you, I expect.'

'Forensics haven't found anything useful in the vicinity of the rock. I was hopeful of some tyre tracks on the path, but the ground's so sandy that any imprints wouldn't have lasted for long. Last night's rain would have washed them away, if there were any to start with,' said Marsh.

Sophie spent a few minutes sipping a hot coffee and looking at the incident board. She was trying to fix the geography of the immediate area in her mind. After a while she felt strong enough to make a phone call that she'd been putting off all day. She perched on the corner of a table in the small office that she'd used during the Donna Goodenough case.

'Archie? It's Sophie. Listen. One of your squads is investigating the Thompson gang . . .'

She listened.

'Yes, I know. Archie, you need to know something, but it's for you only. Please don't share it with anyone else at the moment. The young man's body they dumped down the shaft

outside Gloucester? Archie, please, just be quiet and listen. I'm
going to tell you something and then hang up, because I won't
be able to speak after I've told you. I've been dreading telling
you since I found out. Archie, that young man was my father.'

* * *

The house-to-house inquiries at Studland village yielded no
useful information. Several locals walked their dogs across the
heath, but few went as far as the Agglestone, and even if they
had, the top surface would have been impossible to see from
ground level. No one had seen any vehicles on the heath in
recent days, or any other suspicious activity. The police questioned some of the local teenagers, but none owned up to ever
having climbed to the top of the rock. The weather had been
so wet recently that Marsh and Melsom doubted if anyone
had been at the rock for days.

'Think about it, Jimmy,' said Marsh. 'This wasn't any
normal domestic murder, not the state the body was in. It's
too vicious for that. It'll be some kind of gangland killing, in
which case they'll have known how to cover their tracks.'

'So what's next?' asked Melsom.

'Farms, outhouses. We'll make a start on that tomorrow
morning, first thing.'

Then, Sophie was beside them.

'Does that seem reasonable, ma'am?' Marsh said.

'Perfectly. There'll be a post-mortem in the morning, if
you want to come. Then the forensic examination, though
the initial feedback suggests there's very little to go on. We
can but hope.'

25

CHAPTER 3: THE LOST GIRL

Wednesday, Week 1

Sophie smiled sweetly at Dorset's senior forensic pathologist. 'So what do you have for me, Benny? Sorry to hear about your hip by the way. Martin told me to tell you that rugby and old age don't mix. He said to stick to bird watching in future.'

'I was going to give you a hug, but you really don't deserve one after that comment.'

'Don't blame the messenger. Anyway, what about the body that Barry here discovered yesterday?'

'I can give you the physical stuff, but there's nothing that tells us who he is. Come into the lab and we'll get started.'

In the pathology theatre, the corpse was already laid out on the bench. Goodall's assistant waited at the top end, notebook in hand. Sophie walked around the body, looking at the gaping wounds on the neck and face. She stood aside as Goodall started work. He spoke into a microphone, recording the examination as he proceeded.

'Here we have a young male — Caucasian. His age is probably between eighteen and twenty. Starting at the front, there's some bruising of the forehead, nose and cheeks. This occurred before death, judging by the residual traces of blood. The unusual injury, though, is the removal of the tongue. This was also done before death, sliced off with a very sharp knife. The wound is clean, and shows no signs of hacking. Someone grabbed his tongue, pulled it out as far as it would go and sliced it off with one cut.'

'Would he have died from that if his throat hadn't been cut?' asked Marsh.

'Unlikely, although he would have swallowed a lot of blood, and there will be some in his lungs I imagine. If he was restrained on his back, it probably would have ended up being fatal due to the lungs filling with blood, but my guess is that his throat was cut immediately afterwards. The tongue removal probably has some kind of gangland significance, but that's your area.'

He lifted the head and felt around the skull. 'There don't seem to be any other injuries apart from some more bruising that looks as though it occurred before death.'

He opened the mouth. 'We've taken a DNA sample and it's already off for analysis, but there is some dental work worth noting on his rear right wisdom tooth. It looks a bit crude.'

'What do you mean?' asked Sophie.

'It's not been finished off properly. It's a bit of a botch-up. My guess is that it's been done abroad on the cheap.'

'But my aunt's had dental work done abroad. It saves money, and she reckons it's as good as she could get done here,' Marsh said. 'I think it was in the Czech Republic.'

'No doubt. But she'll have gone to one of their top private dentists. I think I'll get one of our dental experts to take a look. He might be able to give us more information.'

'Could he be foreign?' asked Sophie.

'The DNA profile might give some clues when it comes back next week.'

'That face might have a slightly Eastern European look, ma'am,' Marsh said.

'That's what I was thinking. A slightly Slavic bone structure. The trouble is, it's lost its most obvious features due to the birds. We don't even know the eye colour, and the lips have been pecked as well. It's difficult to visualise.'

She turned to the assistant. 'Did anything show up in the clothing?'

'No. Nothing in the pockets of the jeans. Like the trainers, they're cheap ones that could have come from anywhere. There were no other clothes, just the jeans and shoes. We'll be doing a full forensic analysis of them this afternoon.'

'Well, here's a puzzle then. A body with no identification whatsoever. Benny, I'm not staying for the messy bit. Will you let me know as soon as possible if you find anything of interest?'

* * *

'What do you think, ma'am?' asked Marsh, as they drove back towards the coast.

'It looks as though he was beaten about the head, his tongue cut out, then his throat cut. Probably fairly close together, although we'll need Benny's final confirmation of that.'

'Do you think it was some kind of punishment killing?'

'Nothing else makes sense, Barry. And putting the body up on top of that rock is significant. They were broadcasting it, saying to other insiders, "look what we do to anyone who crosses us." But the tongue removal is important. I'd guess that the victim tried to talk about something that he shouldn't have. Punishment for talking was removing the ability to talk. It's brutal, particularly since he was killed straight afterwards. It was done to hammer home the message to other potential waverers.'

'So who would do this type of thing? It's beyond my experience, ma'am.'

'Extreme gang culture. You wouldn't believe what they can do to someone who breaks ranks. They'll be out there now, watching the press, waiting for it to hit the papers and the TV news. As I said, it's a warning to all the others on the inside. The thing is, Barry, that young lad couldn't have been more than twenty. I'd put him in his late teens. How could he possibly warrant all that being done to him? It's vile beyond words.'

She paused. 'If he is from Eastern Europe we need to think about where he might have been working. The hotel trade, catering and agriculture seem the obvious places to look first. Also the local colleges and the university in case he was a student. This area is awash with hotels, so that's where I want you to start. Get Jimmy onto it as well. Then move to local farms. I'll get in touch with the colleges and university.'

'Will Lydia be joining us, ma'am?'

'Not immediately, Barry. She's on a course this week, and I'm not pulling her out of it. We'll try and cope as we are. I'll send for someone else only if I think it's necessary.'

***

Jimmy Melsom was coordinating the visits to the farms. They were all scattered across the northernmost part of Purbeck, between the ancient chalk ridge and the waters of Poole Harbour. Some of the farms had been worked by the same family for generations, with the owners well known in the local community. Melsom knew some of the farmers himself from his involvement in local sports and charity fundraising events. The officers making the visits had been told to ask about any suspicious sightings in recent days, and were also on the lookout for anything out of the ordinary. The job was over by late morning, just as Sophie and Marsh returned from Dorchester.

'Anything useful?' Sophie asked when they joined Melsom.

'Officially, no. No one has seen anything suspicious either on their land or nearby. But one of the teams was a bit uneasy about one place they called at — Brookway Farm. I asked them to stay around. I think they're out at the cars. Shall I get them?'

Sophie nodded. The farm in question was isolated and close to the harbour. It was reached via a long track that wound across the fields from the nearest public lane. Melsom returned with a tall, thin policeman of late middle age and a younger, woman colleague.

'Jack Holly and Jen Allbright, ma'am.'

'Good morning. I understand something about Brookway Farm didn't seem quite right when you visited it this morning. Could you explain?'

Holly spoke first. 'It's not a working farm, ma'am. There are quite a number in this area that have been converted into holiday homes or even split into apartments. That's not unusual. But I got the feeling that the man who answered the door was waiting for me. I drove into the yard, and he'd have heard that. But in other places, if they'd heard us driving up, the owners would come across to speak before I reached the door. And if they hadn't heard us, they'd be a bit surprised when they opened the door and found a copper on the doorstep. But this guy was neither. He was silent and just looked me up and down. I asked him about the farm and he said the place was about to be converted once the owners could raise the money. Meanwhile it was a temporary let. The fields were going to one of the neighbouring farms. But he was kind of edgy.'

'And while they were talking I was sure that someone was watching from an upstairs window,' Allbright added. 'Jack wouldn't have been able to see, but I was standing by the car. There was a small gap between the curtain and the frame, and I don't think it was there when we drove up. It might have been my imagination, but the shadow seemed a bit deeper there.'

'What did he have to say?' Sophie asked Holly.

'He hadn't seen or heard anything unusual. And that was about it. He didn't say much at all.'

'What did he look like?'

'Middling height and weight. Probably in his late thirties. Mousey brown hair. Denim jeans, grey trainers, blue windproof jacket. Gap in his front teeth.'

'Fine. And well done for being so observant. If anything else occurs to you, tell one of us right away.'

The two uniformed officers left.

Sophie said, 'Let's get out there, Barry. There's no point wasting any time. Grab a coffee to drink in the car.'

The road out of Swanage snaked up the side of the chalk ridge, heading for the Ulwell gap, the only valley west of Corfe Castle. The earlier rain had eased off, but low clouds still obscured the higher ground. They were soon approaching the shoreline of Poole Harbour, although the water could not be seen. There was a thick belt of trees, several hundred yards deep, along the coastal strip. They passed several farms and finally came to the track they were looking for. Potholes covered the surface, which at times was completely broken up. They finally approached the farm buildings and turned into an untidy yard.

The farm looked deserted. There were no windows open and no smoke coming from the chimneys. No one appeared at the doorway as the two detectives walked across the yard. No one answered their knocks, despite Marsh's increasingly insistent hammering.

'Do you think they've gone, ma'am?'

'Looks like it. Let's have a look around and see if anything's been left unlocked.'

There were several outhouses, but they contained little other than aged and rusting agricultural machinery. Beds of weeds, nettles and brambles covered what had probably once been the kitchen garden, and half-rotted gardening implements leaned against a ramshackle shed. A rusty tractor still sat in one of the larger outhouses, but its front wheels were missing and the cabin was dirty. The other sheds were in a similar state. It looked as if the farm machinery hadn't been used in years.

From inside a shed, they heard the sound of a vehicle approaching. They walked out and saw a pick-up truck parked near their car. Two men had climbed out, and were making their way towards Sophie's car.

'Good morning!' she called.

They turned, and the taller of the two walked towards them. He indicated for the other man to stay back. Sophie flipped open her warrant card.

'Detective Chief Inspector Sophie Allen. This is Sergeant Barry Marsh.'

The man nodded.

'And?' His facial expression gave nothing away.

'You may have heard that a dead body was found in the area recently. We're investigating the circumstances of the death.'

'And?'

'Have you seen or heard anything unusual during the past week?'

'Someone called a couple of hours ago and asked that question,' he said.

'Is that right? They're really on the ball, the local bobbies, aren't they? Was it you they spoke to?'

'No. But I heard about it. And my answer is the same. No, we haven't seen anything unusual. But if we do, we'll let you know.'

'How many people live here on the farm?' Sophie asked.

'Three. But we don't work it. And you shouldn't have been nosing about, not without a warrant.'

'We didn't get an answer from the door, so we were just checking to see if anyone was in the sheds or stable, Mr . . . ?'

'Smith. And there isn't anybody else, so there's no need to check further.'

Sophie looked across at the other man, who was leaning against the side of the truck. He was short but very heavily built, with powerful shoulders.

'Who's your assistant?' she asked.

'Mr Jones.'

'Do you own the farm, Mr Smith?'

'No. We've just rented it for a few months. We're leaving soon. The owners are selling up,' he said.

'Who are the owners?'

'No idea. We only deal with the letting agency.'

'And they are?' said Sophie.

'Can't remember,' he said in a flat voice. 'Why is it important to you?'

'Well, you know the police, Mr Smith. Always nosey. Sifters of information, that's what we are. You're fairly close to the shore of Poole Harbour here, aren't you? It can only be half a mile or so.'

'Couldn't say. Never go down there. Anyway, we've got work to get on with,' said the man.

'Well, fine, Mr Smith. I hope you're happy in your work.' She smiled at him, but her eyes were cold. Glancing at her watch, she turned to Marsh. 'We'd better be on our way, Barry. Things to do. Information to sift.' She turned back to Smith. 'Thank you for your help. It's been very illuminating.'

They walked towards the car. Sophie called to the short, stocky man standing by the vehicles. 'Good morning, Mr Jones!'

There was no response, not even a flicker in his eyes.

'What a pair,' Marsh said as they drove away. 'Enough to give anyone the creeps.'

'They're thugs, Barry. Whether they have anything to do with our dead body is another question. Smith and Jones, I ask you. My bet is that they're here to do a final tidying up. Neither of them looked like the man Allbright and Holly saw. Assuming that chap made a quick getaway after the visit this morning, those two are what's known as enforcers. They specialise in getting rid of evidence and loose ends by any means necessary, often using intimidation and violence. When we get back to the station, I want their van traced. And I think we'll get this track watched. I'd like to know where they go when they leave. We'll stop somewhere within sight and call in Jimmy or someone from the station to take over.'

'What do you think they're up to, ma'am?'

'No idea, Barry. But I'm sure it's nothing we'd approve of.'

Once they were back on the more even surface of the lane, Sophie looked for a pull-in that gave a view of the farm track. There was a driveway almost opposite which led to another farm, so she turned into it. Marsh walked up to the farmhouse to ask for information about the occupants of Brookway Farm, while Sophie called for Melsom to take over the watch. Marsh was back quickly.

'He says he never sees them. No one knows anything about them. They don't work the farm, so there's little contact. He won't say anything to them about my questions, by the way. I know him from the local football club. He's a good bloke.'

'According to the database, the pick-up belongs to a hire company. I want the details checked out first thing tomorrow.'

Melsom arrived to take over the watch, and they drove back to Swanage. They spent the rest of the afternoon cross-checking the reports from the house and farm visits, but to no avail. Sophie was pondering her next move. Melsom's call came in the late afternoon, as dusk was falling. Marsh hurried across to Sophie.

'Jimmy says they've gone, ma'am.'

'What? How could they? Is there another track? The map didn't show one.'

'They didn't leave in the pick-up. Jimmy walked down as it began to get dark, and it's still there in the yard. But there are no signs of life in the house or in any of the sheds. He had a good look.'

'What, in the house as well?'

'It's been left unlocked.'

'This is getting weird. Let's get back over there.'

The pick-up was still where it had been left. All of the farm buildings were empty and the farmhouse door was unlocked. Darkness had fallen and the farmyard was inky black.

'I called, but there was no answer. I've had a quick look around and there's no one here, ma'am, not as far as I can tell.'

'How could they have got away do you think? On foot, or by boat?' asked Sophie.

34

'I'd plump for the boat,' Marsh answered. 'I think we should check round the back to see if there's a track that side. I thought there might be when we were here earlier. Do you have a torch in the car, ma'am?'

The three detectives walked round to the rear of the yard, and found a rough track. It passed through a gloomy copse of trees and turned a corner. Spread out before them lay the huge expanse of Poole Harbour. The dark waters lapped close to the bank.

'High tide,' said Melsom.

They could see a wooden jetty thrusting out into the water.

'A vehicle's been down this track and it looks well used,' said Marsh.

Sophie cast her torch beam around the area.

'I think we've lost them.' She walked a short distance along the shoreline. 'There's a smell of smoke in the air. Part wood smoke, but not entirely. Can you smell it, Barry?'

'Now you mention it, yes. It's a bit faint though.'

Sophie continued to walk along the shoreline, shining the torch beam into the trees. Melsom walked in the opposite direction, but neither spotted anything. Marsh had walked a short way back along the track.

'I think it's inland a bit. The smell gets stronger in the copse, up at the northern end.'

They picked their way through the trees and came out in a small clearing, partly lit by the moon. A small fire had been made in a pit where the charred remains of some rubbish gave off the occasional spark.

'Jimmy, could you find a pole of some sort and see if you can rescue some of those remains before they smoulder away completely? I saw some back in the sheds.' Sophie turned to Marsh. 'I think we'll get a small forensics team in, Barry. Could you contact HQ? I want the pick-up fingerprinted as well as the inside of the house. And these charred bits and pieces need to be looked at. There's something odd about this place.'

As she turned, she caught sight of a pale figure watching them from the edge of the trees, half hidden behind a bush. Looking away, she spoke softly to her sergeant.

'Don't look. We're being watched from over on the left. I think it's a young woman. Stay where you are. I'm going to move around to that side.'

Sophie slowly manoeuvred her way around the glowing embers and backed towards the spot where she'd seen the figure. She turned suddenly and found herself facing a pale, shivering teenage girl. She was naked apart from a towel wrapped around her torso.

Sophie held out her hand.

'Don't be frightened. I'm a police officer. I can help you.'

The girl's eyes were wide with fear, and she was shaking uncontrollably. Sophie took off her long overcoat and held it open for the girl to walk into. The girl stepped forward hesitantly. Sophie smiled at her.

'You're safe now. Come and get warm.'

The girl stepped into the thick coat and Sophie hugged her close. Marsh walked over to them.

'Let's get her into the car, Barry. She's absolutely frozen. God knows what she's doing out here, but I think she's suffering from exposure. And she seems terrified. I'll drive her across to the hospital. You stay here with Jimmy and see what you can rescue from that fire.'

* * *

The young woman said her name was Nadia. Sophie turned the heater up to full, and by the time she slowed down at the edge of the town, the car was considerably warmer. The girl was still shaking. As they came down the hill towards the seafront the street lights allowed Sophie to get a clearer view of her face. Her hair was a dirty blonde colour and stuck to her skull, bedraggled and grimy. Her pale face was streaked with tears, and she was still uttering an occasional whimper.

'We're nearly there, Nadia. We'll get you examined, then into a warm bath.'

Sophie had phoned through to the local cottage hospital and the police doctor, Mark Benson. She drove directly to the hospital entrance, and was met by a nurse with a wheelchair.

'Is Doctor Benson here?' Sophie asked the nurse.

'He arrived just a minute ago with Doctor Jenson. They're just washing their hands in the examination area. We're wondering why you didn't call an ambulance.'

'I found her literally ten minutes ago. I got here quicker than an ambulance. I don't want anyone touching her, other than Doctor Benson — for forensic reasons. Now let's get her inside.'

They entered the small A & E area. Mark Benson appeared out of a cubicle and waved to her. He wheeled Nadia into the examination room.

'Maybe you could wait here, please?' said the nurse.

Sophie turned to face her. 'Don't be ridiculous. Don't you know who I am? She remains under police protection until I decide otherwise.'

'It's okay, nurse,' Benson said. 'Chief Inspector Sophie knows exactly what she's doing. She's welcome to be present.' A woman doctor was waiting in the cubicle.

'This is Laura Jenson, one of my partners. She'll do the examination. I'll leave the room if you want me to,' he said.

'I hope that won't be necessary,' said Sophie.

They helped the girl from the wheelchair. Sophie removed the coat and the nurse exchanged the grubby towel for a hospital robe. Sophie held Nadia's hand and stroked her cheek while the doctor examined her. Nadia didn't have any serious injuries to her limbs and torso, just some minor cuts and bruises on her hands, shoulders and knees.

Doctor Jenson spoke softly to the girl. 'Nadia, I must look at your private parts. You must be brave and do as I ask.' Sophie stroked the girl's hair as Laura gently examined her labial area and took a vaginal swab. She also took a blood sample.

'You've been very brave,' said the doctor. 'I think you can have a warm bath now. Would you like some tea or coffee?'

The girl nodded. She was still obviously uneasy, but much calmer now. Sophie held Nadia's hand as she was helped into the bath. She went out of the room while the nurse soaped her.

Laura told Sophie what she had found. 'She has labial and vaginal damage consistent with rape, but she will recover physically. The back of her mouth and throat show bruising and surface tearing. I don't think any of it's been done today but I'd guess it was very recent. She also has rectal tearing and will need some treatment for it. Someone's been brutal to her. She's only a slip of a girl. What do you think? About seventeen?'

'That's roughly what I was thinking. Seventeen or eighteen. She's from Romania. I got that out of her on the way over, but not much else. She's in shock, and was absolutely freezing when we found her. Can you give her something to get her to sleep?'

'Of course. I don't know what else she's been through, but I'd guess she's had so many shocks that her brain can't cope with it all,' said the doctor.

'I'll stay with her until she drops off. I'll have to arrange for an officer to be here for security overnight, but I'll let the hospital staff know. Can you lock all those swabs up for the night? I'll get them collected by the forensic service tomorrow morning. And can you push the blood test through as a priority?' Sophie asked.

'Already done. We should have the results back late tomorrow.'

'Thanks — both of you. I know I can always rely on you, and I'm grateful.'

'It's a pleasure, Sophie,' said Mark. 'Laura's in a hurry so I'll give the girl a sedative in a few minutes, when she's been found a bed. Then I'll be off. One of us will call back to see her first thing tomorrow.'

Sophie went back into the bathroom. The young woman already looked better. Sophie helped her out of the bath and the nurse gently rubbed her dry. The nurse led her over to the wheelchair and took her to a small room set apart from the main ward. Sophie phoned the police station and arranged for a PC to spend the night outside Nadia's room. She sat by the bed, while Nadia nibbled at a cheese sandwich and drank some coffee.

'Nadia, can you tell me what happened?'

'We come to England. They told us jobs in hotels. We pay them money. When we come they did bad things to us. Bad, bad things. Are evil. They kill Stefan. Make us watch.' She started sobbing uncontrollably.

'How old are you, Nadia?'

'Eighteen. I speak a small English.'

'Don't say any more. I just want you to rest. You are safe now. I will look after you. Trust me. You are safe. The doctor will give you an injection to help you sleep, but I will be here.'

Mark Benson gave the young woman a sedative and Sophie stayed with her, holding onto her hand until well after she fell into a deep sleep. Sophie dozed off herself and woke when the nurse came into the room with PC Jen Allbright.

'I thought you went off duty?' Sophie whispered.

'I did, ma'am, but I volunteered for this. I'll be fine, though I might be a bit late in tomorrow morning.'

'I don't want to see you until mid-afternoon at the earliest. And I'll try to have someone else here at six in the morning to sit for a couple of hours until I get back in.'

Sophie tiptoed out of the room.

CHAPTER 4: PINK AND BLUE CLOTHES

Thursday, Week 1

'Jade, I'm really sorry I couldn't eat more of your chicken casserole last night. But it was delicious.' Sophie had been exhausted when she arrived home the previous night. She was still tired this morning.

'It's okay, Mum. Dad's already eyed up the leftovers to take in for his lunch today. It won't get wasted.'

'If the hospital has to discharge the girl and we can't find anywhere to take her, then I might bring her back here for a couple of nights. Is that alright?'

'I don't mind, Mum. I'll look after her.'

'She doesn't have any clothes, Jade. Before you go, do you think you could put out a couple of things that I could take in for her? She's about your build, but a bit shorter. Just informal things like jeans, and maybe a jumper.'

'Okay, Mum. I'll leave some stuff out on my bed before I head off.'

'Jade, in case I do have to bring Nadia back, there's something you need to know. We suspect that she's been the victim of multiple rapes. And she's also witnessed a murder. Don't expect her to be like just any girl of her age. She'll be in shock for a long time to come. She couldn't stop crying last night for all the time I was with her. It was heart-breaking.'

Jade stopped for a moment, facing the door. Then she left the room.

Martin watched her go. 'I know we've already discussed this, Sophie. But I still can't help thinking that it's a lot for Jade to cope with. Trying to befriend someone who's been gang-raped and forced to watch a murder won't be an easy task. I just wonder if it's a suitable thing to ask Jade to do.'

'But what else can I do, Martin? I hope that it doesn't come to it, but I suspect it will. If I go through official channels she'll probably end up in a local hostel somewhere. She'll be safely supervised, I know, but she'll feel alone and vulnerable. She has to stay somewhere close because there's a lot she can tell us. But at the moment she's like a sheet of thin glass that could shatter at any moment. The look she gave me as I helped her out of the bath just melted me. I kept thinking, what if it were Hannah or Jade? What would we want someone in my position to do? And that has to be to give her some warmth and affection. I don't want to lose her trust.'

'If it comes to a trial she will be called as a witness. Won't it be seen as interference by an investigating officer?'

'That's a risk, Martin. But I think we'd get through it okay. Will you trust me on it?'

Martin nodded. 'Of course, as long as it's not for too long. Remember that we're meant to be visiting your grand-parents at the weekend.'

'Yes, Sunday, but it's not certain yet. I have an uneasy feeling about this case. If we do go, I'll find someone else to look after Nadia. By the way, Hannah can get a direct train back to London from Gloucester after we've visited. I'll give her the money to get a taxi back to her flat from Paddington.'

'Good idea.'

Martin leaned over and kissed her cheek. 'I'd better be off. Look, Sophie, you're going to have to speak to Archie Campbell again. He phoned late last night and said that he's been calling

41

you on your mobile every few hours and you haven't been answering.'

'I know. Other than you, he and Harry Turner have been the most influential men in my life. He was a father figure to me for the eight years I was with West Midlands. I phoned to tell him about it on Monday, but I just told him then hung up. I didn't want to tell him at all, but that would have been a dereliction. I just can't cope with it. Not from the investigation side. My brain just seizes up. I'm scared I'll break down if I talk to him about it.'

'Sophie, I know how he feels about you. I expect he's hurting as much as you, just thinking about what you're going through. At least let him know that you are alright.'

He called to Jade, who put her head round the door. 'All done, Mum. There's a bag on my bed.'

Martin smiled at his daughter and turned back to Sophie. 'By the way, I thought you wanted to get to work by eight?'

'Barry took over at six this morning. He texted me last night just before I went to bed. That's why I slept in late. He's a real gem. I hope his girlfriend realises that.'

'Was that the loud woman at the party we went to before Christmas?' Jade asked.

Sophie nodded.

'Didn't like her. A bit shallow. Attention-seeking. And he seemed a nice man. Kind of shy, you know?' said Jade.

'Don't make judgements on the basis of one meeting, young lady,' said her mother.

'But first impressions are often right, aren't they?'

'That's the problem, Jade. Often they are. But not always. So it's always worth giving someone a second chance before making your mind up. They might not be their normal selves the first time around. Anyway, time for you to be going. Have a good day, both of you.'

She tidied up and stacked the plates in the dishwasher. She grabbed the bag that Jade had left on her bed and went out.

* * *

42

Marsh was sitting outside Nadia's room.

'She's still asleep, apparently. A nurse has just been in to check on her and thinks she'll be awake shortly.'

'Fine, Barry. I'll take over from here. Go and get some breakfast, and we'll meet in the incident room at ten. By the way, did you manage to rescue anything from that fire?' Sophie asked.

'Only a few bits and pieces. Some charred paper and remains of burned clothes. We gave it to forensics. They might make something of it. But there are no fingerprints in the house or on that pick-up.'

'What? None at all?' Sophie couldn't believe this.

'No. Every door handle, switch and knob has been wiped clean. They did a slick job. It must have been that pair we saw in the afternoon. Forensics are staying on. They reckon those guys have got to have missed something, somewhere.'

'Professionals, Barry. They're not going to make it easy for us. But if that young lad was killed on the farm, then there will be traces. He must have lost a lot of blood.'

'So you think it's linked? I've told forensics there's a chance of it being the same people.'

'She said that they'd been forced to watch someone called Stefan being killed. I'm guessing that's the body you found,' said Sophie.

Marsh nodded. 'Nearly forgot. HQ phoned the station and said that a Romanian speaker will be with us later this morning. Apparently Kevin McGreedie used her last year in a case at Bournemouth and she was really good. I'll be off, ma'am. I'll get someone else here by nine thirty.'

Sophie took the chair into the ward. She sat beside Nadia's bed until the young woman opened her eyes. Sophie squeezed her hand and stroked her hair.

'Hello, Nadia. You see, here I am. There has been some-one with you all night, making sure you are safe. How do you feel?'

Nadia gave her a sleepy smile.

'I feel I am from bad dream. Men will be look for me.'

'Don't worry about that. I think you need something to eat and drink. Shall I ring for the nurse?'

Nadia had her breakfast and was sipping coffee. Sophie decided it was time to ask about what had happened to her. Nadia struggled to find the right words.

'I go on roof. They were looking. I was hide. I there for all day. I come down in dark and to fire for warm. I saw you.'

'What happened before then, Nadia? How long were you there?'

Tears came to the girl's eyes.

'I not have words in English. Bad, bad men.'

'You said yesterday that they killed Stefan. Was he a young man? Did you know him?'

'He was with them. He saw me. We are . . . how you say?'

Sophie said, 'Friends?'

Nadia shook her head.

'Family?'

She nodded.

'Brother? Is he your brother, Nadia?'

'No.'

'Cousin?'

'Yes. Cousin.'

Sophie decided to wait until the interpreter arrived before she tried for any more information. She showed Nadia the clothes that Jade had left for her.

'These are for you, Nadia. My daughter has given them to you.'

Sophie had expected there to be one set of clothes, but Jade had included underwear, a pair of faded blue jeans, a pair of pink trousers, two T-shirts, two jumpers, one pink and the other blue, and socks. She'd even thought to include a jacket, a hairbrush, a pair of gloves and a pair of trainer shoes. Sophie was surprised at the thought that had gone into the selection.

'Is very kind,' Nadia said. 'What is name?'

'Jade. Don't change into the clothes yet, Nadia. The doctor is coming back to examine you. You must wait. How are you feeling now?'

'I am sleepy. But I safe now.' She looked intently at Sophie and squeezed her hand. 'Thank you. With my heart.'

Mark Benson arrived a few minutes later to examine Nadia. Sophie sat and watched.

'Now you,' he said.

'What?'

'You looked a bit peaky yesterday evening. I'll just give you a quick onceover.' He winked at Sophie and mouthed, 'Good for her to see.'

She sat on the end of the bed while he took her blood pressure and listened to her chest through his stethoscope.

'Fully fit,' he solemnly announced.

'I should bloody well hope so, you cheeky devil. You look as though you've wanted to do that for ages.'

'All part of the Benson service.'

He and Sophie went outside for a moment so he could speak to her. 'Now, Nadia is physically already on the road to recovery. Some good food, exercise and time to relax are all she needs. I'll prescribe her some more sedatives to help her sleep. I imagine that will be a problem. Psychologically? She will need some counselling once things settle. Today, though, we've got to decide what we do with her. There was an overnight fishing boat accident and the hospital really needs her bed.'

'I can put her up myself, Mark, but only for a couple of nights. It would be convenient while we're questioning her. But we'll have to find somewhere for her to go after that.'

'Do you think the Romanian embassy might have some suggestions?'

'Possibly, but I'm worried about her safety. I think she'll be in extreme danger, though I don't know any of the facts yet. We've got an interpreter coming in this afternoon. I have to let the embassy know that we have her, so that they can

45

inform her family back in Romania. But if any information leaks out, the gang that did this to her could find out where she is. And I'm not having that happen.'

'Sounds fair to me, if you're happy to do it. I'll come back in after lunch to do another check, and I'll discharge her then if all is okay. Suit you?'

'Fine. And thanks.'

* * *

When Sophie arrived at Swanage police station a little later, Marsh told her that the forensic team was still at Brookway Farm.

'We'll have to leave them to get on with it, ma'am. They'll let us know the instant they find anything. David Nash is in charge again.'

'Fine. It's just that with so little to go on, I feel as if I'm in limbo. Until we interview Nadia this afternoon we can't really make any progress.' She paused. 'Let's work through the probable order of events yesterday, okay? Take me through it, Barry. We'll see if anything occurs to us.'

He began. 'Jack Holly and Jen Allbright called at the farm at about ten thirty in a marked squad car. The man who answered the door raised their suspicions, but not in any direct way.'

'Okay, stop. That probably means he wasn't either of the two men that you and I saw in the afternoon. Their attitude would have made anyone suspicious. How did they describe him?'

'Late thirties. Gap in his front teeth. Medium height. So you're right. The one who talked to us didn't have a gap in his teeth, and the other one was short and bulky. So there are at least three,' he said.

'And Holly didn't comment on his accent, so it's unlikely that he was foreign. Let's move on.'

Marsh continued. 'They decide to leave. They decide to move the girls out? I'm guessing here. You probably know more than me from your talk with the girl.'

'She did say "we", as if she was part of a group. I got the impression that it was a group of women or girls, but I might be wrong. Somehow she escaped, and I'm guessing it was during the move. But why didn't she have any clothes on?'

'Maybe they were stripped. It would reduce the chances of escape. It's a well-known method of intimidation, isn't it?' said Marsh.

'She says that she hid on the roof. Do we have any photos of the place?'

'I asked Jimmy to take some while he was over there first thing this morning. I'll get him to print them out.'

While Marsh was gone, Sophie went in search of Jack Holly. She asked him to start examining photofit images on the national police database to see if he could pick out the man at the farm. When she returned Marsh was back with Melsom and the prints.

'Can either of you remember where the bathroom was?' she said.

'Top floor, back wall, halfway up the stairs,' replied Melsom.

'So is that its window, do you think?' She pointed at one of the images. 'It's like a little dormer, sticking out from the building.'

'I think so, ma'am,' he replied.

'So if she got out, she could clamber up using that down-pipe, then onto the small roof, and from there up onto the main roof?'

'Looks like it could be done if someone was agile enough. I wouldn't like to have chanced it though. And it explains the towel. And once she was missing, they'd look for her on the ground or hiding in one of the sheds. Maybe it didn't occur to them that she'd gone upwards. They'd expect her to make a run for it,' he said. 'Clever girl.'

'That's my Nadia,' Sophie said. 'Now, what happened next?'

'They'd spend some time searching for her, but it would have to be quick. The other girls would have to be guarded while they were doing it, and maybe there were only the three of them,' said Melsom.

'We know they didn't find her, so what would they do?'

'Get the rest of the girls away then come back to make a more thorough search,' he said.

'But you and I turned up, Barry. That probably spooked them even more. Once we'd gone they burned the stuff they didn't want to take, and left by boat. So the big question is, where could they have gone?'

'Poole Harbour's vast, ma'am. Isn't it the largest natural harbour in Europe? It's got three or four inhabited islands and dozens of small ones. The shore this side is a maze of creeks and inlets, and the far side is one huge built-up area. They could have gone anywhere,' Marsh said.

'Yes, but they didn't, Barry, did they? They probably went somewhere very specific. We need to think it through. Let's move back to the body on the rock. We've already said it was a very public statement. They knew the body would be found, and that we'd start making enquiries when it was discovered. They'd guess that we'd do exactly what we have done and start a house-to-house. They knew we'd get to their place sooner or later, so they'd have another ready. In fact, my guess is that they were going to move anyway. That's why they put the body where we found it. A twisted sort of farewell gift. Didn't they say that the place was rented from an agency and was up for sale? I think they've got somewhere else, somewhere better. Now comes the guess work. Criminals don't change their habits much. That applies to most people by the way, not just the slime balls. So the new place won't be vastly different from the old one. Let's assume that their system, whatever it was, was working for them. They'd want to keep it going. So their new place is likely to be near the harbour.'

'But Poole Harbour has a coastline of thirty-six miles, ma'am, so I'm told. And that's not counting the islands,' said Marsh.

48

'Bear with me, Barry. Let's look at the map. The islands wouldn't be any good for them. They'd be a trap. I think we can also discount all the residential areas. I don't think they'll want to be too close to their old place either. They'll still be based at a farm, or maybe industrial buildings of some kind. That's my guess, anyway.'

'I can't fault your reasoning, ma'am,' said Marsh.

'I think they'd been planning this move for some time. You know, if it hadn't been for your Mr Kirby's new binoculars, and you getting off the mark so quickly with the house-to-house, we might have missed them entirely. Maybe they thought they had plenty of time for a leisurely move, and then Allbright and Holly came calling. If so, Nadia owes her life to their prompt action. If the gang hadn't needed to get away so fast, they would have taken their time searching and they'd have found her.'

She turned to Melsom. 'And you, Jimmy. You deserve a ticking off for deciding to wander down to the farm yesterday afternoon without my say-so. But you may just have saved that girl's life.'

'So do we start looking along the coastline? It'll take a long time, ma'am,' asked Marsh.

'We'll wait until this afternoon. I want to hear what Nadia has to say before I decide. If she confirms my thoughts, then I'll get the go-ahead from HQ to assign the manpower to it. Meanwhile, Barry, you and I have to make an attempt at identifying those two heavies from the photofits. So fetch yourself a coffee and get stuck in. Jimmy, the tongue-cutting may give us a lead. Start digging to see if there are records of any previous incidences. By the way, I think the victim might be Nadia's cousin. If so, his name is Stefan.'

'The pick-up truck is a dead end. They hired it from a company in Poole, but gave false details. An address that is no longer there for a man who doesn't exist,' said Marsh.

'Well, it was worth a try.'

Sophie called Archie Campbell again. This time she managed to speak for longer.

CHAPTER 5: HORROR STORY

Wednesday, Week 1

Nadia was discharged from the hospital and she and Sophie drove to the police station. As they entered they passed someone waiting in the reception area who Sophie vaguely recognised. She led Nadia to her temporary office, and called Marsh to sit with the girl.

'The interpreter's arrived, ma'am. She's waiting in reception,' he said.

'That's what I was afraid of. Okay, you stay here with Nadia. I'll go and get her. Or not. Oh, why did it have to be her?'

Marsh looked puzzled.

'We have a history. I didn't realise she was a Romanian speaker. I may have to abort this, Barry, and get someone else. So be prepared. And this cubbyhole is too bloody small. Is there any chance of getting somewhere a bit more spacious and comfortable?'

Sophie returned to reception and approached the visitor.

'Doctor Porter.'

The woman smiled awkwardly. 'Hello again, Chief Inspector. I suspect that you might not feel very positive about taking me on as your interpreter. And I can understand that. You left me feeling humiliated and ashamed last time we met. I have to say that I deserved the tongue-lashing you gave me. It was only after your harsh words that I fully understood how badly I'd let that young woman down. It made me rethink my approach to what I was doing. I suppose I really owe you my thanks. I offer you my apologies over what happened, even though they can never bring that poor girl's life back.'

Sophie nodded. 'I didn't know you were a Romanian speaker.'

'My husband is Romanian. I met him on an exchange of Business Studies students. I'm fluent in spoken rather than written Romanian. I imagine that's what you want? That's why I'm registered with the local police in Bournemouth.'

'Yes. To get someone in from UCL would take days, and whoever they did send would be vastly overqualified for the interpreting I want them to do. But I'd be prepared to wait if necessary. Do you understand that?'

'What you're in fact saying is that you'd prefer to wait rather than use someone in whom you had little confidence?' Dr Porter said.

Sophie nodded again.

'I'd like to regain your goodwill, Chief Inspector, if I can. You won't regret using me, I promise.'

'This is another murder inquiry, Doctor Porter. Please realise that you will be bound by absolute confidentiality. Not a word of what you learn can be spoken outside these walls without my permission. And the confidentiality extends to chatting with your husband. Not only no mention of what you hear, but no mention of the fact that you have even been here until I say otherwise. It won't be easy.'

'I think I can understand that.'

'It's probable that the girl in question has been gang-raped, Doctor Porter. I also believe that she was forced to witness a sadistic murder. I need the details from her, but she must be treated with the utmost delicacy. I found her last night, so she hasn't had much time to recover. She was naked, nearly dead from exposure and absolutely terrified. Knowing all this, are you sure you still want to continue?'

Mary Porter was silent for a few moments.

'Yes,' she said finally. 'I want to make amends. To show you that I'm a better person than you think I am. And, if you do decide to use me, will you please call me Mary?'

'Okay, we'll give it a go, Mary. We'll do it gently and calmly. If necessary take your time to get the translation exactly right. Nadia speaks a little English, and may think that she understands my questions. I want you to translate even if it looks as though she understands what I ask.'

The desk officer called across. 'Ma'am, Barry Marsh just phoned down. You can use Inspector Rose's office. He'll be out of the station for the next hour or so.'

'Thanks, Tony.'

Sophie left Mary Porter in Tom Rose's office while she went to fetch Nadia and Marsh. She had begun to care about Nadia as if she was her own daughter. She could not easily forget how careless Mary Porter had been the previous year. Donna Goodenough had also been subjected to abuse, which Mary Porter had chosen to ignore.

'The chief inspector's very focused, isn't she?' Porter said to Marsh.

Marsh was arranging the chairs for the interview. He pointed to one of them. 'That'll be yours.'

'Do you know about me?' she asked.

'No. All I know is that you met when we were investigating Donna Goodenough's murder. She never told me what happened between you. My DC was there, but he was told never to talk about it. So no one else knows in case it's worrying you.'

* * *

The first stage of the interview lasted for over an hour. Sophie sat beside Nadia and held her hand, occasionally stroking

52

her arm. Barry Marsh took notes. Nadia described a chilling scenario. She was one of a group of six teenage girls and young women. They were lured away from college or jobs in Romania with the promise of work in the hotel industry in Britain, attendance at local colleges and the chance to study for a degree course at a British university. They and their families had paid for the transport to the UK. Things were wrong from the outset. The promised luxury coach had been replaced with a minibus. Conditions during the drive across mainland Europe deteriorated rapidly. By the time they stopped at a remote farm on the Normandy coast, their documents and passports were in the hands of the two drivers. Nadia did not know how many trips the men had made before hers, but she suspected there had been many. Conditions deteriorated further after they were transferred to an old motor launch for the cross-Channel trip. They travelled overnight, and the girls were locked in a cabin. They had waited in France for several days until stormy weather cleared to a patchy mist.

They moored to a small, rickety jetty in Poole Harbour, where they were let out of the cabin and led ashore. Nadia recognised one of the trio of men who met them. He was Stefan, her second cousin. They were roughly bundled into the back of a van. It was then that the girls knew they had been duped. When one of them objected to their rough treatment a man punched her twice in the face. The girl spent the short drive to their final destination sobbing in the corner of the van, while the others tried to clean up her face with paper tissues. They were all hurried inside a farmhouse and taken to a room on the first floor, furnished with three old double beds.

Nadia stopped talking and began to cry. After a while she continued speaking, her voice catching, shaken with sobs.

The rapes started that night. After they had eaten, the girls were hauled out and taken to a larger room on the ground floor. Five men were waiting for them, including Stefan. The girls were each given a drink of fruit juice. Nadia refused hers and spat it out. One of the men slapped her hard across the face and Stefan tried to intervene. She couldn't follow everything they said, but she thought Stefan was trying to protect her. An argument ensued, and Stefan left the room, slamming the door behind him. Then the horror began. Each of the men grabbed a girl and hauled her to his room. The man who took Nadia had a gap between his teeth.

Sophie glanced across to Marsh. The man at the farm.

When her ordeal ended, this man led Nadia back into the first floor room. One by one the others joined her. All of them were shocked, confused and tearful. The girls who had finished their drink seemed distant and unfocused. They comforted each other and tried to rest. A short while later they were disturbed again. Two men they hadn't seen before entered the room and looked around at the girls cowering in their beds. They selected Nadia and hauled her out, kicking and screaming. They took her to a warm, well-furnished bedroom. And then her real nightmare began.

'Had you seen these two men before?' asked Sophie.

'No. And except for the next morning, I didn't see them again.'

'I think we all need a breather,' said Sophie. 'Nadia, you have given us a great deal. You've done so well. I'm proud of you, and you should be proud of yourself. We will bring all these men to justice. Would you like to go for a walk? The fresh air might be good for you. We could go to the seafront for a few minutes. It won't take long to drive there.'

The three women walked along the front, and then out onto the stone jetty. They sat on a seat facing towards Ballard Down and the chalk cliffs.

Through Mary Porter, Nadia said, 'It is so beautiful here. Romania only has a small coastline. I think you are lucky in your country to be surrounded by water. And to have such peace. I think I would like to remain here in Britain to study if it is possible.'

'Don't you want to go home and see your family?' Sophie said.

'Oh yes. More than anything. But I mean after that. I don't want what those men did to stop me doing the things I want. If they do, they will have won.'

'We will arrange for your family to fly across to see you soon,' said Sophie. 'I would like you to stay while we hunt for these men and bring them to trial. I need you to be safe and secure. But only come back if you are sure it is really what you want to do. You can rely on me if you do decide to come back. I will always be your friend if you need me.'

The young girl gave Sophie a wonderful smile and threw her arms around her.

* * *

The three women returned to the police station to continue the interview.

The next morning the girls, all of them naked, were taken out of the farmhouse, and across the yard into a shed. They stood huddled against a wall, cold and fearful of what might happen next. The two men who had taken Nadia came into the barn. They were followed by a Romanian man, dragging Stefan. Stefan's hands were tied behind his back and he had clearly been beaten about the face. He was forced to kneel in the middle of the floor. What happened next was so rapid, and so horrifying, that at first Nadia thought she was hallucinating. One of the men lunged forward and grabbed Stefan's tongue, pulling it out as far as he could. He then sliced it off with a knife blade. In the horror-stricken silence that followed, he stepped behind Stefan's back and sliced the blade across his throat. Blood spurted out across the stone floor and Stefan toppled forward. Several of the girls fainted and all of them screamed. Nadia fell to her knees and vomited. Then she blacked out. When she came to, she was back in the girls' room in the farmhouse.

The girls were left alone for the rest of the day and that night, but their clothes were not returned. Food and water was brought to them, and they were allowed to go to the bathroom, but only one at a time and under guard. The two men who seemed to be in charge were not seen again. The girls were left with the gap-toothed man and two Romanians.

The following day three of the girls were taken out and raped in the middle of the afternoon. Nadia was left alone. In the evening the girls could hear noises in the rooms below, as if objects were being moved. They also heard the sound of vehicles coming and going outside. None of the girls were taken out of the room that night.

The next day the sounds of activity continued until the middle of the morning when the noises suddenly ceased. One of the Romanian men came in and stood guard. He kept looking through the net curtains that were draped across the window. He told them he would kill anyone who made a noise. In the early afternoon, the men collected the girls and pushed them out down the stairs. They seemed nervous. Nadia pleaded to be allowed to pay a visit to the toilet. Inside, she grabbed a face flannel and a towel. She forced open the fanlight of a window above the sink and, clambering onto the basin, was able to haul herself up and force her thin body through the gap. She stood on a narrow outside ledge, clinging to the window-handle and listening to the noises from the yard at the front of the house. She realised that she couldn't escape by going down. Instead, she began to climb up. She rested for a while on a small dormer roof above the bathroom window, and deliberately dropped the small flannel onto the ground below. She returned to the vertical rainwater pipe and inched up, finally managing to haul herself onto the roof and into a drainage gulley. She crept forward up the gulley until she reached the top ridge and crawled along it. She settled against the chimney-stack, and lay in the deep shadow at its base.

Not long afterwards she heard raised voices. Someone ran around the outside of the farmhouse and a shout told her that the flannel had been found. The sounds of running feet below continued for some time, but at last she heard the vehicles driving away. It was silent now, but Nadia decided to remain where she was until dark. She was terribly cold.

Nadia saw Sophie and Marsh arrive in the early afternoon. She sat huddled with her back against the chimney breast, trying to catch some warmth from the weak midwinter sunshine. She lay down again when she saw the pick-up truck return. She waited while the two men carried out a hurried search of the house and its immediate surroundings. One of the men was the younger of the two who had raped her. The other was a short, heavily built man she hadn't seen since the boat trip across the Channel. The men carried some boxes into the trees, and Nadia caught sight of the fire. In the late afternoon the two men hurried down the track and Nadia saw a small boat move away from the jetty. No one came, but the pick-up truck still stood in the middle of the yard, and Nadia was afraid to move.

The temperature dropped further as the sun began to set, and Nadia realised that she would die if she stayed on the roof for much longer. She slid back down the roof gulley and found a handhold that allowed her to drop her legs over the gutter to the drainpipe. Somehow she found the strength to hold onto the pipe as she slowly lowered herself to ground level. She could hear no sounds. She made her way through the copse to where she'd seen the fire, and crept as close as she could. She knew she would be silhouetted if she came too near the fire, so she stayed behind a bush for most of the time, occasionally venturing closer to gain a little warmth. But the fire was dying. She was wondering whether to return to the farmhouse when she heard the three detectives approach. She recognised Sophie and Marsh from their earlier visit. She listened to their conversation, but couldn't understand much. She was sure they were police officers, but didn't know what would happen to her if she showed herself. Then Sophie spotted her.

* * *

It was late afternoon when Nadia finished. She described the other girls and what she remembered of their captors.

Sophie thanked Mary Porter for her careful interpretation.

'It's a privilege, Chief Inspector. It's probably been the most harrowing afternoon of my life, and I won't forget it. I did try my best.'

'I know, Mary. Thank you. Can you make it back tomorrow morning? I need to find out more about her life in Romania. Family, friends, that kind of thing. But I now need to get Nadia to somewhere safe and secure for a few days. Barry and I will get our heads together to work out where we go from here.'

Mary Porter left.

'Barry, I'm taking Nadia away with me now. She's too tired to wait around here. We'll make a fresh start in the morning. Can Jimmy keep trawling through the records for a while? I also wonder if any of the coast watch organisations have records of boat movements. These men probably sneak across under cover of darkness or mist, but someone may have spotted the boat at some time. It's not urgent but if you have any ideas, that would be great. Call me if you find anything. But don't stay late. It'll be better if we're all fresh in the morning.'

CHAPTER 6: BODIES IN THE FIELD

Thursday Evening & Friday, Week 1

Jade Allen was chopping vegetables in the kitchen when her mother arrived home with Nadia.

'Hi, Mum. Hi, Nadia. I've just made a pot of tea for you, and thought I'd start on the dinner. I'll show Nadia her room if you want, Mum.'

Jade hugged them both and held Nadia's hand as she led her out of the room. Sophie could hear her chattering fade as they went up the stairs.

Sophie set out cups and saucers and poured the tea, adding a plate of chocolate biscuits. She carried the tray through to the lounge, kicked off her shoes and settled into one of the comfortable armchairs. She shut her eyes, trying to dispel her fatigue. She took a sip of hot, refreshing tea. She'd always thought that Jade was the less sensitive of her two daughters, more likely than Hannah to blunder into situations. Today she had revealed a completely new side to her character. Maybe she might become a good doctor after all. Sophie was annoyed with herself for underestimating her own daughter.

The sound of girls' voices came through from the hallway. Goodness, she'd drifted off to sleep. She took another sip of tea. It was still hot so she hadn't slept for long.

The two young women came into the lounge. Nadia was a good three years older than Jade, but they looked almost the same age. Jade's sleek, dark hair was tied back into a ponytail and she was a couple of inches taller, but they were both slim.

'Nadia's offered to help me with dinner, Mum. We'll take our tea through to the kitchen if that's okay.'

'Of course.' Her daughter just went on surprising her.

'You can doze off again, if you want to,' said Jade.

'Was it that obvious?'

'Slightly pink cheeks, Mum. And you've been doing it for a few months now. But don't worry, I won't tell anyone. I don't think Dad's noticed. He does it himself. Either that or he keeps quiet about it.'

'We've struck a deal, Jade. Neither of us reminds the other about the onset of middle age. The one who breaks the deal first gets to pay for the next meal out.'

'Cool.'

Sophie finished her tea and settled back into the chair. She picked up the daily paper. It wasn't often that she managed more than a quick glance at the headlines. She yawned again. The emotional turmoil of the last few days had affected her sleep. She was James and Florence's closest living relative and this unexpected discovery, wonderful as it was, meant that she now had their health and wellbeing to think about. But discovering the circumstances of her father's disappearance had stunned her to the core. She turned the pages of the newspaper without reading them. She put it aside and thought about the coming Sunday and the planned visit to Gloucester. Maybe she could ask Lydia to come across and spend the day with Nadia. The young detective would be home from her training course by then.

She finished her tea and walked through to the kitchen. Nadia was showing Jade how to chop an onion at high speed.

'I learn in hotel kitchen,' she explained.

'Nadia is doing a hotel management degree, Mum. Sounds interesting.'

'Well, if there's food involved, Jade, I can understand your interest. What are you making?'

'Mixed grill. I've halved the steaks, there's some bacon that needs to be used up and I've decided to introduce Nadia to the joys of black pudding. Dad bought some at the weekend.'

'I might have known. Any excuse for you and your father to eat that foul stuff.' Sophie laughed.

'There's white wine in the fridge, Mum. But I think Dad would have a fit if we had it with this. Do you want to open a red so that it's ready?'

'You're too young to know all these things, Jade. We've ruined you.'

'Yeah, well, don't worry about it. It's all cool.'

* * *

Martin did his best to appear relaxed when he arrived home, but Sophie could sense his tension. He was too conscious of Nadia's story, she thought. And she was aware of the frustrated anger he felt towards abusive men.

'Jade's chosen some wine that she claims will be appropriate for black pudding,' she told him. 'She sounded like a real expert.'

'It's all Dad's fault. He's the one who tells me all about choosing wines to go with the food. All that stuff about real ale and getting the hoppiness right. I could never be a binge drinker. All my mates'll be knocking back the booze by the pint, while I'm still sniffing the bouquet. Do you realise how much you've ruined my future? I'll be mentally scarred for the rest of my teenage years. I'll get to my mid-twenties and all my friends will have passed through the binge drinking phase. I'll have missed a whole important phase of my development, and he'll be to blame. Wine-tasting. Huh.'

'What have I done to deserve this?' asked Martin.

'It's alright, Dad, I'm only kidding. Nadia's going to help me with the dinner. It'll be ready in about half an hour, okay? Now kindly leave us alone to get on with our work.'

Sophie and Martin dutifully returned to the lounge, a little shell-shocked. The sound of giggles drifted in from the kitchen.

'How did you and I manage to create that girl?' asked Martin.

'Maybe there was a full moon on the night in question. I can't think of any other explanation. But I tell you what, I feel a whole lot more cheerful than when I first came home. She does wonders for my mood. And she's looking after Nadia so well. That cheerful prattle is just what the girl needs, and no one could do it better than Jade. In fact, I'm not sure anyone else could do it at all. We're all treating her with kid gloves, and maybe all she needs at the moment is light-hearted chatter with someone her own age. Jade seemed to know that instinctively. I keep thinking that I might have underestimated her, you know.'

'One of the staff from her place was across at my school today. He looked at me in amazement when he found out who I was. "But you seem so normal," was his first comment. Apparently Jade did a song and dance routine at school assembly which brought the house down. Everyone loved it apart from the head, who thought it lacked a moral message. Jade told him that it did have a message — have a good time. He added that she is far and away the brightest kid in her year, so we must be doing something right.'

'So that was the reason for all the thumping from her room. Do you think we should ask her about it?'

'Probably better not to. We don't want her to think we're spying on her.'

Sophie's mobile phone rang. She told Martin what Mark Benson had said.

'Rohypnol traces in her blood. We'd guessed that they'd used something like that on the girls.'

'What do you plan to do with her for the next few days?'

'She'll be coming into the station with me tomorrow, and possibly Saturday morning. I may ask Lydia to look after her on Sunday if we go to Gloucester. They might have to stay here if she's still fragile. Is that okay?'

'I've no objection as long as she's with someone you trust. Remember that we don't really know her, Sophie. We don't know what she was like back in Romania. We don't know anything about her family.'

'We'll be pursuing all of that tomorrow. I'll make some more decisions then.' She paused. 'By the way, I phoned Archie today and reassured him that I was alright.'

'And did he believe you?'

'Not really. He's like you. You can both see below the surface.'

* * *

As Sophie expected, Nadia's next interview was far less draining. She went into the girl's family and social background, and then the contact that had lured her away from her college course. Sophie wanted as much detail as possible so that she could alert the Romanian authorities. The girl described the other young women who had been brought across to England with her. She was worried for their safety, particularly the youngest of the group, a sixteen-year-old called Sorina with whom she had formed a close friendship. Sorina had been an only child in her home country and had been lured away from a job in a hotel restaurant with the promise of formal training as a chef in the UK. According to Nadia the girl had spent most of the journey in terrified silence and had found the ordeal at the farmhouse hard to bear. Nadia doubted whether she would last very long under the brutal treatment of the gang.

Sophie called the Romanian embassy in order to check on progress. She then arranged for Nadia to call her parents, with

Mary Porter listening in to the conversation. She'd advised Nadia to keep the details of her ordeal to a minimum at this stage. After talking to her daughter for a few minutes, Nadia's mother spoke to Sophie through Mary Porter.

As the conversation finished Sophie's mobile rang. She heard tension in Barry Marsh's voice and walked out into the corridor.

'We've found a body at the farm.'

'Where?'

'One of the fields adjoins the copse and there's a strip of rough grass between the two. The body was there. We wouldn't have spotted it, but we had a dog with us, as you suggested. It started pawing at the ground and whining, so we started digging. Forensics are on their way. It must have been there for some time because there are weeds and stuff growing on top of it.'

'Can you tell anything about the state it's in?'

'No. We stopped once we realised what we had. It's wrapped in a rug, and we just uncovered the feet, so we can't tell yet whether it's male or female. The thing is, ma'am, the dog is behaving the same way in another spot. We think there might be more.'

'I'll be over directly. I'll get someone here to look after the girl. Is David Nash still there at the farm?'

'He's gone, but the rest of his team are still here. They were about to pack up but now they're staying around. Nash is on his way back.'

'Leave everything until he gets there. He's the expert, so he can decide the best way of extracting the body. And well done, Barry. It was a good idea to take the dog out of the yard.'

Sophie left Nadia in the care of Tom Rose's assistant, and drove out to the abandoned farm.

* * *

Sophie was thankful for the dry weather. Even so, the area around the grave was beginning to get churned up.

'We've kept everyone away from the site, apart from the marked path,' Marsh told her. 'We've also marked out the other area where the dog was sniffing.'

Sophie looked around. 'It's a well-chosen spot. That low ridge at the top of the field means it's out of view from the farm. And the copse hides it from this side.' She turned back to Marsh. 'How deep?'

'About a foot and a half. That's when we reached the upper part of the rug. We uncovered it, opened it up and found a foot.'

Sophie had a quick look at the excavation.

'We'll just leave it now for forensics, but keep someone here on watch. What else did you find?'

Marsh pointed to one of the sheds. Traces of blood had been found on the floor.

'We'll have a chat with David Nash before he starts.'

The forensic chief was busy instructing the squad who were to extract the body. They had spread large sheets of plastic on the ground nearby, ready to receive the extracted soil, and they were erecting an open sided forensic tent. Nash greeted Sophie with a wave.

'We're just about ready to go. I did wonder about bringing in a mini-excavator, but if there are other graves nearby I wouldn't want them compressed with the weight of the machinery. So we'll use the old fashioned method. The soil's not too heavy at the moment, so we won't lose too much time.'

'Are there enough screens up there on the rise to prevent Joe Public from seeing what we're up to?' Sophie said.

'Yes. I've just walked the area, and we're as private as we can be. Your people up on the road can keep their eyes open for anyone trying to trek over here from the lane.'

'Well, let's get started.'

It took less than thirty minutes to extract the first body. The rug was still intact enough to be lifted out without difficulty. Inside was the body of a young woman. She was in an advanced stage of decomposition and they could not tell her age. She was laid out on a trestle bench, and the digging team moved a few yards away to the second spot identified by the dog.

Marsh took Sophie into one of the farm buildings. They ducked under the tape stretched across the entrance.

'In here,' Marsh said. 'Blood in some of the cracks between the stones. And quite a lot, from what Nash said.'

'So this is where he was killed. If Nadia was telling the truth there would be traces of her vomit as well, probably against one of the walls. Did he say anything about that?'

'Not to me, but he was going to get a summary to you this afternoon. Maybe it was in that.'

They walked back to the grave site. As they arrived, one of the diggers called out, 'found something!'

Sophie stood beside Nash and they watched the team brush soil from another rug-encased bundle.

'Dave, were there traces of vomit found in that shed? Probably against a wall?' she asked.

'Yes. Someone had used farm disinfectant but we found blood between the flagstones in the middle of the floor and some traces of vomit over to one side. We've got a sample. It's on its way back to the lab for analysis. You look relieved.'

'It confirms her story, that's all.'

By the time darkness fell, two bodies lay beside their graves. Both of them were young women. Nash estimated that they'd been buried for periods of between two months and a year. The dog showed no signs of having found any more graves, so the forensics team started to pack up. They planned to return the following day for a sweep of the area using the latest technology.

'But it won't find more bodies,' Nash said. 'That dog's a marvel. If it hasn't detected any more, then there aren't any. But we have to be certain.'

The two corpses were secured in body bags and manoeuvred into the vans, ready to set off for Dorchester and the waiting Benny Goodall. Sophie didn't envy him his job for the next few days.

She turned to Marsh. He looked devastated.

'Have you anything planned for this evening, Barry?'

He shook his head.

'Come up to Wareham and have something to eat with us. I have to go into Swanage to collect Nadia. You can pick up your car and follow me up the road. Martin or Jade will be cooking something, and one more won't be a problem.'

'I don't know, ma'am.'

'You need company this evening, Barry. You should be with someone who's seen what you have. Which means me. Thank God we left Jimmy back on the road. You're in a mild state of shock and I can't afford to let it get to you. I don't want you hitting the bottle either, which is what'll happen if you're left on your own. Please trust my judgement. We can also talk things over if we feel up to it. I'll have to give a report to Matt Silver, and it might help if you were there too. I'll ask him to pop over to my house. You can drive back to Swanage later tonight if you feel up to it. Or, if you want to kip down for the night, then that will be okay. Believe me, it will be better for you.'

'Thanks, ma'am,' he murmured.

Sophie walked outside and took out her mobile phone. She'd been dreading this call for days. She had to tell her new-found grandparents that she and her family could only visit for an afternoon. They sounded disappointed. Sophie was utterly frustrated. She knew they'd started to plan for Graham's funeral now the remains had been released. They were all hoping that a date could be fixed for the end of the following week.

CHAPTER 7: BLOSSOM

Friday, Week 1

Benjamin "Blossom" Sourlie stalked out of the block of condemned flats, slinging a small backpack over his shoulder. He hated its sour smell and the grubby, washed-up people that squatted there. He wouldn't be seen dead in the place if it wasn't for the monthly supply of drugs and other paraphernalia he had to pick up. He was glad when he reached the fresh air of the street outside. How could people choose to live in such filth? He shook his head, and crossed the road to a narrow lane that led to the car park. His short, squat form cast a shadow as wide as it was tall.

It was very dark. Blossom didn't see the thin, hunched form standing in the shadows. The figure stepped out in front of him and drew a knife.

'Gimme your fucking cash,' the stranger snarled.

Blossom stopped walking and looked at the man who stood scowling in front of him. He stepped a little closer and slipped his right hand inside his jacket pocket as if to fetch out a wallet. Then his left fist, encased in a soft leather glove, shot out and hit the man hard in the abdomen. The man jerked forward. Blossom's right fist came up and hit the side of his jaw, breaking it. There was a gurgle as blood filled the mouth. The stranger crashed against the wall and slid to the ground. Blossom didn't even stop to look at his would-be assailant. He walked past and into the small car park at the end of the alley. There, he unlocked his car, slung the backpack under the front seat and drove away. He smiled in satisfaction. Who needed drugs to get high?

* * *

He arrived back at the farmhouse a little after midnight. In some ways the new place was more convenient than Brookway Farm. For a start, it was a good deal closer to Poole. The main problem was a longer boat journey inside the harbour. Brookway had been relatively close to the harbour entrance at Sandbanks. Now the boats would have to navigate right up the harbour, a distance of about six miles. There had been a suggestion that they move to the northern shore. But it was too built up and they could have been spotted, particularly now the police were on their trail.

Blossom had never understood why that lad's body had to be put up on top of the rock. Why couldn't it just have been dumped at sea somewhere, weighted down so it would never be found? Ricky was getting out of control. Blossom didn't like Ricky's sadistic streak and his hunger for the big, public show. At some point he'd have to speak up. Either that, or just up sticks and go.

He unlocked the door to the old farmhouse and went in. All was silent. He locked the bag of drugs into a cupboard, walked through to the kitchen and poured himself a beer. The kitchen range was still warm from when he'd stoked it up earlier in the evening. No one had bothered to put any more fuel on since. Lazy sods. If it hadn't been for him and Charlie, the whole scheme would have collapsed months ago. Now, with the boss's sporadic illness, it was beginning to look as if their days were numbered. Who would have thought it? Charlie's nephew, Ricky, had taken over the operation but success seemed to have turned his head. Maybe Blossom needed to sit down with Charlie and spell out the problems. But how would he react? Blossom shook his head wearily. The trouble was, he and Charlie weren't getting any younger. Ricky had started to form his own alliances and wouldn't be easy to overthrow. Blossom had the uneasy feeling that, when it came to the crunch, Charlie would side with his nephew — and Blossom would end up floating face down out in the Channel somewhere. After all, he'd never been anything more than Charlie's enforcer.

He opened a porn magazine and began to flick idly through the pages. Maybe he'd screw one of the girls a bit later. The others were always telling him to take one, but he'd never gone through with it. He felt uneasy about the one who'd escaped. There had been no news on the local radio or in the press about her being found. Maybe she was dead, but somehow he doubted it. She could even be in the hands of the cops by now, although he and Ricky had done a good job of cleaning the old place up. They'd left nothing that could lead the cops to this new location, and even this one was temporary. Ricky had started talking about a complete change of plan, moving much further east where the Channel was narrower, the boat trip much shorter and access to London quicker. Blossom was unsure about it. He'd crossed swords with one of the big London gangs many years before, and it hadn't been a nice experience. He'd escaped without injury, but some of his mates hadn't been so lucky. Muscling in on that market could prove a step too far unless it was planned properly. He doubted whether Ricky would be bothered to do the necessary homework.

He switched on the television to get the latest news before turning in for the night. There might be something about the missing girl. When the main headline was announced Blossom watched aghast. The partly decomposed bodies of two young women had been found buried on an abandoned farm near Poole Harbour. What? Blossom couldn't believe what he was seeing and hearing. What bodies? He didn't know of any bodies. What the fuck had been going on when he was away from the place? He stormed up the stairs, crashed open the door to Ricky's room, and switched the light on. A white-faced girl sat up, pulling the duvet up around her neck, her eyes wide with fear. Ricky opened his eyes and snarled at Blossom.

'What the fuck are you doing, you stupid pillock?'

'You'd better come down and see what's on TV. You've got a lot of explaining to do.'

Blossom turned on his heel and stalked back downstairs. He was standing in front of the screen, swallowing the last of his beer, when Ricky walked in. Blossom pointed at the screen, and the headline scrolling across the bottom. "Two women's bodies found buried on farm near Poole Harbour."

'Jesus,' Ricky said. 'They're lying, Blossom.'

'What do you take me for, you stupid fucker? They wouldn't lie over something this serious. I know that. You know that. Every Tom, Dick and fucking Harry knows that. If they say they found two bodies, then they found two bodies.' He pointed his stubby thumb at Ricky. 'And you put them there, didn't you? When I was off looking after the business and didn't have my eye on you. You psycho bastard. Charlie'll be going mental.'

Ricky looked Blossom in the eye.

'Charlie knows. He was there. He and that crazy Romanian, Barbu. So you see, Blossom, it's all three of us. And now you know. What are you going to do?'

Blossom heard a noise. Barbu was standing in the doorway watching them, impassive.

'Well, I know what we have to do, and I mean *we*. Get away from here, for a start. Do you think for one moment that the cops won't be looking all along the shore for us? You just had to play the cool gangster when those two cops came calling, didn't you? Why couldn't you just act innocent for once and not raise their hackles? I saw the way that blonde one looked at us once you'd started your spiel. She knew you had something to hide all right. They must have been back there pretty quick with sniffer dogs or something. They'll have every cop in the area out looking for us, and this place is too much like the last one. I reckon we've got twenty-four hours at most before they come knocking on the door, and this time we won't get away. They'll bring a snatch squad and go through this place like a tornado. So I suggest we all start packing right now and get away before it gets light. And for fuck's sake don't let any of the girls get away this time. I'm gonna call Charlie. You two can start getting everything together and loaded into the vans.'

'And what makes you think you're giving the orders now?'

'Because all this,' Blossom waved at the TV, 'means you're incapable of doing anything that isn't totally stupid. Sulk about it if you like, but none of you seem to have a sensible thought in your heads. We're not in some crappy backwoods country where the cops take months to get moving, then turn up as a couple of cretins in uniform who can be bribed into turning a blind eye. I suppose that's what Barbu thinks. Fuck it all, Ricky, they'll have people a lot cleverer than you or me involved now. So for fuck's sake get moving. We'll shift everything and everyone across to Charlie's empty depot in Poole.'

* * *

This time the move was completed rapidly and without mishaps. A lot of the stuff brought from Brookway was still in bags and boxes. Blossom had phoned Charlie and told him what they were doing and why. Charlie sounded hesitant and Blossom wondered if the gang leader was out of his depth. Things had moved too fast for him. Maybe it was the medication he was on, but he'd failed to keep on top of things. Everything started to go wrong after Hazel died, thought Blossom. He knew Charlie had taken her death badly, but hadn't realised quite how much. Ever since then Charlie had let Ricky take the lead.

Blossom stood still, struck by a sudden thought. Maybe Charlie wasn't ill. Was it drugs? It fitted. He'd probably been out of his head, along with Ricky, when the girls had died. Christ. What had gone on? So Charlie was as crazy as his nephew. God knows, he, Blossom, wasn't exactly an angel but he had some limits. Did Charlie and Ricky realise how much they'd changed over the years? They wouldn't have killed young girls or sliced the throats of lads like that Stefan when they'd started out all those years ago. Sure, violence had been a part of all their lives. But it had always been necessary violence, only what was needed to get a job done. And he, Blossom, had been the main provider. He had done the mopping up of leakages and the tidying up of any loose ends. And he'd never gone further than he'd had to. But now? God knows what road they were on.

As far as he could tell, that lad had been murdered in front of all the girls. In front of six fucking witnesses, for Christ's sake. Girls who were intended for the streets, who might end up talking to the cops at some point. Ricky said it would frighten them into silence. Silence my arse.

Blossom heard a noise behind him. Ricky and Barbu had walked into the loading bay from the office corridor. Blossom didn't trust that Barbu at all. He had the eyes of a snake.

'Okay, Blossom?' asked Ricky. 'How long do you reckon we're safe here?'

'Shift those girls on as soon as you can, Ricky. Make sure they end up a long way away from this area. Do you know anyone up north who's looking for girls? Manchester, or Liverpool?'

'No contacts that far away. It's either move them out quick to our normal customers, or keep them here longer while we find new people. Do you know any?'

'I'll think about it. Maybe Charlie'll have some ideas. Is he coming over?'

'Not till later. We all need some sleep.'

Blossom felt uneasy. 'We need a guard on those girls, Ricky. We ought to take shifts. I'll do the first one. And let's leave the girls be for a while.'

'You giving orders again?'

'No, I'm not, Ricky. Just making some sensible suggestions.'

Ricky Frimwell ran a hand through his thinning hair. 'Okay. Barbu and I'll get some kip. Wake me up when it gets light.'

'It's January, Ricky. It doesn't get light until nearly eight. We all need some sleep, and that includes me. I'll wake you at six. That gives you almost four hours.'

He turned aside, pretending to be busy. He felt angry and betrayed by Ricky. All crap and no cooperation. When the two men left the loading bay he rested his head against the door of the van. This was all going nowhere. Did Ricky have a sensible thought in that selfish head of his? After a few minutes he settled into a chair in the small office. The girls were in a large storeroom next to it, bedded down on a line of mattresses. Blossom had found them some old sleeping bags. He found himself hoping they were comfortable and wondered if he was getting soft. Maybe he was getting old. He punched the cushion in a vain attempt to get comfortable, and settled back to think things through.

CHAPTER 8: HELP US

Saturday, Week 1

Marsh looked more cheerful as he drove Sophie and Nadia from Wareham to Dorset county police HQ. After the meal the previous evening, his mood had lightened. As she'd said, being with her family was just what he'd needed. Matt Silver had arrived mid-evening and the three detectives had discussed the discovery of the bodies, and how this affected the case.

Marsh waited in the reception area with Nadia while Sophie met with the chief constable and his deputy.

The meeting was short and Sophie grumbled to Marsh as they made their way to Swanage. 'I know these meetings have to be done, but it's always one-way traffic. I tell them what's happened and what our plans are and they ask a few questions. Then I might get a promise of some extra resources. That's the way of the world, I suppose. Don't quote me will you, Barry? At least they've been handling the contacts with the National Crime Agency and the Romanian authorities.'

Mary Porter had arrived for their third session. Reluctantly, Sophie was beginning to warm to her. She had done everything asked of her without complaint, and Sophie was beginning

75

to feel as if she were part of the team. An official from the Romanian embassy was due to arrive from London later that morning to interview Nadia, and the girl was understandably nervous. Sophie promised that she and Doctor Porter would be present at the interview. The embassy had assisted Nadia's mother to fly across from Romania. She was due to arrive in the next couple of days, and this cheered the young woman considerably.

Sophie still regretted having to cut short her family's visit to her grandparents. It had been a hard decision to make. She was aching to see the elderly couple again and make up for all the lost years.

The embassy official arrived, along with DCS Neil Dunnett, Matt Silver's boss. He'd kept well away from Sophie since the end of the Donna Goodenough case, so she was surprised to see him. All she'd been told was that someone senior from HQ would bring the official down to Swanage. She led them along to Tom King's office.

'Is there a problem?' Dunnett asked quietly, once they had sat down in the office. 'You were very quick to get us out of the incident room. I thought he might be interested to see progress.'

'It's a live investigation, sir. The gang is still out there. We don't know how far their tentacles spread and who their contacts are inside Romania or even here in the UK. We don't know whether these girls are coming in without papers, or whether someone is supplying them with false papers. We don't know whether the gang bringing them in is working entirely by itself or whether it has someone on the inside giving them a helping hand. As far as I'm concerned we tell their embassy officials only what they need to know, and that doesn't include the details of our suspects. Now, if you'll excuse me for a moment I'll collect Nadia and our interpreter.'

'Do we need one? He speaks very good English.'

'No doubt. But Nadia doesn't, so he'll probably talk to her in Romanian. I want to know everything that's said. I also want to ensure he only asks her questions relevant to the embassy's needs. I need Mary in here to check that he does just that, and to translate his questions for our benefit.'

She turned to the official.

'Mr Dodrescu, as you are aware, I am the senior investigating officer on this case. At the moment the young woman, Nadia Ripanu, is our only witness. We are now investigating three probable murders, so she is of the utmost importance to us because of the information she has. You may ask her questions about her welfare, about her family, about her treatment by us since we found her but you may not ask her questions about anything to do with the investigation. I'd like you to arrange for a visit from a senior police officer from your country to liaise with us over the case, since part of the gang operates within Romania. Is all of that acceptable to you?'

The official looked puzzled and stroked his nose as he talked. 'But the chief superintendent didn't tell me any of this. I understood I could ask her anything. I do have her best interests at heart.'

'I'm sure you have, but are you a trained police officer, sir?'

He shook his head.

'As I said, I will happily talk about the details of the case to a fellow detective from your country. In fact we need to do so, in order to carry out investigations in Romania. But that is not your role, so please stick to the areas I have explained.'

'I see from the press that two bodies have been found. Are these likely to be Romanian women?'

'The forensic service has only had time to carry out some cursory checks. Full post-mortem examinations will start on Monday, so we won't know until midweek. They'll be looking at dental work and anything that might give us an idea of who they are and where they come from. Tissue has already been sent off for DNA analysis, and we should get those results back in a day or two. I'm assuming that the bodies are those of young women from Eastern Europe but I'm not releasing that to the press until we are sure. That information is just between ourselves, Mr Dodrescu. Please don't mention it to anyone. Is there anything else you wish to know before I collect Nadia?'

He shook his head and Dunnett nodded. Sophie went to collect the two women. Her words might possibly have generated some friction, but she was the one in operational charge. They would play by her rules or not at all.

She returned with Nadia and Mary Porter. Dunnett sat at Tom Rose's desk, which suited Sophie. The rest of them would be grouped around a low table. Sophie placed Nadia opposite Dodrescu, with Mary Porter on one side and herself on the other. Seated at the desk, Dunnett was a mere spectator. Sophie wondered if the ACC had told him to stay out of her hair.

'How have you found your medical care?' Dodrescu asked.

'It has been beyond what I expected. I was kept in overnight on Wednesday, and I have seen the doctor for an examination at the hospital every day. He tells me that I am healing well. I have a special cream for my injuries and tablets to help me sleep. I have no complaints. Everyone has been so good to me.'

'And your accommodation? Where are you staying and is it satisfactory?'

'I am in safe police care. My room is lovely and I have made a good friend. Someone is with me at all times. I feel safe.'

'Can you give me the names of the other young women who were with you, Nadia?'

The girl looked at Sophie.

'The list of names is already with your embassy's undersecretary for police matters, Mr Dodrescu. Surely you have it?' Sophie said.

'Yes, you are right. I do. I wondered if Nadia had remembered anything different about them,' said Dodrescu.

'We should not be testing Nadia, Mr Dodrescu. We are here merely to satisfy the embassy that Nadia is being well looked after. Don't translate that, Mary. If you'd like to continue?'

'Have you been well treated by the police?'

'Yes. They have been very kind. The chief inspector has been so thoughtful. I could not have asked for better treatment. I just worry about the other girls who came with me.'

'We are doing everything in our power to find them, Nadia. Trust me,' said Sophie.

Dodrescu asked a few more rather pointless questions to satisfy the bureaucratic needs of interstate cooperation. He declared himself satisfied with the care that Nadia was getting. He told Sophie that he would be back in two days' time with Nadia's mother. He and Dunnett left the office.

'I can't wait to see her,' Nadia said. 'But I won't know what to say to her. How can I tell her what happened to me? I am so ashamed.' She started crying.

Dunnett popped his head around the door.

'What are your immediate plans?' he asked Sophie.

'We're narrowing down the list of places they could have moved to, by contacting agencies that rent out old farmhouses. We should get the list down to a couple by later today, then we'll visit them. We're also ploughing through photofits, trying to identify the men that were at the abandoned farm. We've contacted most of the CID departments across the south and asked them to look out for Romanian girls on the streets. We might be able to get more information by speaking to some of them.'

'Fine. I'll be on my way.'

He looked at Nadia's tear-streaked face and raised his eyebrows.

'She's worried about telling her mother the full story of her ordeal. Maybe you could skip the details until she sees her. I may need a session with her using our interpreter so that I can explain the situation calmly.' She turned to Mary Porter. 'Can you come in again on Monday, Mary? I know it's a lot to ask, but I have no choice if Nadia's mother is coming then.'

'Yes, I can manage that. But later in the week may be more difficult. I have a series of seminars and lectures to give from Tuesday onwards. I'll only be able to spare a few hours here and there.'

'That's fine. Monday should be the last of the big sessions. And I'm so grateful for what you've done. Neil, we owe Doctor Porter an enormous vote of thanks. She's been just perfect. I thought you'd like to know.'

'Of course. I'll be off. See you tomorrow.' He disappeared.

Sophie turned back. Mary Porter was smiling at her, blushing slightly.

'It's time I said it, Mary. I've changed my mind about you. For what it's worth, this mere DCI holds you in high esteem.'

She held out her hand. Porter took it, then leaned forward and gave Sophie a quick peck on the cheek.

'Thank you,' she said. 'You're a very lucky person, you *mere DCI*. You inspire such loyalty in the people who come into contact with you. Though luck is probably the wrong word to use. Whatever you've got, I'm glad I've been exposed to it.' She glanced at her watch. 'I'd better be off. What time do you want me on Monday?'

'I'll let you know but I doubt it will be before late morning. Have a good rest tomorrow, Mary. You've earned it.'

Sophie took Nadia to the hospital for her daily check-up, and then drove her back to her house for lunch with Martin and Jade. Nadia remained there while Sophie returned to the incident room in Swanage in order to clear up a backlog of paperwork.

Later that afternoon she was sitting in her office, trying to gather her thoughts, when Barry Marsh hurried in.

'We've traced two possible locations, ma'am. Both are small farmhouses close to the shore, in similar settings to Brookway, but further north. Both have been rented out in the past week or two as holiday lets, the first for a month with an option to stay longer, the second for a fortnight.'

'Good work. We'll pay them a visit, but not without backup and a watertight plan. That includes having the marine section out in the harbour to watch for any escape attempt by boat, and a firearms unit nearby. I'll warn HQ. Get us some coffee, Barry, while I'm on the phone. Then we'll sit down and produce a plan. We'll go to the one with the longer letting first.'

* * *

Everything was in place. The first farm was to be visited at eight in the evening. Sophie, Marsh and Melsom drove along the farm track, followed by an armed unit and a backup team. Both remained out of sight as Melsom drove into the small yard and stopped, with the car facing the front door of the farmhouse. Sophie and Marsh climbed out, leaving Melsom in the car. They wore bulletproof jackets under their coats. A uniformed officer from the backup squad came with them. There was a single vehicle parked in the yard — a blue Range Rover with a small trailer alongside it. The three officers took a good look around before walking to the door. Sophie spoke into her radio and waited until she was sure that the squad members were in their agreed positions. She rang the doorbell. Footsteps approached along a wooden floor. The man who answered the door was middle-aged with greying, sandy hair.

'Yes?'

Sophie held up her warrant card. 'Sorry to bother you, sir. I'm DCI Sophie Allen from Dorset police. I wonder if you've seen any unusual activity in the area over the past few days.'

'Nothing out of the ordinary, no. What kind of activity do you mean?'

'Boat movements close to the shore of the harbour. Unexpected vehicles using the approach track. That type of thing. How many of you are staying here?'

'Myself, my wife, our daughter and her family. Four adults and three children. And as I said, there's been nothing unusual.'

81

'May we come in, sir? It would be very helpful if we could have a quick look around.'

He stepped aside, looking rather puzzled. Marsh spoke into his radio and followed Sophie into the house. The uniformed man waited outside. They followed the tenant down a short hallway and through a doorway into a large farmhouse kitchen. A small group of adults and children were seated around the central table playing a board game.

He introduced the two detectives.

'Two police officers, everyone.' He turned to Sophie. 'This is my wife, Janet, my daughter Karen, her husband, Peter, and their two older children, Amelia and Rachel. Their little brother, Lawrence, is asleep upstairs. I'm Kenneth Jackson.'

'Cluedo, I see,' said Sophie. 'So we haven't got here in time to prevent the murder, then?' She smiled at the two girls.

'I know who did it,' replied the younger one, solemnly. 'But that's all. I don't know where. Can you help me?'

'That would be against the rules. I'd probably get told off by my chief constable if I gave you any clues.'

The girls giggled.

'How long have you been here?' Sophie asked, turning back to Jackson.

'Just since the weekend.'

'Is this about those farm murders?' asked his wife. 'It's been in the news since this morning. I wondered if it was a bit ghoulish playing Cluedo this evening, but the girls insisted. Are you visiting all the farms in the area?'

'It's partly reassurance, Mrs Jackson,' Sophie said. 'But I'd really appreciate a quick look around the other rooms if you don't mind.'

'But not the room Larry's asleep in,' added the daughter.

'Just a peep.'

'And if we refuse?' Karen's response was sharp. Her cheeks coloured slightly.

'Please don't. I'd have to consider returning later with a warrant. Don't think you are under suspicion, because that isn't the case. But I do need to check the rooms and the out-houses. I promise not to wake him.'

The detectives looked briefly into every room. A few minutes later they were back outside, thanking the Jacksons for their cooperation. Two of the uniformed officers had already checked the barn and outbuildings.

'I bet that added a buzz to their holiday,' Marsh said as they drove away. 'They'll probably be talking about it for months. And they didn't even know that the hit squad was lurking in the shadows. They'd have had a fit if they'd spotted those guys.'

'Now, let's move on up the coast to the second place. We'll do it the same way. Can you radio the boat and tell them what's happened? We're moving on to Marsh Copse Farm for a ten o'clock visit.'

* * *

As the police vehicles turned off the main road onto the lane leading to Marsh Copse Farm, they saw a dull red glow in the night sky ahead of them. At the same time they received a garbled radio message from headquarters. There was some kind of emergency at the farm, but as yet there were no details. They arrived to find it was ablaze, several fire appliances were hosing the front wall and roof of the building. The detectives hurried across to the senior fire officer. Sophie flashed her warrant card.

'How bad is it?' she asked.

'Could be worse. It would have burned down completely if it hadn't been for your guys spotting it and phoning in double quick.'

She looked blankly at him. 'Who?'

'Your guys on the police boat. Apparently they'd just arrived offshore to keep an eye on the place when they saw the first flicker of flames. They came haring up here while they radioed in. They managed to get in the back of the building and close some internal doors before the fire took hold. They didn't think there was anyone still inside.'

83

'Where are they now?' she asked.

He pointed in the direction of a group of dark-clad figures standing beside one of the support vehicles.

She turned to Marsh. 'Let's go and find out what's going on, Barry. The rest of you wait here.'

They walked across and found the two officers sipping coffee.

'I hear that you two are to be congratulated,' Sophie said. 'The fire chief thinks your quick thinking probably saved the farmhouse from total destruction. Can you tell me what happened?'

'We'd just arrived in the boat and were lying a couple of hundred yards offshore,' replied the woman officer. Her face was flushed and blotched with particles of soot. 'Unlike the last place, this one is very visible from the water. We could see it silhouetted against the skyline. I had the binoculars out and was sweeping across the building when I saw light flickering. I asked Joe here to take a look and he guessed straight away what was going on.'

'I've seen it before, ma'am. Flickering light in several windows, getting stronger. So I phoned in for the fire service, then reported to HQ while Mary brought the boat into shore. We hoped that HQ would tell you, but our first priority was to check the place over to see if anyone was still inside.'

'And?'

'We don't think so. The back of the building seemed okay, so we broke down the door and did a quick recce. The worst of the fire was at the front, facing the harbour, so we shut as many doors as we could and called out to see if anyone was trapped. Joe ran up some stairs at the back to check a few rooms but didn't find anything. I tried to use a fire extinguisher that was in the back kitchen, but it was no real use. It was really blazing by then and we had to get out. The thing is, ma'am, there was a reek of petrol about the place. My guess is that it was deliberate, and some of the fire crew agree because of the way the fire's spread. It's in several pockets apparently.'

'I can't be sure that there was no one in there, but between us we must have checked well over half the rooms, and there was no answer to our calls.'

'You did brilliantly, both of you. It just frightens me that you may have put your own lives in danger.'

'I don't think we did, ma'am,' the male officer replied. 'We're both pretty cautious types, and there's a lot of stone in that old building. Not many carpets, rugs, bits of furniture or other stuff. I'd guess that the main damage will be around the front stairwell and I didn't go near that.'

'Well, get yourselves home now and get a report to me tomorrow please. Include anything at all that you think might be useful for the investigation, and phone me if you remember anything important. I don't suppose you caught sight of any movement when you arrived?'

'No. My guess is that they'd just left.'

Sophie sent most of the police team home. The fire was now largely out and several of the men were getting kitted up for a search of the building. She and Marsh waited until the search was over. There were no bodies inside the building, just the charred remains of furniture and fittings at the seat of the blaze.

The rest of the fire team carried out a check of the sheds and outhouses. The buildings were all empty.

One of the firemen said, 'There was some food in the fridge and bits and pieces of clothing in some of the rooms but there really wasn't much. We did find one odd thing, though. Someone had written two words across the wall of one of the upstairs rooms. It says "help us". We think it's written in lipstick.'

Sophie looked at the fire chief. 'At the moment this place is your baby. But I'd like a criminal forensic team here as soon as you're happy that it's safe for them.' She turned to Marsh. 'We nearly got them, Barry. I could kick myself. My guess is that we might have just arrived in time if we'd visited this place first. I wonder what put the wind up them?'

'Maybe when the news about the bodies at Brookway hit the TV screens,' said Marsh. 'I wonder if that means they didn't expect them to be discovered? But surely they must have known we'd find them sooner or later? It's standard procedure to bring in a dog in a farm search.'

'You're overestimating the average criminal mind, Barry. Thinking isn't their strong point. Most crime is opportunistic and short term. And that's the way most criminals think. There are some smart scams around, but they'll always be in the minority. And those thugs you and I saw a couple of days ago are most certainly not in that class.' She yawned. 'Let's go home. We'll leave a couple of the uniformed crew here to stand guard overnight and I'll arrange for the forensic unit to get here early tomorrow morning. We'll need to do a check on the surrounding properties.' She turned to the fire officers. 'Thanks, everyone. You've all done a brilliant job.'

CHAPTER 9: BLOSSOM QUITS

Saturday Morning, Week 1

'How do you fancy a move to Weymouth, Blossom?'

Blossom looked across the sparsely furnished office at Ricky.

'Don't really know it. I've been there a few times, but all I remember is the girl I was with. She was a cracker, so maybe my memories are a bit vague. Can't remember much about the town. Why? Is it on the cards? Because we've got to get out of here, and as soon as fucking possible. This place stinks.'

Ricky settled his flickering eyes on the man facing him. The short, squat figure always seemed about to explode into violence. 'You're not happy, are you?'

'No, I'm fucking not. This is meant to be a business. What's been going on lately, it's just too much. Bodies being dug up by the cops? A body left on top of a rock? What's all that about? And look what's happened. Having to move our shit out of two perfect places. You need to get on top of it, Ricky. It has to stop. We'll have cops breathing down our necks for months now.'

'Well, this new place we've spotted will be perfect. We can lie low for a while, then restart when things have calmed down. Charlie's chopped the link with the guys in Romania in case they start talking. There's no way they can finger us now. He had a plan ready in case that end of things fell through.'

'What about the girls here? What happens to them?'

'There are two ideas. We could run them ourselves once we're in Weymouth. I've got a contact in the town who could look out for a good place to base them. Or we could shift them on somewhere, like you suggested. We were thinking of somewhere in Wolverhampton or that area. Charlie's still got contacts there.'

'It's a better idea than taking them with us to Weymouth,' said Blossom. 'I don't fancy being a pimp again. Let's face it, none of us knows fuck all about it now. It's been years since me and Charlie ran girls ourselves. Everything'll have changed. Listen, do you fancy going to the pub? Just for a quiet chat, I mean. Just you and me? Things need to be said.'

* * *

Blossom stood at the counter watching the barmaid return his partner's change. It was only twenty pence, for God's sake. Why not let her keep it? But that had always been Ricky's way with money. He could remember once seeing him scrabble around on his hands and knees in thick, wintry fog because he'd thought he'd seen a fifty pence coin lying beside a muddy path. It had turned out to be a milk bottle top. Understandable in a kid, but not a grown man.

They took their pints across to a table in a secluded corner.

'All the better for dark skulduggery,' Blossom said.

'What? I've never understood you, Blossom. I never will. I've always thought you're too fucking smart to be in this line of work. But you can be a prize prick at times. You do know that we sometimes feel like topping you?'

'Why doesn't that surprise me?' Blossom downed half of his beer in one long swallow. 'Charlie would never let you do it. The two of us go back too far.'

Ricky grunted. 'He thinks the outfit wouldn't survive without you. He says when you add it all up, you're the one who does the hard graft. We'd have to find someone to replace you, and he says they wouldn't be half as good.'

'And what do you say?'

'Just stop riling me, Blossom.' Ricky picked at a spot on his nose as he spoke.

'I don't rile you, Ricky. Not like you make out. I just tell you what I think. When you've done something stupid, I tell you. What the fuck's wrong with that? I used to do the same with Charlie.'

'Yeah, but you two grew up together. You have a bond. To me, you just sound as if you're always whinging.'

'I can see where this is going, so I may as well say it right now. Why did you have to kill that lad, Ricky? All our trouble started then. If I'd known what was going through your head, I'd never have gone back over to France and left you to manage things. It felt like I arrived back in the middle of a hurricane. And Charlie would never have put up with it, not in the old days, not when Hazel was alive. So what's changed?'

'You're pushing your luck.' Ricky leant forward to spit the words into Blossom's face. His knuckles clenched.

'Fucking sit down, you pillock. What are you going to do? Try and land one on me here? It's me, Blossom, not some lowlife skank-head. You've had years of seeing what I can do to people, and what people can't do to me. But Charlie knows I don't do violence without a reason. We've survived because we haven't made too many enemies. People trust us. They'll do business with us, whatever that business is. Girls, protection, fencing, whatever. All the other guys know us, and they know me. My name means something. But now all that's changed. They'll all be wondering. So what is the story behind those bodies? I need to know.'

There was a pause. Ricky said, 'We made some snuff movies.'

'Oh, Jesus. I'm out of here.'

Blossom finished his beer and headed for the door. He walked across to the quayside and stood looking out across the wind-ruffled water, his insides churning. Ricky joined him but Blossom didn't look at him. He continued to stare across the harbour to the Purbeck hills beyond the south shore.

'I was out of it, Blossom. I was taking stuff that Smiffy got for me. I didn't know what was going on and I didn't want to. It was Barbu's idea and Charlie went along with it. I'm starting to get it together now. I know it was a mistake.'

Blossom turned to him. He looked up at the pale face as if seeing it for the first time.

'A mistake? Is that all you can say about it? Well, maybe it's just too late.' He looked into those cold eyes. 'It's the murders, Ricky. You know how I feel about killing. It's always been a step too far for me. And now you tell me that you killed them just to satisfy your sick wish to film it and flog the footage to other sick minds? I might be bad, but I'm not a pervert. I thought I knew you both. We've been hanging around together for so long. Now, with all this, I wonder if I ever did. And Charlie must have gone sicker in the head than I thought. He wouldn't have done it while Hazel was alive. Well, I've had enough. Count me out from now on.'

He turned away and walked back along the quayside in the direction of their temporary base. He didn't see Ricky take his mobile phone out and make a call.

* * *

Five minutes later Ricky sauntered into the cold, damp warehouse.

'Where is he?' he asked Smiffy.

'He hasn't come back yet.'

'What? But where else would he go? He'd only just left me when I phoned you. What the fuck is he up to?'

Ricky's phone rang. He looked at the display.

'Hello, Blossom.'

'Just to let you know I won't be back. I guessed you'd arrange a little Ricky and Barbu type welcome party for me when I got back. Well, I'm not that stupid. But don't think I'm out of your hair just yet. Just to warn you, I've got my eye on you. And on the rest of them. I expect to see those girls delivered safe and sound to wherever you decide to offload them. If they end up buried or dumped at sea I'll know, and I'll find a way of getting to you. If you do everything by the book, as we planned, I'll be off your back. Don't try and trace me, Ricky. Remember — if the girls stay alive, I don't go to the cops. And say goodbye to Charlie for me, will you? We go back a long way and we had some good times together.'

The call ended.

'Fuck,' Ricky said to no one in particular. 'He guessed. He must have had this planned, and kept his car nearby.'

'What did he say?'

'We offload the girls in the normal way. He's fucking paranoid about us killing any of them. He says he'll be watching us.'

'What's got into him? Why has he turned into such a goody-two-shoes all of a sudden?'

'Charlie said Blossom always had this thing about what he calls "unnecessary violence." He's got a soft spot for women. Always has. You've seen what he can do with his fists. He can afford to be picky. Working with him has always been a bit of a bastard, he's always been an oddball. But he got on well with Charlie's wife, Hazel. They were cousins.'

'I always wondered why Charlie stuck with him. There's a word that describes someone like him, sort of snooty and picky at the same time.'

'Charlie and Blossom came down from the Midlands together a long time ago, along with Hazel. And the word you're looking for is fastidious. That's what Hazel used to say about him.'

'Yeah, that's it. How can a fucking hood be fas-ti-dious? When he lost his rag he was more violent than anyone else I know. Even Barbu kept his distance.'

'It was all controlled, Smiffy. That's what he'd say. He used to go on and on about it. Controlled violence. It was his answer to everything. But I've got to give it to him, it worked for years. No one dared cross him. We've put up with him because of it.'

'Maybe it's better this way. Fewer of us. What does he mean, we've got to leave the girls alone? They're not softened up enough yet. Whoever we push them on to won't be best pleased.'

Ricky looked troubled. 'We can't keep them here. Blossom was right on one thing. This place does stink. Maybe we'll move to the new place Charlie's found, keep them there and then send them on their way when we think they're ready. I still wonder about running them ourselves.'

'We've got a few days yet, haven't we? It'll take that long for you to find someone to offload them onto. We could work on them here for a bit longer. Leave it to me and Barbu.'

'We don't have a few days, you twat. Blossom's playing his own game now, and I don't trust the bastard. He's been up to something for months, and I was too mixed up to spot it. We move to Weymouth right now if Charlie gives the go-ahead. Blossom could be phoning the cops this minute.'

* * *

They reached the lonely cottage outside Weymouth late in the afternoon. Yet again they had loaded everything into several vans and made a hurried exit. Their human cargo was sick and weak, but the girls were allowed no recovery time. Barbu and Ricky fed them crack cocaine. They were gradually converting them into addicts. Once out on the streets they would be obedient to their pimps. The feistiest of the girls still resisted. They silenced her with vicious punches to her face and kicks to her body. One of the men would hold her down while the other poured a Rohypnol-laced drink down her throat. After that, she was easy to manipulate. The happy, optimistic bunch that had set out from Romania only a few weeks earlier were now pale, grubby and half starved. Their faces had a perpetual expression of dulled hopelessness and fear, but at least the rapes had stopped temporarily. Even their guards had become exhausted by the continuous, rushed moves from one place to another and just wanted to eat and sleep.

'Where does Charlie find these places?' asked Smiffy. The gap between his teeth made him whistle slightly.

'It was Hazel. She found them all years ago. Her list is out of date now, but she knew loads of people, and Charlie's just going through them. This place'll be okay. It's warm. A bit cramped, but we'll cope,' Ricky said.

'Why doesn't Charlie spend more time with us? It's only you, me and Barbu now. There's no Stefan, and Blossom's legged it. It's gonna be hard keeping it all together.'

'Stop fucking whinging. It's not as if these slags are hard work, is it? They're out of their heads half the time. It'll be harder once we start working them.'

'When's that gonna be?'

'Maybe next week. We'll see how we get on. If we need more help we'll get it. But that means less dosh for us. Now Blossom's fucked off, his share of the money comes back into the pot. You didn't think of that, did you? As far as I'm concerned, we're better off without him. Prickly bastard.'

CHAPTER 10: A NEW FRIEND

Saturday Afternoon, Week 1

Anger, frustration and bewilderment all swirled around in Blossom's head. He stood at the window of his small bedsit, looking out at the pouring rain. He felt safe here. He'd never told the Duff family, or anyone else, about this small bolthole near Bournemouth's attractive town centre gardens. His tiny apartment was at the top of an old building. The other flats were all much larger and the occupants included an attractive, brunette accountant; a middle-aged male college lecturer; a newly qualified doctor; a dapper store manager and the rather overweight owner of a betting shop. He made sure he got on well with all of them. He always greeted them with a smile and a cheerful remark whenever he passed them on the stairs. This was his home, alongside normal people, not the twisted and mentally stunted types he had to work with.

Blossom had bought the small flat two years previously. Once Hazel's illness became serious and she was incapable of moving out of her bed, he began to realise that she was the lynchpin of the whole operation. He guessed that things would probably head downhill once she died, hence his decision to buy the flat. He'd rarely stepped outside the twisted criminal world, and buying this little place had proved to be a pleasant surprise. Normal people, doing normal things. His neighbours chatted about the weather, the flower displays in the landscaped gardens, the state of the economy, and so on. Violence played no part in their lives. They were all innocents, and Blossom thought it was a wonderful thing.

He'd drifted into crime directly after leaving school. He'd been sucked into a life that revolved around lawbreaking and violence, and had never left it. The people here were a revelation to him, and he loved them. He was particularly fond of Jennie, an attractive accountant with a ponytail who had moved in only a few months ago. She was just a wonder. Blossom's eyes twinkled at her whenever they met, and she smiled back. Not that he had any hope with her. He wasn't stupid. He'd noticed how she juggled her evening dates between two boyfriends. He kept an eye out for her, to make sure she was safe. He also looked out for Agnes, the elderly widow who lived on the ground floor. She was a dear, and so trusting. She liked the fact that he was called Blossom. It was a nickname he'd been given as a teenager, when he'd had to read his only poem out loud to his class. He'd loved that poem, and so had his teacher, but the rest of his class had mocked him. He'd told Agnes that part of the story but not the rest. The ensuing fist fight had sealed his future. He discovered that he had a natural way with his fists. He seemed to be immune from any damage his opponents tried to inflict. Unlike his nickname, the punches and kicks just bounced off his stocky frame.

For a time he'd drifted between various unambitious and loose-knit gangs. Then Hazel, his rebel, tearaway cousin, had introduced him to her fiancé. Tall, bony Charlie Duff and short, stocky, Blossom Sourlie were made for each other. Blossom provided the muscle and Charlie the plans. Or so it seemed. Then Hazel had been struck down by her illness and Charlie's nephew, Ricky, had started to play a more prominent role. Uncle and nephew began to make decisions that were just plain crazy. Blossom started saving hard, adding to the money left to him when his mother died. Now he owned this little flat and was able to walk away from the Duff gang. As he stood at the window, looking out across the rain-sodden flower beds, his anger faded and he felt something he hadn't experienced for many years. Possibility. He could start afresh. He'd have to look for some kind of work. A bouncer at a nightclub? Or would that attract the kind of trouble he wanted to avoid?

The heavy rain shower was passing. Blossom decided to go out for some fresh air. He'd walk down through the Winter Gardens to the shore. Out in the fresh air, watching the pounding waves. Just what he needed. He was on his way down the last flight of stairs when Jennie, the ponytailed accountant, emerged from her flat.

'Hello, Blossom. Haven't seen you for a while. If you're going to town, I'll come with you.'

They walked out of the front door together and crossed the road into the gardens.

'So what have you been up to?' she asked.

'Sorting out some work problems. I know I haven't been around much recently, but I'm here for a while now.'

'All okay, I hope? I think you said you worked in private security. Is that right?'

'Yeah. I'm changing my job, though. I've had enough of that crew. Is there a word for lying, cheating, two-faced gits?'

'None that describes it the way you said. It sounds as though you're better off out of it, if that's how you feel. Have you found a new place?'

'Not yet. I'll need to start looking soon, but I'm fancy free at the mo.'

He looked across to the stream flowing through clumps of grass and bedraggled-looking shrubs. The water was almost overflowing its banks.

'That was heavy rain this morning.'

'Got to get used to the occasional wet spell, Blossom, living on the coast. Listen, are you doing anything this evening?

I've been invited out to a bar in town. They're people I don't care too much for and I could do with some company.'

'What about your boyfriend?'

'Which one?' Jennie laughed. 'I know you know. Everyone in the house does. Believe it or not, they're both away at the moment. I could do with someone reliable with me this evening. But don't get the wrong idea, Blossom. Two boyfriends are enough.'

He grinned. 'We wouldn't fit. I'm only five two. And what are you? Six foot or more? Thanks, I'll come. It'll be great to get out.'

That evening Blossom sat in a bistro, chatting happily to the kind of people he might have considered mugging not so long before. He also landed a job. A close friend of Jennie's owned a small business and was desperate to hire someone reliable to fill in as a security guard while their usual watchman was in hospital. Blossom could start the following Monday.

'Not bad,' said Jennie, as they clambered into a taxi for the short trip home. 'I enjoyed it more than I expected, and you landed a job. We ought to celebrate. Coffee and chocolates at my place?'

CHAPTER 11: ANAGRAM

Sunday, Week 2

'Any luck with the photofits, Barry?'

Sophie had expected to be first in on a Sunday morning, but her DS was already present. He sat hunched over his computer with piles of folders and documents littered across the floor beside him. She perched on the corner of his worktable.

'It's possible, ma'am. There was no complete fit, but several looked vaguely similar. The most promising is the taller one we talked to. Do you want to check?'

He brought up three images on the screen.

'I see what you mean. I'm not sure about the first. The head is too bony, but I'd agree that the other two are possibilities. Isn't that last one a bit young, though?'

Marsh looked at the date of the picture.

'It was taken more than ten years ago. He was lifted for drug dealing and suspected extortion.'

'What happened?'

'Suspended sentence for the drugs. The other charges were dropped because of insufficient evidence. One of the witnesses disappeared and the case fell apart.'

'So who is he? Where was he based?'

Marsh ran a hand through his tousled red hair. 'Richard Frimwell. Based in Bournemouth. But the address on his file no longer exists. It's been redeveloped.'

'So we don't know where he is now?'

'Well, it's possible he might be in Poole, down near Sandbanks, but I can't be sure. I've got a possible address.'

'Well, if it is him, he's moved up in the world. Or made some cash. What about the other one? He looks closer to the right age.'

'Someone called Simon Brooks. But as far as I can tell, he's locked up at the moment. That's still to be confirmed though.'

'Any luck with the short, thickset guy we saw? He was a bit older, wasn't he?'

'Nothing at all in any of the official records. I phoned a colleague over in Poole and he reckons it sounds like someone they've heard about but not come across. Apparently they've picked up whispers of someone who looks like him who goes under the name of Blossom, of all things. But he's never been lifted, and they know nothing else about him. No name, no address, no details at all. But they suspect he's a hard man who just has to show his face and things get done.'

'Do you have an address for the younger one?'

Marsh nodded.

'Well, let's pay him a visit. I need to be gone by midday. We're visiting my grandparents in Gloucester.'

'I thought you came from Bristol, ma'am.'

'I've just discovered my grandparents from my father's side, Barry. It's why I've been a bit preoccupied all week. And there's an awful lot more that I've found out that's left me reeling. I'll give you the short version in the car.'

* * *

There was no answer at the small villa, and the place looked closed up.

'Let's take a stroll round the back,' Sophie suggested.

They walked around the bungalow, peering in the windows. There were no signs of life, but the property was furnished. Sophie knocked at the back door but there was still no response. Marsh looked around the garden. It didn't have much in it, but it was tidy.

'We're being watched,' he said. 'Man in the garden on the right. I'm not sure he wants to be seen. Maybe he doesn't want anyone to think he's a nosy neighbour.'

The villa next door was significantly larger, with a bigger garden. The man was watching them through a gap in the hedge. He was standing several yards back, so it was difficult to make out his features clearly, but he was tall.

'You know how I love nosy neighbours, Barry. Let's have a word.'

Marsh waved and they went over to the fence.

'Good morning. We're from the police. We're trying to trace the owner of this property. Can you help us?' he asked.

'Not sure I can,' came the reply. 'They're away a lot and I hardly know them.'

'Is the owner a Mr Richard Frimwell?'

'Yes, but as I said, I haven't spoken to them much.'

'You said "they". So if it is Mr Frimwell, he's with a wife or partner?'

'I think so. But I don't know for sure.'

Marsh took the photo out of his pocket. 'Could you just have a look at this photo for us, please? I need to be sure we are talking about the same man.'

'He's older than that,' said the neighbour.

'Yes, this is an old photo. But could it be the same man, eight or nine years ago?'

'Hard to say.' The man scratched his head and smoothed his thinning hair. 'Could be, but people change with age, don't they?'

Sophie, silent up to now, said, 'You have a nice garden, sir. It looks oriental with that little pagoda by the pond and the small courtyard in front of it. Did you design it?'

'Hazel. My wife.' The voice was flat.

'So she's the green-fingered one, is she?'

'She died three years ago. I pay someone to keep it up now.' He turned to Marsh. 'Is that all? I need to get on. Do you have ID? Anyone could say they're police.'

Marsh flipped open his warrant card. 'DS Barry Marsh. This is DCI Sophie Allen.'

There was a pause. 'I didn't mean to be rude,' the man said to Sophie.

'No, of course not. Your wife had a real eye for garden design, sir. You must miss her, Mr . . . ?'

'Black. Of course I miss her.' His voice was dismissive.

'Barry, could you look out a contact card, please?' Sophie turned back to the neighbour. 'We need to speak to Mr Frimwell quite urgently. Could you contact us if you see that he's returned? Or if there's anything else you think might be of help?'

Sophie looked again at the little garden within a garden. She began to intone:

'No more footsteps in the moonlight.

The pavilion door lies ajar,

but the only sound is of dry leaves rustling in the court-yard . . .'

'What?' said the neighbour.

'It's from an old Chinese poem. It's about the loss of a loved one. It always makes me think of a small courtyard in front of a pagoda.'

He looked at her as if she were mad. The two detectives made their way back around the villa to the small front garden.

'What was that all about, ma'am?'

'My mum says it was one of my father's favourite poems. It's based upon some old Chinese writings, and is about the absence the poet feels when he revisits the courtyard after the loss of his lover. Telling you about my dead father must have put it into my mind. When I saw that little Chinese area with the dried leaves and he told me that his wife had died, the words just popped into my head.'

Sophie looked at the neighbour's house.

'Look at the house name, Barry.'

'Chez Lahar Lei. It sounds kind of Chinese,' said Marsh.

'His wife's name was Hazel. It's an anagram of the words Hazel and Charlie. Don't you think he was a bit cagey? He was on edge for some reason.'

'You were quoting Chinese poetry at him, ma'am. That would confuse the best of us. Maybe you're just too suspicious.'

'Goes with the job, Barry.' She glanced at her watch. 'Let's get back. I've got to get to Gloucester this afternoon, and we still need an hour or so back at the station.'

She spent the rest of the morning with Marsh, planning their strategy for the next few days. They intended to speak to as many street girls as possible, looking for a Romanian connection.

Sophie drove back to Wareham shortly before noon. Lydia Pillay had just arrived, ready to take charge of Nadia for the rest of the day. They had a hurried lunch together and Sophie, Martin and Jade set off on the two hour drive to Gloucester. Sophie slept most of the way.

CHAPTER 12: CHARLIE DUFF

Sunday Morning

The girls were still asleep. Smiffy left them and went down to the kitchen to make some tea and toast. He looked out of the window at the countryside around the isolated cottage. The trees of a small, wooded vale glinted as the winter sun lit the frost on their branches. A crow lazily lifted itself from the ploughed field that lay on the other side of the track, and flew off in the direction of the coast, which could be seen beyond the tree line.

'One thing about the places Charlie finds, they're always pretty.'

Smiffy turned to find Ricky standing behind him.

'It's good, apart from being further away from the coast. But maybe that's not important?'

'No. Charlie's chopped the links with his Romanian contacts until this fucking mess blows over. We won't be bringing any more girls across for a while.'

* * *

Blossom woke from a deep sleep. For a moment he wondered where he was. It had been weeks since he'd last slept in his flat.

He threw off the duvet, slid out and padded to the shower. He dressed and, as they had arranged the previous night, went downstairs to Jennie's apartment. He tapped on the door.

Jennie was wrapped in a towel. 'Be a sweetie and make a pot of tea, would you?'

Blossom walked through to a well-fitted kitchen and filled the kettle. Life had taken a major turn for the better. He switched on the radio and found himself listening to some classical music. He checked the dial. He'd never listened to Radio Three in his life before, and he sat down and let the classical music wash over him. He searched for tea and mugs in the cupboards and took milk from the fridge. He placed the items on a pine table in the middle of the kitchen, then sat waiting. She came in, towelling her hair.

'What's that music?' he asked.

'Umm, sounds like a string quartet, but I don't know which one. Why do you ask?'

'I've never listened to anything like it before. It seems kind of right for my mood. You know, sort of light and airy.'

'Probably Mozart or Haydn by the sound of it.'

'Don't you listen to pop music?'

'Not much. I quite like folk. The boyfriend I had when I was first at university was heavily into the folk scene and I used to tag along. In fact my all-time favourite song is an old one from my parents' time. *The Last Thing on My Mind*? Tom Paxton?'

Blossom looked blank, so she began to sing.

'You've got a lovely voice,' he said.

'It's my middle-class upbringing. Singing and music lessons, brownies and guides, A levels, university. All the usual stuff.'

'I suppose you did accountancy or something?'

'Not at first. I studied medicine, because my parents always wanted me to be a doctor. I made it past the halfway point and then realised I hated every minute of it. So I took a year out, travelled for most of it. When I came back I started a degree in management and accountancy. Much more my type of thing. And that's how I am what I am.'

'What, you mean being a greedy banker and having two boyfriends for the price of one?'

'I've just finished with Paul — the tall one. We started going to one of the local bondage clubs. The deal was that we wouldn't go too far or get too heavily involved with anyone else. But I found out that he'd started meeting someone on the quiet at one of those hard-core London clubs.'

Blossom laughed. 'But you were two-timing him, weren't you?'

'No. Everyone here thinks I was. I quite liked the idea of that sort of reputation, and I played along with it. But James, the other man in my life, is just a very close friend. We go out for meals and to the theatre together, but we're not an item.'

'So there's hope for me yet?'

She smiled. 'Play your cards right and you never know.'

'But I'm not into bondage. I do boxing and I've done a bit of wrestling. I do all kinds of gym exercises, but I couldn't do S&M. It's mostly a bit of a dabbler's lark, isn't it?'

'That's all I wanted, and I kind of enjoyed it while it wasn't too serious. I've always liked being in charge, it suits my bossy nature, I suppose. But Paul was getting in too deep. I was getting worried anyway, even before I found out he was seeing someone in London.'

'My old boss was into it. It was his wife who was keen, but he's been a few times since she died.'

'Was this the guy you described as a two-faced git?'

'That's the one. Charlie Duff.'

'What was his line of work?'

'He does lots of things. He owns a car repair workshop, a couple of rundown hotels, a pub, a couple of second-hand shops, a couple of sex shops and a chain of cafés. It's all shady. He's basically a criminal. And I ended up working for him.'

'Should you be telling me this, Blossom? I'm not sure I want to know, anyway.' She shook her head in amazement. 'I've just helped you get a job as a security manager, for Christ's sake. And now you tell me you've been working in some kind of underworld gang. What have I done?'

'It's all in the past, Jennie. I've been planning this break for some time, ever since I bought my place a couple of years ago. I've had enough of it. There's no honour among thieves, believe me. It's dog eat dog, and the people are all sick in the head.'

'Well, okay. But this is a side of you that I never suspected. It's going to take me a while to get my head around it.' She finished her tea and looked him in the eye. 'Have you thought of going to the police?'

'Yeah. I probably will, but there's a lot I have to think through first.'

'Okay. That's good enough for me for the time being. But don't put it off too long. And let me know when you've done something about it, okay?'

'Message received loud and clear, boss.' He glanced at the clock. 'Do you fancy going out for a big breakfast? I've found a really good café in town.'

'Sounds yummy.'

* * *

Sorina, the youngest of the girls, had become close to Catalina after Nadia had escaped. Now she was worried about her. The previous evening she'd been sick twice in the van, and then had been forcibly drugged by two of the gang members. She was sharing the same bed as Sorina, and had disturbed her several times in the night, tossing and turning. Sorina tiptoed to the window, pulled the curtain aside and glanced out. It was a beautiful scene. The cottage was situated at the head of a shallow valley that led to the coast, several miles to the south. The copses of trees along the valley were coated with frost that glinted silver in the low, morning sunlight.

She returned to the bed. Catalina was flushed, with a sheen of perspiration across her face. She moaned softly. Her breathing didn't seem right. It was laboured, with a pronounced rasp. The younger girl gently placed her hand on her bed-mate's forehead. It was burning. She walked to a sink in the corner of the room, wetted a flannel and gently wiped Catalina's face. The older girl groaned and opened her eyes.

'I don't feel well, Sorina.'

'I will tell the men. Maybe they have some medicines. What is wrong?'

Catalina tried to haul herself up into a sitting position. 'My head is so sore and I feel sick and weak. Maybe it was something in that horrible food they've been giving us.'

'Just stay in bed. I will do what I can.'

A few minutes later the door was unlocked and Barbu's head appeared. The men had got into the habit of unlocking the doors to give each pair of girls ten minutes in the bathroom.

'Catalina is unwell. She has a fever,' Sorina told him.

He came into the room and glanced at the older girl. 'Get her into the bathroom anyway. We'll take a look after breakfast.'

'Can't she stay in bed?' Sorina asked.

'Do what I say.'

She helped Catalina up, and drew back the bedclothes to allow them to air. Barbu waited at the door for the two women to make their way along the narrow landing to the small toilet and washroom. He stood outside while they cleaned themselves. Catalina shivered as they dressed and made their way to the kitchen. She refused all offers of food. She sat with a mug of coffee, shaking. Sorina overheard Barbu talking to one of the gang leaders, but could not understand what he said. One of them placed a small packet of paracetamol tablets on the table in front of Catalina. She shook her head.

'Take them,' Sorina whispered. 'It is the only medicine you will get. They may help you to feel better.' Catalina took two.

'Can she go back to bed?' Sorina asked. 'Please? I am worried about her. She has a fever.'

'Make sure she's better by the end of the week,' Barbu snapped. 'Otherwise it will be the worse for both of you. If you need more medicine, tell me.'

She led Catalina back up the stairs and into their room. She helped her friend back into her nightclothes. Sorina looked through the cupboard shelves and found a couple of old, thin blankets. She lay beside Catalina until her breathing slowed, then she crept out of the room and back downstairs.

'I will look after her,' she told Barbu. 'Some soup would be good at midday. I will take some water for her. She must keep drinking.'

He merely curled his lip and glanced across at Ricky.

'Charlie's going to have a fit,' Ricky said quietly to Smiffy. 'We can't afford to lose another one. Speaking of Charlie, that looks like his car now.'

A black BMW was making its way slowly along the icy road. Ricky unlocked the door and walked out to greet his uncle. His cheery welcome was not reciprocated.

'The fucking cops have been at your place,' said Charlie.

'What? The bungalow?'

'What other place have you got, for Christ's sake?'

'There's nothing there to finger us. It's as clean as a whistle.'

'I should fucking hope so. But they shouldn't have been there at all.'

'Maybe it's for something different. Plods come calling for all kinds of reasons.'

'What do you take me for, you prick? Do you think I'd come rushing across here just because some thicko cop in a shiny hat has paid a visit to ask if we're happy with the colour of their nice new uniforms? It was two clever-clogs detectives. I reckon it was the same two that Blossom said you saw at the farm. A ginger-haired guy and an older woman. And she gave me the fucking creeps. She started talking about Hazel's garden and then spouted poetry at me. She's either off her rocker or playing silly games. What was it she said to you at the farm?'

'Something about sifting information.'

'Well, she's been sifting alright, and you've come to the top of the heap, you pillock. Why didn't you just stay natural and not raise any suspicions? She knows your name now. How long will it be before she gets mine?'

'Did she ask?'

Charlie gave his nephew a withering look. 'Course she fucking asked. But that doesn't mean I told her. And there's no reason to think she'd make any connection between us. But you're gonna have to stay out of sight for a while. Christ, this whole business is disappearing down the plughole.'

'Do you think Blossom's been talking to them?'

'I don't know what to think any more. One thing's for sure, we can't just leave him out there. He knows everything. If he decides to talk, we're all for the high jump. We've got to find him.'

'And?'

'What do you think?'

* * *

Sorina spent the rest of the day looking after Catalina. She visited her every hour and, if she was awake, encouraged her to swallow some water. She spooned some thin soup into her mouth at lunchtime and managed to get her to chew part of a slice of toast. As dusk fell, she helped Catalina out of bed, wrapped her up in a blanket and sat her in a chair while she changed the damp bedclothes. Sorina then sponged her down, dried her and helped her back into bed, giving her another two tablets.

That night Catalina's moans disturbed her, and her own dreams were filled with images of sickness and death. The next day Sorina kept a close watch on her friend.

On the second morning she awoke to the sound of birds fluttering in the eaves. She turned and realised that Catalina was lying on her side, watching her. The older woman smiled weakly.

'Are you feeling better?' Sorina asked.

Catalina nodded. 'But I am still weak. I know what you did for me, Sorina. I am so grateful to you. You are a true friend.'

Sorina smiled happily at her roommate. 'I was so worried about you. And I need you to be well if we are to escape together and join Nadia.'

'We will see,' said Catalina.

CHAPTER 13: THE VISIT TO GLOUCESTER

Sunday Afternoon

Susan and the Allens' elder daughter, Hannah, had arrived together earlier than the rest of the family, travelling direct from Bristol. Sophie hugged her grandparents and introduced them to Martin and Jade.

'Hannah's been telling us all about her life in London at drama college,' James said. 'It sounds fascinating.'

'What are your plans, Jade?' said Florence.

'Medicine. I want to be a doctor. I always have. Do you approve?'

'Oh yes, but why do you ask?'

'I've only just met you, but you are already two of the most important people in my life. I've been thinking about you all week. I couldn't talk to Mum about it because she's been so busy. I don't really know what to say. I'll probably keep putting my foot in it, but I want you to know that I already love you loads.'

'That's just the best thing you could say, Jade.' Florence's voice was quivering.

'A cup of tea, please, someone. I'm gasping.' In her present mood, the last thing Sophie wanted was a repeat of their emotional first meeting.

'On its way,' said Susan. 'And Hannah has bought a big box of cream cakes and scones, so we can have a proper English cream tea.'

'There's something you must know about the three women in my life,' Martin said. 'It's their love of food in general and cream cakes in particular. Sophie might be a senior police officer, but I'm convinced she'd turn to a life of crime if it meant getting into cake shops. Even her love for me only extends as far as the supply of cream buns. I have no illusions.'

Hannah gave him a hug. 'Poor Dad, having to put up with us. But you love us really, don't you? Here, have another cream cake.'

Martin sat down beside his mother-in-law. 'How are you, Susan? You're looking really well.'

'I feel wonderful. I've found the parents I never had. After what my real ones did I could never bring myself to try again with them. It's too late now, they're both gone. But James and Florence are such kind and thoughtful people. It must have done them a world of good to discover all of us, too, after forty years. They're just a bit worried about Sophie's workload.'

'Aren't we all,' he said. 'But you know what she's like. The problem is that there's another huge case at the moment.'

'Is it the one I think it is — those bodies dug up on the farm?'

He nodded. 'That's all I can say. Part of the problem is that she doesn't know how far it extends, and where it might go.' He sipped his tea. 'Let's talk about more cheerful things, shall we?'

His two daughters were having a whispered conversation.

'I wonder what those two are up to?' he said.

They soon found out.

'Ladies and Gentlemen!' announced Hannah. 'Please take your seats for a short entertainment provided by that talented duo, Sisters-a-GoGo, song and dance duo extraordinaire.

We sing. We dance. We sometimes fall over, but so far we've always managed to get up again. This has been long in the planning . . .'

'Three telephone chats in the past two days,' interjected Jade in a stage whisper.

'. . . And short in rehearsals.'

'None,' added Jade. She made a zero sign with her thumb and forefinger.

'But what we lack in practice, we more than make up for in enthusiasm and energy.'

'She supplies the enthusiasm, the cream cakes supply the energy.' Jade suddenly looked puzzled. 'What do I supply, Han?'

'The glamour and charm?'

'That'll do nicely. Shall we start?'

The two girls sang, danced and joked their way through two of their own songs, and finished off with a humorous rendition of "Sisters".

'That was just perfect,' said Florence. 'How on earth did you manage to put it together in so little time?'

'We are just so talented, it doesn't bear thinking about,' answered Jade. 'Sisters-a-GoGo is set to take the world by storm. Eat your hearts out, Beyonce and Lady Gaga, your time is up. Start looking for new jobs now, because—'

'We did it for Mum and Dad's twentieth wedding anniversary party,' interrupted Hannah. 'It was only last year, so it's still fresh in our minds.'

Jade was still striking a dramatic pose, one hand on her hip, the other pointing in the air. She turned and gave her sister an exaggerated glare.

'Spoilsport,' she said.

* * *

After tea they discussed Graham's funeral.

'We've been offered late Thursday morning,' James said. 'There's a slot available because of a postponement. We've

113

been assured that the pathologist will have freed his body by then, so we're thinking of taking that booking. What do you all think?'

They all agreed and began to make plans.

As they were leaving, Florence drew Sophie aside.

'This has been one of the happiest days of my life. I never dreamt I would feel like this ever again. To discover you all and to find what lovely people you are is just so perfect. I can't put into words what it's meant to me.'

'Gran, this hasn't been just a one-off. I hope that we'll see each other regularly. Martin and I would love the two of you to come and stay with us down in Wareham. It will have to wait for a few weeks until my workload has calmed down a bit. But we'll continue to pop up and see you here, if that's alright.'

'I'd love it, more than anything else in the world. Susan's going to call on us later in the week, but she lives a lot closer than you. I already love Hannah and Jade. You must be very proud of them.'

Sophie nodded, tears in her eyes. 'I am. Fiercely proud. That's how my mum described her feelings for me.' She gave Florence a kiss. 'We have to go. I have an early start tomorrow.'

* * *

Soon after they arrived home Sophie received a phone call from Benny Goodall, the pathologist.

'What? Are you sure?' Horrified, she lowered herself into the nearest chair.

'Jesus, Benny. I didn't expect it to be this bad . . . Okay. Will you keep me informed? I'll come across tomorrow if that's alright. We need to talk about this.'

Sophie sat staring at the phone for several minutes. Then she looked up at her husband.

'There are signs of multiple deep knife wounds on both of the bodies, even though there's not a lot of tissue left.

Benny saw nicks to the bones and joints consistent with a sustained knife attack. And each body had similar knife marks on the small bones in the neck. Benny thinks they both had their throats cut to finish them off after they'd been stabbed or slashed.'

CHAPTER 14: INTO THE SAFE HOUSE

Monday, Week 2

Sophie had an early morning meeting with Marsh and Matt Silver, her boss from headquarters. They discussed how to proceed and the deployment of the forces at their disposal.

'Let's summarise, then. What are the main issues we have to deal with?' said Silver.

'One: the body on the rock. We think it's a cousin of Nadia's, called Stefan. We hope that she and her mother will identify it today. Two: the two bodies dug up from the field. We think they were smuggled across from Eastern Europe for prostitution. Why they were killed, we don't yet know, but it looks as if they'd been buried for two or three years. We have to wait for the post-mortem reports to confirm that. Three: follow up on Nadia's recollections. Four: look for street girls from Romania, to see if they were part of the same chain. Five: follow up on the few descriptions we have, particularly the two men Barry and I saw at the first farm. We're pretty sure one of them was a Richard Frimwell but he seems to have vanished. That's suspicious in itself. The other may have been called Blossom of all things, but there's not much else known about him. One of the local constables has also been trying to identify the gap-toothed man, but with no success yet. Six: follow up on the farm bookings. We need to trace whoever organised the rentals, but the information trail is a bit convoluted. Brookway Farm was a long let. They've used it for at least five years, we think. We've traced the lettings agency but the booking was done by phone via another agency. There aren't any names as yet, and no one there can remember a face-to-face meeting. The gang were going to move out anyway, because the owners were selling the property. We've traced them and one of the team has been across to Bournemouth to speak to them. They're an elderly couple and we've discounted them from any involvement. Seven: try to find where the gang has moved to. It'll be somewhere fairly local, I'm sure. But they must have got wind of our plans, because they'd been gone for less than a day when we visited that second farmhouse.'

'More likely they saw on the news that you'd found the bodies. That would have panicked them into moving further out,' said Silver.

'It's proving to be a bit gruesome, Matt. Benny called me yesterday and said that the two women might have been slashed and then stabbed to death. He needs a bit more time to confirm it.'

'Do you need extra help?'

'It would be useful.'

'No problem. The chief's given us carte blanche because of all the publicity. I can get you some extra people.'

'It's quality, not quantity, Matt. I've got Lydia back from her course, and that'll be a bonus. We mostly need people to go through the records, checking details, contacting people and that kind of thing. A dozen will be enough.'

'Fine. Leave it with me. I'll come down as well.' He held up his hand. 'But don't worry, I'm not taking over. You'll still be the boss. It's just that you'll need someone here to keep everything ticking over when you're out and about. And you know how you like to bounce ideas off me. I promise not to get in the way.'

* * *

Nadia was sitting in the incident room with Lydia Pillay when the message came through that her mother had arrived, and would be with them soon.

Sophie called Mary Porter, and she set out immediately.

'Nadia, there's no need to be anxious, surely?' said Lydia.

'But when she knows what they did . . . I wish you do not say. Sometimes I think I would rather die.'

'But if she doesn't know, she won't understand what you went through. And she will guess at some point, even if you deny it. No lies, Nadia. That's what the chief inspector said. We know it will be hard for you both.'

Mary Porter was the first to arrive. The small group assembled in Tom Rose's office, and Sophie had a few minutes to try and calm the distraught girl.

She needn't have worried. As soon as her mother appeared at the door, Nadia flung herself into her arms and the two women stood hugging each other and sobbing. Then Nadia introduced Sophie to her mother, Gabriela, who embraced the detective. She was a short, dark, stocky woman, unlike Nadia, who was slim with fair hair.

Gabriela said, 'Thank you from the depths of my heart for rescuing my daughter.'

Mother and daughter sat next to each other, holding hands. The single sentence Gabriela had spoken proved to be the only English she knew, so Mary Porter translated as Nadia described her ordeal to her mother.

They then discussed Nadia's future plans. Her mother wanted her to go home.

'Mother, I want to stay and help the police,' Nadia said. 'I want to help find the others. I feel so sorry for Sorina. She is only sixteen. She was crying all the time. I must help them search for her. And the doctor here has been so good. The nurse sees me every morning and says I am recovering well. I would not get such good treatment back home. I have made friends with the chief inspector's daughter. But most of all, I owe it to the chief inspector. She is the best person I have ever met. I must help her find the men who did this. Can you understand?'

Sophie said, 'If you can remain for a few days, Gabriela, we can find somewhere for you both to stay. I can put you under police protection so that you have someone with you all the time. Nadia is an important witness. We really want her here to help identify the men who abducted and assaulted her, once we find them. I've been in touch with your own police in Romania, and someone is coming over to visit. They will want to know how Nadia was tricked into coming to England, so that they can look for the gang members still in Romania. I hope that you can stay until then.'

'Please, mother,' said Nadia. 'It would be like a holiday for us. I really want to stay and it would be perfect if you could be with me for a few days.'

Gabriela agreed. They then talked about how the gang operated in Romania. Gabriela talked about how she had been misled. She had thought it too good an opportunity for her daughter to miss, and had encouraged Nadia to take the trip to Britain. Her eyes flashed angrily as she described the men. When they finished, Sophie called in to see Silver, who was still in the incident room. He was able to arrange safe accommodation for Nadia and her mother.

* * *

Sophie drove Gabriela and Nadia to the pathology unit at Dorchester for the identification, along with Mary Porter. Sophie always hated this task, especially when the victim was young. The bewildered look in the eyes of the identifiers, a life lost, potential unrealised, just the absolute waste of it all.

Stefan was the son of Gabriela's older sister. She told them that she'd watched him grow up, had looked after him during her sister's later pregnancies, and had taken him on picnics and outings. And here he was, pale and lifeless, laid out on the cold surface in the mortuary's small viewing room.

'How am I going to tell my sister?' Gabriela whispered.

Sophie had no answer.

* * *

Sophie left Nadia, her mother and Mary Porter with one of the assistants while she went in search of Benny Goodall. He was waiting for her in the main theatre. For once, neither of them had any small talk.

'This is what you need to see, Sophie.' He handed her a theatre mask.

He took her arm and steered her across to a table where a skeleton was laid out under bright lights. He angled one of the lights to illuminate the ribcage, and leant across.

'Look at these nicks on the ribs. Do you see them? This body has fifteen in total. Up here at the top of the thoracic vertebrae there are another three similar marks. There are also signs of similar nicks at the front of the skull, near the nasal cavity.'

'What does it mean, Benny? What could have been happening to cause marks like these?'

'I've only seen such marks once, many years ago when I was still a junior. They were on the body of an old tramp who'd been slashed to death by a group of drunken teenagers. But I've seen photos and I spent time yesterday checking some reference works. I think it's probable that this poor woman was tortured. They used a knife to inflict a succession of cuts, stabs and slashes. She was losing more and more blood as time went on and more wounds were inflicted. The marks on the front of the skull could indicate that she had her nostrils sliced. I shouldn't hazard a guess, not in my position, but the marks on the top vertebrae are consistent with having her throat cut, probably as the final wound.'

'And the other body?'

'Very similar. In all likelihood they were tortured to death using sharp knives. And there's something else,' said Goodall.

'You sound as if the something else is even worse. What could be worse than this, for God's sake?'

'Two of the bodies show similar nicks on the front edge of vertebrae in the sacral and lower lumbar area. They might have had a knife pushed up inside them.'

'Are you sure?'

'I don't know what else could have caused the marks, really I don't. It's just appalling.'

'I don't know what to make of it all, Benny. Why, for God's sake? Why do this? What else have you got to tell me?'

'The autopsy references I checked against were from the States. The bodies were victims of some murders in California where young homeless women were killed on camera. Snuff movies, isn't that what they're called?'

Sophie was silent for several minutes, looking at the two bodies. She took hold of the pathologist's elbow.

'I need to go, Benny. But can I get a coffee first? I need something to calm me down.'

'I'll join you. I really wasn't looking forward to telling you this.'

'Do you know if forensics have managed to get DNA samples yet? A Romanian police officer is due sometime this week. I'd like to keep him informed about progress in identifying these poor girls.'

'We've sent off samples. I don't know when the results are due. If I find out I'll let you know.'

'Thanks, Benny. This is so awful. I just can't take it all in.'

Sophie was silent as they drove to Wareham, and the safe house set aside for Nadia and her mother. Once they had arrived, she told the two women that they were not to leave the house. They could not risk being seen if any gang members happened to be about. She promised to bring Jade over to visit Nadia as often as she could.

As they parted, Nadia flung her arms around Sophie.

'I can never thank you enough for what you've done for me. I wonder if I should change my plans and become a police officer like you. You are such a good person.'

Sophie smiled at her. She said nothing about the anguish gnawing away at her own heart.

* * *

Back in Swanage, Sophie said goodbye to Mary Porter, who agreed to return at short notice if she was required.

'Maybe we can remain friends?' Mary said.

'Yes, I'd like that. It's difficult for me to think about anything other than the investigation at the moment, but once it's over we could meet up. Maybe an evening out?'

'You're on. Leave it with me.' She gave Sophie a peck on the cheek.

Sophie was only left to her thoughts for a few minutes before Jimmy Melsom interrupted her.

'We've had a bit of a curious report come in, ma'am,' he said. 'It's from an old resident of Studland.'

'Do you mean old as in elderly or old as in long-standing, Jimmy?'

'Both. He's in his seventies, I think, and has lived in the village since the year dot. He said that something like that first body happened once before. Up on top of the Agglestone, I mean. But it wasn't a person. He says that about twenty-five years ago they found the body of a cat up there, then a dog. The cat had been strangled. The dog had its throat cut. Do you think it's worth following up?'

She pondered this for a while.

'Yes. Go across and get the details, but I want them corroborated by someone else. See if he can think of another local who's also likely to remember it. If it's all just hot air, which is

122

more than likely, then cut it short and get back here. It's only useful if it can give us a name. We can't afford to waste any time on wild goose chases.'

* * *

Sophie was speaking to Barry Marsh. 'Any luck?' she said.

'No. There's nothing else on a Richard Frimwell, and no mention of anyone with the nickname Blossom. They've either been very lucky or very careful.'

'Probably both. But that assumes they do exist and are our men. I can't believe there's nothing more known about them. I hope we're not barking up the wrong tree. The problem is, those two are the only real lead we've got at present. We really need some kind of break. Will you keep plugging away at those farm rentals for the time being?'

Marsh sensed desperation in Sophie's tone, but said nothing. Things were not that bad, surely? It was only a few days since they'd discovered the bodies in the field, and they'd picked up on several possible leads. Any one of those could yield the vital piece of information that would set the case rolling. She'd appeared strained right from the start of this enquiry, almost brittle. He wondered if there was more to the discovery of her grandparents than she was letting on. At times he'd seen her sitting at her desk with her head in her hands, looking as if she was about to collapse under a weight of worries. He suspected that these concerns might not be linked to the case, and were due to something entirely different. But what? Surely, finding her grandparents would be a cause for celebration, not extreme tension? One thing was certain, she would not take kindly to any questions. He'd keep quiet for the moment and hope things didn't get worse.

He wondered if Bob Thompson in Bournemouth would have any contacts that might provide a clue about this Blossom character. A photofit image would be something, since there didn't seem to be anything on file. He phoned through to headquarters.

* * *

Lydia Pillay was fresh to the case. The previous week she had been away on a course on 'Modern Trends in Intimidation.' Violent crime had become more subtle in recent years. Despite the general perception, levels of violence had decreased, but there were some worrying trends. Intimidation and bullying were becoming more overt, particularly when coupled with antisocial behaviour. Pillay was expected to share her new knowledge with colleagues. But it would have to wait for this case to be closed first. She was reading through the dossier when she had an idea. She walked across to Marsh.

'Barry, if a boat's been used then shouldn't we be checking with other boat owners? Surely someone must have noticed if a small cruiser or whatever has been going in and out?'

'We contacted the harbour authorities and have asked them for their records. But Nadia's boat came in at night, when there was a mist. If they always chose those kinds of conditions, then the chances of being spotted would have been minimal. But I take your point. We should check to see if anyone's spotted suspicious movements. Come up with a plan, check it with me and we'll put it to the boss. By the way, you probably know her better than the rest of us. Does she seem okay to you?'

'What do you mean?'

Marsh chewed his pen. 'It's hard to explain. But she seems anxious at times. Not so much when we're involved with the case, but I've caught her a couple of times sitting with her head in her hands. I've backed out before she's seen me. I wondered if you'd spotted it too, or if it's just my imagination.'

'Yes, I have. I don't know what to make of it either. Let's just keep our eye on her, sir. Maybe something's happening that we don't know about.'

'Okay. But tell me if you find out anything, won't you? Meanwhile, we just keep on crosschecking. Jimmy and I are still ploughing through the property booking records. The farmhouse ones all seem to come from forwarding or non-existent addresses, but I'm still hopeful they might yield a clue. But you know me. I always live in hope.'

'Where is Jimmy, by the way?' Pillay asked.

'He's off to Studland to follow up a report from a resident.'

* * *

Jimmy Melsom was sipping tea from a bone china cup. The saucer, which was equally ornate, did not match the cup. The cup across the other side of the table, in front of the elderly man he was interviewing, matched Melsom's saucer.

'It must have been a good thirty years ago. Mebbe longer. But it were the cruelty, you see? It were wicked.'

'So why do you think it's linked to our present case, Mr Potts?'

'The first one were a young kitten. Strangled, if I remember right. Nothing else, but it were thrown up onto the rock. It were my workmate, Harry, that found it. Well, it were actually a little lass who'd climbed up the rock, but Harry was walking his dog nearby. He heard her scream like, and he went across. Her family were having a picnic under the rock. Holidaymakers. Harry brought the body of the kitten back and I remember the vet saying it had been strangled. Anyways, a couple of weeks later it were a puppy's body up there, with its throat cut and its tongue missing. And that's what made me phone you lot up. 'Cause I heard, on the quiet like, that that lad's body had its tongue missing. Is that right?'

'I can't confirm or deny it, Mr Potts. We don't release details about a suspicious death, for obvious reasons. Are there any more details? Like who found the dog's body?'

'Well, that were me. I kept my eye on that rock after the cat were found. Thought it might be black magic or sommat.

But we didn't find anything else afterwards, like. But what I can tell you is that there was a camp at the back of the village at the time. You know, Scouts or Boys' Brigade or sommat. And when they went, it stopped.'

'But there were only the two incidents?'

'From what I know, aye. And I get to know most of what goes on around the village. Not that I'm a nosey bugger, don't think that.'

'Right, Mr Potts. We need to try and get an accurate date for this. It's not going to be easy, is it?'

The old man shook his head glumly.

CHAPTER 15: THE KITTEN AND THE PUPPY

Monday Afternoon, Week 2

'It's a good lead, Jimmy.'

'I can't see it, ma'am. He hasn't a clue which year it was, so I don't see how we can make any progress on it.'

They were sitting in Sophie's office. Jimmy Melsom's features wore a hangdog expression.

'In the account you've just given me there's one official person mentioned. Think about it.'

She watched. Melsom's face didn't alter.

'Sorry, ma'am. I must be particularly thick today. I still can't see it.'

'The vet, Jimmy. Your Mr Potts told you that the dead kitten was taken to the vet. Now let's assume the same for the dog, though it may not be necessary. Vets would keep records, wouldn't they? So get onto the practice that's nearest to the village and go through their records for summers around the years he's thinking about. Then find out the name of his pal who found the cat. See him and try and get a date out of him. And use the reminder trick on both of them. You know, was there a wedding anniversary or some special occasion the same year? Was something else going on at the same time? Could the camp have been there for a special event? If we can get two corroborative dates, it will be worth following up. Just keep probing, Jimmy. All you need is to find something that tickles their memories. But go for the vet angle first. You might even find someone who was on duty, like a nurse or receptionist who might remember.'

'Thanks, ma'am. I just couldn't see it.'

'That's my job, Jimmy. You'll learn with experience.'

Melsom was back with Ray Potts in less than half an hour. This time he made better progress. The elderly man had been thinking, and had decided that the incidents had probably occurred sometime in the late eighties or early nineties. Melsom obtained the address of his ex-workmate, Harry Mowbray, and that of the vets' practice where the dead animals had been taken.

Harry Mowbray's memory was vague, and his daughter, who lived with him, informed the detective that her father suffered from significant memory lapses. Melsom saw the vacant expression on the old man's face and didn't pursue the matter. He returned to Swanage to visit the veterinary surgery. Here he made better progress and spent the rest of the morning searching through old records with the aid of Shona, the receptionist. It was Shona who found the entry, dated July 1989. Both animal corpses had been examined within a week of each other.

'Those initials are for Mr Eastways. I think he was the senior partner until he retired. It was quite a long time ago,' said Shona. 'I only came here three years ago when the last receptionist moved away. She'd been here for yonks. She doesn't live locally anymore but we still have her phone number. I can phone her if you like. Apparently she knew everything that went on.'

'If I can just have her name and number please, that will be fine. And for the vet, if you have it.'

'Good luck,' said Shona with a smile. 'Let me know how you get on. Please?'

* * *

128

Colin Eastways still lived locally and kept in touch with the practice and many of the farmers he used to serve. He ushered Melsom into his lounge and offered him some coffee.

'I wouldn't normally remember cases involving pets from that long ago, but these two incidents were most peculiar. They should both still be on record at your place because the local police were involved.'

Melsom cursed himself for yet again missing the obvious. Why hadn't he checked the records at the station? It was obvious that the incidents would have involved the police in some way.

'Anyway,' the retired vet continued, 'none of us doubted that the same culprit was responsible for the two incidents, though the second was more serious. The kitten had just been strangled as far as I remember, but the puppy had been partially strangled, then had its throat cut and its tongue sliced off after death.'

'And both had been thrown onto the top of the Agglestone?'

'Apparently, yes. We didn't see that. The bodies were brought to us by whoever found them. Why the interest now?' asked Eastways, then said, 'Ah. It'll be that body found on the rock last week. I understand. But surely there's no connection after all this time? These incidents with the animals were twenty years ago. Maybe more.'

'I can't comment, sir. But we follow up every lead. Were the owners of the animals ever identified?'

'I really can't remember. But I can tell you who may be able to help. Our receptionist at that time was Maria Ogamba. She lived in Studland and knew everything and everybody. The trouble is, I don't know where she lives now.'

'That's fine, sir. I already have her details from the current receptionist. She had the same idea as you.'

'Nice to know they've still got staff who are on the ball.' He paused to take a sip of coffee. 'I miss it, you know. I try to keep in contact with some of the farmers and clients, but it gets more difficult each year. So many people have moved away or died.'

Melsom didn't know what to say to this. He finished his coffee and stood up.

'Thank you, sir. You've been most helpful. Please contact us if you remember anything else, no matter how trivial it may seem.'

He phoned the former receptionist as soon as he got back to the car, but there was no answer. He returned to the station. Marsh and Sophie were both pleased with the information he'd obtained.

'Do you seriously think there's a link?' he asked Marsh.

'Well, it seems a bit peculiar, doesn't it? But the similarities with the dog are really unusual. The slit throat and the tongue removal. And the vet said that it was reported to us? Go down and see Tom Rose and find out where the records might be. With a bit of luck they'll still be around.'

It took Melsom the rest of the morning to find the details of the animal incident. They told him nothing new. The investigating constable had made minimal notes. There was no record of the owners.

'It doesn't show us in the best light, does it?' he said to Marsh over lunch. 'I mean, I can get more information from vet records than from our own.'

'They might have had other priorities, Jimmy. We don't know what else was going on at the time. Maybe he never managed to find out anything else. Look on the bright side. You've still got the receptionist to contact. And if that doesn't work, get back over to the village and pick the brains of some of the old people. Someone will remember something, believe me.'

He didn't need to make another visit. He tried the phone number he'd been given for Maria Ogamba again and this time she answered the phone.

'Of course I remember it, Officer. It was very weird, and there was a bit more to it than most people realised.'

She now lived in Dorchester. Melsom made arrangements to call on her that afternoon.

* * *

'Well! What a handsome young man!'

Maria Ogamba gave a throaty laugh. 'You're safe to come in, Constable. I don't bite. Leastways, not much.'

She led Melsom through to a small sitting room, and went to make them a pot of tea.

'You know, it's about time that some of you lot followed up that wicked crime. But it's not exactly recent, is it? What's taken you so long? Was the paperwork a bit difficult?' She laughed.

Jimmy smiled rather nervously and took out his notebook.

'Mr Eastways said you'd probably remember what happened better than anyone. Could you just tell me, and what your thoughts were?'

'Of course, Jimmy. You did say your name was Jimmy, didn't you? My memory isn't what it was, you know . . .'

She looked at him from under lowered lashes. 'Only joking!' Her grey curls shook as she laughed.

'Where shall I start? Well, it was Harry Mowbray that brought the little kitten in. He worked in one of the timber yards, so he walked across the heath to work some days and so did Ray Potts. Harry lived in the same row of cottages as me, four doors along, I think.'

Not again, thought Melsom. Why hadn't he thought to ask how they knew the heath and what they did for a living? He was becoming a little depressed about his deficiencies as a detective.

'You can tell I've been thinking about it, can't you?' She laughed. 'I wouldn't normally remember something in this much detail, you know.'

'You're doing very well, Mrs Ogamba.'

'Ms, Officer. I never got married. My man was a real rascal. He fathered my children and then buggered off. Fancy leaving a beautiful woman like me, eh? Can you believe it?' She roared with laughter.

Melsom smiled weakly.

'It was me that made the entries in the records, you know. Neat writing, eh? Did you read them? But that was only the medical details. The poor kitten had been strangled, then a week later the puppy came in. It was terrible. What kind of person could do that to a poor young animal? But you know all this already, don't you?'

Jimmy nodded.

'I think the animals were from the farm, you know, and had been taken onto the heath deliberately. One of the men who found them said that they'd seen an old sack thrown away by the rock. There were lots of kittens on that farm. The cats lived in the barn and kept the rats and mice away. They had dogs as well, and the one that came in was about the right size for a litter of collies that had been born a good few months before.'

'But who would have done it? Killed them, I mean?'

'And in that horrid way. It was just awful to see that puppy's injuries. I remember hoping that it hadn't suffered much.' Maria's face had lost its cheer. 'There was a camp on the farm at the time. Some kind of youth group. They were using the field closest to the heath. I reckoned at the time that it was one of the lads from there. No other animals were ever found after they'd gone. They were a bunch of tearaways from some estate in Southampton. Most of them were fine, but there was a small group that went out looking for trouble. They were there for nearly two weeks.'

'Can you remember anything else about them? The organisers? Anything like that?'

'You're asking a lot, young Jimmy. I think the organisers came every year for about three or four years, but with a different bunch of lads each time. I remember that they were from a church, but the lads weren't. They were probably from the local parish, maybe a youth club or something. There was no problem any other year, but that group had a couple of nasty types in it, so I heard. The leader's name was Paul. That's all I remember. He was there each year. The church? I don't know. It was somewhere over on the east side of the city in a rough area. I think it was a modern building. Well, that's the picture I have in my mind, so it must have got there somehow. Maybe

132

from talking to him, cos I can't think how else I'd get a picture in my head.' She stopped. 'And that's it. I can't remember anything else. So do I get my kiss now?'

She looked at him solemnly, and then burst into laughter. 'Your face is priceless. You can come visit again anytime, young man.'

Melsom finished his cup of tea and left hastily.

* * *

'This might be leading somewhere, Jimmy,' Barry Marsh said. 'It looked like a no-hoper when that old chap first called in, but something's coming out of it. Well done. Look, I could leave it all to you since it's really your baby, but I do know a DS in Southampton. It might save time if I contact her to see if she can identify the church. Is that okay by you? If she can't help us then I think the boss knows a DI there.'

'Sure. Go ahead.'

Marsh phoned through to Gwen Davis, a detective sergeant in the Southampton city force. He told her what they knew about the church and the youth group and asked if she could help narrow down the possibilities.

'From what you've described I'd guess three, Barry. Two Anglican and one RC, and all in the East End. The area was flattened by bombing in the last war, so most of the buildings date back to the fifties. The two Anglican ones are St Crispin's and Oakfield Parish. The RC one is St Bede's. They're your best bets. Get back to me if they don't work out, and I'll have another think.'

'Thanks, Gwen. How are you, by the way?'

'I'm fine. Let me know if you fancy meeting up for a meal or a drink. I'm still around, you know.'

'Okay, Gwen.'

Melsom was grinning at him when he looked up.

'You didn't hear that, Jimmy. But you're allowed to have heard the earlier bits.'

'Sorry, boss. Didn't catch any of the church information. Selective hearing.'

Marsh tore off the page of notes and passed it across. He waved Melsom away and settled back to his own work. He was still trying to make sense of the complex web of contacts for the farmhouse bookings and harbour records. The two farmhouses had been rented out by different letting agencies and to different clients. An agency in Poole let Brookway Farm and one in Bournemouth let Marsh Copse Farm. This latter farm had only been occupied for a few days. Those agencies had been acting on behalf of different clients who turned out to be a small finance and loan company based in Kidderminster and an estate agent office in Weymouth. Marsh had contacted all the organisations in the chain so far, but had made little progress. Each time he moved one level back in the complex web he merely uncovered another level that gave up no really useful information. Each organisation claimed to be merely acting on behalf of another, with all contact being done by telephone. He decided to follow the trail of payments. Bank accounts wouldn't lie.

The money trail for the bookings took him back over exactly the same ground, with each agency paying the next for rent, deposits and any other bills. Finally he began to get somewhere, because the convoluted trails for each of the two farmhouse rentals led back to a single organisation, a small insurance company with an office in Wolverhampton. He phoned the number he'd been given only to hear the familiar 'number no longer in use' message. He swore and slapped his hand down hard on the desktop.

He looked up to find Sophie standing in front of him, peering over the top of her reading glasses.

'Sorry, ma'am. I'm just getting frustrated. They've tangled up the trails for these bookings really well. I don't feel as if I'm getting anywhere.'

'But you are, Barry. What does all this confirm?'

'That whoever did these bookings had something to hide.'

'Exactly. If these lettings were totally innocent they wouldn't have hidden the details so well, and you'd have got some names hours ago. The fact that it's so complex shows that it's all been carefully planned. So keep digging. Any luck with the boat, by the way?'

'Not yet. I had a brief chat with Lydia about it earlier, and she's taken it on. We've got it narrowed down to about five possible registrations. She's out with one of the local guys right now checking up on owners, insurers and harbour records. We should know more by the end of the day.'

'Get yourself a cup of tea, stretch your legs for five minutes, then give it another go. It will unravel at some point, I'm sure, and then you'll be cheering rather than cursing.' She glanced at her watch. 'In fact, I'll join you. I need to keep you updated on the latest information from Benny Goodall. It really isn't nice.'

* * *

Across at the harbour offices in Poole, Lydia Pillay was trying to make sense of the boat records. She'd also managed to get hold of VHF radio registrations and was working her way through both, with the help of two local officers. In the end, her task was made easier by the fact that owners of boats carrying out legitimate business had no reason to hide their traces. Owner details for small to medium-sized cruisers were clearly listed and matched the records for the radio transmitters. No more than three or four had anything suspicious about them. She checked the details for these against sightings of boats on the quieter, south side of the harbour. And there it was — a medium-sized blue cruise boat with ownership details registered with an agency and its radio registration logged at a different address. She called through to Barry Marsh with the details.

'I'm coming back in,' she said. 'I'll follow them up myself unless there's something else you want me to do.'

'No, that's fine. I've been going back through the lettings for the farmhouses and it's turned out to be a really tangled web. There's no daylight yet, but the boss thinks I need to keep at it. I hope something might connect your strand with mine at some stage.'

'How's Jimmy getting on?'

'He's across in Southampton, trying to identify something that's cropped up from the dead kitten lead that came in this morning. It looked such a no-hoper that I was set to file it in the 'waste of time' section. But the boss was right again. Something in the report must have tickled her interest and it seems to be paying off.'

CHAPTER 16: MIDWINTER TIDE

Monday Evening, Week 2

The trouble with redbrick church buildings, thought Jimmy Melsom, is that they just don't look the part. A few scraps of litter were blowing about in the wind and graffiti was scrawled across the end of a terrace wall opposite the church. Suddenly the sun came out, and the grass in front of the church sparkled. The brickwork seemed to glow as the sunlight caught it. Melsom stepped out of the car, keen to get this over before the rain started again.

The vicarage was the first building after the Oakfield Parish Church. Melsom rang the bell, which was rather ornate for the plain house. A middle-aged man wearing a dog collar came to the door. He was in the middle of a conversation with someone inside the house, but managed a smile. Melsom held open his warrant card.

'Come in, Officer. Sorry to be so rude. I've just come back from the shops and seem to have forgotten the single most important item that my wife asked me to get. Old age, I suppose. By next week I expect I'll be wandering round in my pyjamas, dribbling.' He laughed.

Melsom was shown into a neat sitting room and asked if he wanted a cup of tea. He declined. He had drunk enough tea during his visits that day to fill his bladder several times over. He explained the purpose of his visit.

'That was me,' the minister said. 'I'm Paul Benfield. I was the curate then, and was offered the position of vicar when my predecessor retired ten years ago. Ruth and I were newly married, and we ran the local youth group for quite a few years. We took them away somewhere every year, and I think we were in Studland about five times. We switched to a scout campsite in the New Forest after that. It had better facilities. Ruth will remember. I'll get her.'

He left the room and came back with a petite, neatly dressed woman who was drying her hands on a towel.

'There was one year in particular that the locals remember for a variety of reasons,' said Melsom. 'One of them told us that you had a more troublesome group than usual. Is that right?'

The couple glanced at each other. 'Yes,' replied Benfield. 'That was the last year we were there. The farmer was not happy with the behaviour of a couple of the lads, and I couldn't blame him. It's not as though they were really bad, because then I would have brought them back early. But they were uncooperative and sullen. And we were aware that they were sneaking off without permission. They were seen in parts of the farm that we'd clearly explained were off limits.'

'The trouble was that they just didn't see the need to follow rules,' Ruth added. 'We'd forbid something, they'd accept, then we'd find out later that they'd gone and done it anyway.'

'Is there any chance you can remember their names?'

'I'm not sure I'd want to, Officer, even if I could. People change, you know. Everyone deserves a chance to redeem themselves for their childhood misdemeanours. And it was a very long time ago. Twenty years or so.'

'June, 1989, sir.' Melsom fidgeted. He felt awkward. 'And I have to insist, sir. This is a murder inquiry, so the normal niceties don't apply.'

'Where did you say you were from?' Ruth asked.

'Dorset,' he replied.

'Oh. We've seen the news.' There was a silence and the couple looked at each other. Ruth nodded to her husband.

'We may still have a list, officer. We used to keep stuff in an old filing case when we lived in a local council flat. We dumped it in the storeroom when we came here and haven't opened it since.' He paused. 'This will take some time, so I'll need to postpone my next appointment. Please give me a minute or two, then we'll move to the study.'

He left the room and Ruth took Melsom through to a small room at the end of the hall. It was stacked with boxes, cabinets and cases.

'I know what I'm looking for,' she said. 'But it may take some time to find it.'

Her husband came in and they soon unearthed a small attaché case. They moved to the study and spread the contents out on a desk. Paul and Ruth flicked through the neatly stapled collections of documents, until Ruth suddenly stopped.

'Here it is! June, 1989. This bundle has all the details relating to that year's camp. I'll find the page you want. If it's not in here, then it won't be anywhere.'

The vicar and his wife leant over the pack and flicked through the stapled pages.

'Yes, here's a list of the teenagers we took. I'm not sure, but I think it was these two that caused the trouble.' He pointed at a couple of names. 'I'll take this page out.'

'No, please don't separate it. I'll take the lot. I'd prefer it if we did the final searching back at the station, if you don't mind. It's possible that more than one item might end up as evidence.'

'I suppose we ought to get rid of all this stuff,' the minister said, looking at the rest of the packs taken out of the case. 'It's probably breaking some kind of information law, keeping it this long.'

'Maybe,' Melsom replied. 'But at least you've got it under lock and key. And when you do dispose of it, it's got

139

to be done properly. Shred or burn it. Don't just dump it for recycling.'

'You sound like an expert,' Ruth said.

'Well, you can imagine how much documentation we create and have to get rid of,' Melsom replied. 'We'd be hung drawn and quartered if we just dumped it somewhere.'

He took the file, thanked his hosts and left. He phoned through to the incident room straight away. He'd got something right at last.

'Ma'am? I've got a file with names in it. I'm bringing it in now!'

'Okay, Jimmy. Stay calm, drive carefully and get across here in one piece. You may just have the single most vital clue so far.'

He was back within the hour. He put the papers down on Sophie's desk and traced down the list of thirty names with a finger. Marsh looked over his shoulder.

'Here it is, look. Ricky Frimwell, age fourteen.'

Sophie turned and threw her arms around Marsh, and then hugged Melsom.

'Oh, Jimmy, you little beauty!' She stabbed her finger down on Frimwell's name. 'You thought you'd got us beaten, didn't you, you slimy toe-rag? Well, we're getting closer. And we're going to get you, wherever you're hiding.'

* * *

'What's going on?' asked Pillay when she returned. 'Everyone looks cheerful.'

'Jimmy's thread turned up trumps. There was a name on the camping list. It was Ricky Frimwell, the one I picked out a few days ago from the photofit system. So we're all feeling happier, particularly the boss. Corroboration.'

'I bet she's relieved. I've got the boat records with me, so I'm going to start crosschecking them now. Let's hope they show up something and it fits in.'

She got to work and Marsh returned to his desk to make more phone calls. He'd made a diagram on a large sheet of paper which looked like a tangled web, but it was narrowing at the top. The threads of the complex booking system were all beginning to merge.

It was nearly seven in the evening when he finished. At last, a single name sat at the top of the page with every strand leading back to it: Midwinter Tide. It was a company name, with a registered office in a side street near Poole quayside. He took the diagram through to Sophie's office, where she was discussing boats and radios with Matt Silver and Lydia Pillay.

'Here we are,' he said. 'Traced back to a single company. Midwinter Tide.'

'What?' said Pillay. 'Are you sure?'

'It's taken me nearly two days, and I'm as sure as I can be. Why?'

'Sorry, sir. I didn't mean to doubt you. It's just that the name of the boat is Midwinter Tide. The one I think has been smuggling in the girls from across the Channel. It's certainly the most likely candidate.'

'I've got an address', Marsh added. 'Do you think we might have time to drop in on them this evening?'

Sophie looked at Silver.

'Absolutely,' he said. 'I'll get on the blower right now.'

'That's the spirit, Matt,' Sophie said. 'One armed unit should be enough as backup, don't you think?' She glanced at her watch. 'Let's go for nine o'clock. The heavy mob should be ready by then.'

* * *

The small warehouse was dark, dank and uninviting. It was also empty. The uniformed squad forced open the door and poured in, with the detectives following close behind. No one was lurking in the shadows or hiding in the store cupboards. They did find several bin bags of rubbish, just inside the staff entrance door, which they emptied out onto plastic sheeting.

'Don't touch anything directly,' said Sophie. 'Just a little poking with your pens, please. I want to confirm that we've got the right place, and once we're sure we'll call in the forensics squad.'

She left Marsh and Pillay picking through the rubbish while she, Silver, Melsom and some of the uniformed officers searched the building.

The main part of the building had once housed a vehicle repair depot. This was obvious from the inspection pits and hoist fittings, the empty tool racks fitted to the walls and the oily stains on the concrete floor. There were three offices and two storerooms, all empty. There was a small boiler room at the end of a short corridor. Sophie put a hand on the boiler's surface. Was it her imagination or was there still a vestige of warmth in some of the outlet pipes?

'Ma'am! Something here', called Melsom from further along the corridor.

She followed his voice into a small toilet. In the corner was a small rubbish bin. Melsom was pointing to the item on top. It was the empty packaging from a box of tampons.

'Now that is interesting. And it looks fresh, don't you think? We'll leave it there for forensics.'

They returned to the entrance area and had a look at the rubbish, now spread out. There were empty sandwich containers, a couple of beer cans, soft-drink packets, biscuit wrappers, used paper tissues and empty milk cartons.

'I think it's only been here a few days, ma'am,' Pillay said. 'The cartons are only just past their use-by date. If they were really old they would smell worse than they do.'

Matt Silver appeared beside them. 'There are some traces of white powder on the floor in the corner of the far store room. Looks as if it's been spilt. Could be the hard stuff,' he said.

'I think we have enough to confirm we've got the right place, Matt. We need to get Dave's forensic team in now. Let's secure everything and get back outside. We'll organise a door-to-door for the area tomorrow morning and see if anyone working nearby can tell us anything. We'll leave an unmarked car to keep an eye on the place overnight, just in case someone returns.'

CHAPTER 17: THE BODY IN THE YARD

Tuesday, Week 2

The disused warehouse building didn't look so intimidating in daylight, although it still reeked of old motor oil, mouldy rags and rancid milk. Sophie turned her nose up.

'Odd. I didn't notice the smell quite as much last night. I suppose all my other senses were more active.'

She and Marsh found David Nash in one of the offices. He'd arrived an hour earlier and was directing members of his team to different areas of the grubby building. The two detectives went outside and joined a small team of police officers who were gathering, ready for a check on the neighbouring premises. There were only six other buildings in the immediate vicinity, and they divided them between the four detectives, working in teams of two. Little came out of the visits. No one reported anything suspicious. The warehouse had been largely unoccupied in recent years, with only an occasional visit from what appeared to be a maintenance crew.

'I want you to stay around for the rest of the day, Jimmy,' Sophie said. 'We'll leave you one of the cars. Take an occasional wander and keep your eyes peeled. It's possible that someone might come back for a look, or to get rid of that rubbish we found. Report anything suspicious back to Barry.' She sniffed. 'You know, that smell is worse once you get outside. Barry, could you organise that dog team to come down and have a nose around? I want that stink checked out.'

The forensic chief phoned through with an interim report during the late morning. The spilled powder was crack cocaine, most surfaces had been wiped so there were few fingerprints, and the smell was caused by a partially blocked drain.

'It's probably been blocked for ages, but recent use of the toilets has resulted in a backup. I don't think there's anything suspicious about it,' he said.

'That's a nuisance. I've organised a dog team to check it out. Maybe I'd better cancel.'

'It's too late, ma'am,' said Nash. 'They've just arrived. They may as well go ahead and give the place the onceover now they're here.'

Sophie went through to see Marsh.

'Quick work with the dog squad, Barry. They're at the warehouse already. But it may be a false alarm.'

She gave him Nash's explanation for the smell.

An hour later, Melsom called.

'Ma'am, the dog's acting funny. There's an enclosed patch of ground out at the back of the building. The dog's whining and pawing at the ground. Dave Nash wants to dig. Is that okay?'

'Of course. Tell him we'll be over directly.'

The piece of ground was a square of compacted earth and stones. When Sophie and Marsh arrived they found that the digging had just started, with the top few inches taken off a spot in the centre.

'It's tamped down hard,' Nash told them. 'Whatever it is, it's been there for some time, I'd guess.'

They watched two members of the team labour at shifting the heavy soil, trying to probe each layer carefully. While they were working, Sophie went over to have a word with the dog handler.

'That's some dog you have,' she said. 'It's amazing that it could pick up scents from under such a hard-packed surface.'

'Floyd is the only dog in the division that could have done it,' replied the handler. 'It's his speciality, ma'am. The force even loans us out to other counties. There's no other dog in the South West that can come near him.'

'Well, if we find anything I won't forget you both, not after finding those other bodies at the farm. We weren't expecting them either.'

Just then one of the forensic diggers called out and they walked across. There was a small piece of bone protruding from the exposed surface. The team switched to smaller hand tools. Finally a full skeleton lay exposed.

'What do you think, Dave?' Sophie asked.

'I'm no expert — you'll need a pathologist for that. But I'll stick my neck out and say it's an adult male. What I can tell you is that it's been there some time, more than just a few years. There's no organic matter left.'

'I'll get Benny Goodall across.'

'There's no need, ma'am. We can lift it out. We'll do it once we've photographed it in situ. Then we can have a look underneath for any other remnants. I'd guess that the clothes have rotted away completely, but there might be traces of one or two things left from the pockets. That's if he was wearing any clothes when he was buried. We'll get the body taken across to Dr Goodall's lab directly.'

'Okay, Dave. You're the boss.'

'My guess is that it's been there for at least a decade, possibly more. That soil hasn't been moved for a very long time. Sometimes the surface can look solid, but it's just been tamped down. But this stuff was hard all the way down.'

'Could it be historic and nothing to do with us?'

'No. The dog picked up the scent, and got the exact position. It has to be thirty years or less. Whether it's linked to your current case or not, I wouldn't know. But my guess is between ten and thirty years. With Dr Goodall's help we should be able to narrow that down a bit.'

Sophie nodded. She walked through the warehouse and out into the street. Was this latest discovery somehow linked to the others? It hardly seemed credible. The answer would depend on how long the premises had been owned by Midwinter Tide, whoever they were. More digging through the records would be required. She sighed. Had there ever been a time when a police officer's job was straightforward? Probably not, despite what the television programmes of the seventies and eighties would have had us believe. She'd grown up watching them and remembered how simple everything had been. Put a bit of pressure on a few obvious suspects, get a few clues, follow a few suspicious characters and suddenly the case was solved. The reality was this sense of being almost overwhelmed by the sheer number of possibilities, each one just out of reach. Then there was the huge volume of facts, reports, statements, records, documents and assorted bits and pieces, any one of which could hold the single clue that might unlock the case. Consider the snippet that Melsom had found from the church people in Southampton. On another day, and in a different mood, she might well have turned down his request to follow up this lead.

Story of my life, she thought. A seeming breakthrough one day, then on the next something that makes the fog come down again. She looked towards the quayside, where the harbour water rippled in the chilly breeze. She knew why she was so tense. It was now only two days until her father's funeral and the thought was making her feel nauseous. She had never told anyone about her true feelings for her father. The events of the past week had turned all her emotions upside down. She was still in shock, reeling from the realisation that all the thoughts she had had about him throughout her life had been utterly wrong. In some ways a complex case like this was the best thing that could have happened. It occupied her mind and prevented her from thinking about her father.

She heard footsteps approaching. Barry Marsh.

'I don't think there's much more we can do here, ma'am. The dog seems to be happy, so it doesn't look as though there

147

are any more bodies. But I wonder whether there's any scanning equipment that might confirm it for us? You know, like you see on TV programmes about the past?'

'Bournemouth University has an archaeology department. I wonder if they could advise us. We'll get Jimmy to contact them when we get back.'

* * *

They returned to the incident room and continued probing into the tangled world of Midwinter Tide. The company had been in existence for at least twenty years and its registered address, at the Poole warehouse, had remained unchanged during all that time.

'Are the directors listed in the entry?' Sophie asked.

'Yes, there's five. A. Hazard, E.D. Inch, E.L. Luff, R. Frimwell, B. Sourlie. No first names, just initials. The only address is the place we've just left. And, interestingly, that bungalow we visited at the weekend is mentioned in one of the records I found. So do we start looking at these other names?' Marsh said.

'Yes. More time in front of those blessed computers. Get Lydia onto it as soon as she's tied up all the boat stuff. Does that company registration say anything about what the company does?'

'Nothing useful. It just states "General Trading." Not giving anything away, are they?'

Pillay joined them. 'The boat isn't in the harbour, ma'am. The harbour police and the marine unit have been out searching all morning. They think they've covered all the marinas and jetties. Either it's been hidden in a boathouse somewhere or they've moved it completely. Shall I contact the other harbours along the coast just in case they've moved it further afield?'

'Yes, do that, Lydia. Have any names turned up yet?'

'Just the company. It's registered to them, but there is a signature on one of the VHS radio forms. It's just a scrawl and difficult to make out.'

'Take a look at these names. Could it be any of them?'

Pillay looked from the names to the form in her hand.

'It could be that last one, B. Sourlie. It's the closest, but it's hard to be sure.'

The other two detectives came in. Sophie sat staring at the list of names. There was something odd about them. They already knew the name Frimwell, and now Sourlie seemed to match the record that Pillay had found. She looked at the other names, and suddenly it struck her. It couldn't be. Jesus. Surely it couldn't just be coincidence? She made herself a coffee and walked through the incident room to the office where Matt Silver sat.

'Look at this, Matt.'

She handed him the list.

'So how does this help?' said Silver.

'Take out the names Frimwell and Sourlie. They've cropped up elsewhere, so we know they exist. Look at what's left.'

He stared at the list.

'What am I looking for?'

'Anagrams, Matt. The first three names, A. Hazard, E.D. Inch, E.L. Luff, form an anagram of the words Hazel and Charlie Duff.'

'Surely that's coincidence?'

'No. And do you know what? I've spoken to the bastard without realising it. Barry and I went to visit Frimwell's house on Sunday and chatted to the neighbour. He told us his surname was Black, but I thought he was uneasy when he said it. He's a widower. He also said his wife's name was Hazel. The name of their house was Chez Lahar Lei. That's an anagram of Hazel and Charlie. I noticed it as we drove away. This fits in. Someone, and I'd guess it was the dead wife Hazel, liked anagrams. She was probably a crossword addict.'

'Do we go across to pay him a visit?'

'No. Let's just keep a watch on the place for the time being. This can't count as substantive evidence, can it? I don't want to alert him by calling again. As far as he's aware, we only know about Frimwell. Let's keep him in the dark but watch his movements. By the way, Matt, has there been any luck with the search for street girls from Romania?'

'We've got teams out in Bournemouth, Poole, Weymouth and Dorchester. I've asked our colleagues in Hampshire for their help. Southampton and Portsmouth are much bigger markets, so it's more likely they will have ended up there. That's if they haven't moved them further afield to the Midlands or the north. I'd guess that most of the trafficking for the whole country comes in through the South Coast ports and then the women are distributed around some kind of network.'

'It's appalling, isn't it? What you've just said describes these women as goods for consumption in the market, not human beings with lives to fulfil.'

'I know. But that's the reality of how they're treated by the men who run them. A commodity, just like any other. It's a dreadful truth, Sophie.'

'From what Nadia said, the gang appears to start with a softening up process in which the women are beaten, raped and intimidated. It's likely to be carefully planned, even though it might not appear so to the girls on the receiving end. How long do you think this stage might last, before they're shipped onwards to start work?'

Silver drummed his fingers as he thought. 'The drugs would make them more acquiescent. So my guess is a couple of weeks. Maybe three at the most. It wouldn't be too long because while they're not working, they're not earning. And it's the money that drives it all. It's lucrative once they start working, once they're out on the streets, but before then they're using up money rather than making it.'

'So we need to trace the batch Nadia was in by the middle of next week? I'm assuming they'll have been delayed a bit because of the moves.'

He looked at her. 'Do you realise that you used the word "batch" just then? But your logic is right. We probably have a few more days at most. They won't be working a five day week.'

Sophie stiffened. 'Nadia has her heart set on us finding the youngest one, Sorina. Let's focus on her, Matt, if you think I'm in danger of not seeing them as individuals. She's sixteen. She's slightly built and looks younger than her years. How do you think she must be feeling right now? Terrified, weak, exhausted, sick to the heart? Again, I'm only guessing, Matt. It's so far outside my experience. But she's there in my heart, in my mind and in my soul. She isn't just another item on a list for me!'

'Sophie, I know that. I didn't mean my comment in the way you've taken it . . .' Silver's reply was too late. The door had already slammed shut behind her.

* * *

Silver didn't follow her. He'd never seen her so edgy. It couldn't be the case, since progress was steady and the whole team knew they were starting to home in on the perpetrators. Today's discovery of a body was probably a one-off, someone who'd crossed the gang and paid for it. So what was causing her moodiness? The funeral was in two days' time, but she'd never known her father anyway. If anything, the discovery of the truth behind her father's death had led to an unexpected blessing in the form of her grandparents. So what was going on?

Down the corridor in the ladies washroom, Sophie was bent over a toilet, vomiting.

151

CHAPTER 18: THE GUN

Wednesday, Week 2

Barry Marsh decided to visit the quayside warehouse early in the morning, before the GPR team arrived from Bournemouth University. He'd woken early, too agitated to go back to sleep. After an early breakfast he was ready to take the first ferry across from Studland to Sandbanks. The warehouse was almost deserted now that the main forensic team had finished their work. A solitary squad car was parked at the entrance. He had a quick word with the constable on duty, then unlocked the small staff door and walked inside. There was no point in carrying out another search. The forensic team would have gone through the place more thoroughly than he could. But was there something else, something less obvious, which might yield some insight into the premises and the company that owned it? He spent several minutes looking idly through the rooms and corridors. Nothing. He sighed and went back outside, stopping to speak to the officer in the car.

A man in his sixties came wobbling by on an ancient, squeaking bicycle and came to a halt beside him.

'Found summat interesting here, then?' he said.

'Can't be sure, sir,' Marsh replied.

'Ricky Frimwell's place. But you probably know that.'

Marsh looked at him with more interest. 'Do you know him, sir?'

'Not really. Surly bugger. I tried saying good morning a couple of times as is only polite like, and just got ignored, so I didn't bother from then on. I come past most days, see.'

'When was the last time you saw him here?' asked Marsh.

'It's been empty for months, years more like. There was a van here a couple of days ago when I came by, with a couple of men loading it with boxes from inside, but I didn't stop.'

'We haven't heard that from any of the other people around. They said they haven't seen anything.'

'That's because these other places don't open up their doors till nearly nine. I come past between seven and seven thirty most days.' He glanced at his watch. 'I'm a bit late today.'

'So when did you see this? Which day?'

'Not in the morning at all. It were nearly dark. Must have been Saturday afternoon. I live up yonder.' He pointed in the general direction of the nearest housing estate. 'I've got a dinghy. My pal and me use it for a spot of fishing and just mucking about in. Keeps us out of trouble.' He gave Marsh a toothy grin.

'Anything else you can tell us about Frimwell?'

'No. Don't even know why I knows his name. But there used to be an older bloke who was here, and a woman. She was a cracker. But I ain't seen them in years. I used to think it were them that owned it. They had a posh car, like.'

Marsh took out his notebook. 'Can I have your name and address, sir? I'll need to arrange for someone to visit you and take a formal statement. Anything at all you can remember would be very useful to us.'

He phoned the incident room and asked Melsom to contact the old man. He'd only just finished when a van arrived with the GPR team and their equipment.

He chatted with the geophysicist in charge, and she explained how ground penetrating radar worked, and what they might expect to see if there were any more bodies buried.

153

'I don't think we'll find any more,' Marsh said. 'The dog we used is the best in the business and after sniffing out the body we dug up, it lost interest completely. But we have to check, and there could be other stuff.'

The technician set up the equipment and the team started their survey. It took only half an hour to scan the small yard, and Marsh was impatient to see the results.

'As you said, no bodies,' the team chief reported. 'But there are a couple of other things down there that show up as slight disturbances on the readings. There's no detail on the radar, so we'll go over the ground again using some different techniques.'

The second run confirmed that a small, dense object was buried under the ground. The expert explained that it might be natural, possibly an unusually solid rock. Marsh phoned the information through to Sophie, and requested for two of the forensic officers to carry out the dig. The archaeology team found nothing else, so they packed up and left. The chief remained to give advice. While they waited they looked at the printouts.

'You say it might just be a large stone?' Marsh said.

'It's possible, although the readings indicate something metallic. But we won't be sure until it's dug up. There are all kinds of variables at work in this kind of survey.'

Two of the forensic officers were back within an hour and, with a specific location to dig, it wasn't long before they found the object. Inside several layers of heavy-duty plastic was a handgun, wrapped in an oily rag.

* * *

'It hadn't just been chucked away, ma'am,' Marsh informed Sophie. 'It'd been well wrapped and carefully buried. My guess is that with a good clean, it would still be usable. And we found a bag of bullets beside it. I looked at the arrangement of fence posts around the outside of the yard. The place where the gun was buried was lined up exactly with one of the posts

154

at the side and another at the back. The body was in the same position on the other side.'

'Was there any clue as to how long it had been there?'

'The woman in charge of the unit thought about ten years for the gun. She had a look at the hole where the body was, and thought that it had been there longer. Maybe up to twenty years. But forensics will be able to give us a date on that, won't they? Isn't there a time-scale for different stages of decay?'

'Yes, but it's not exact, Barry. It depends on the type of ground and the organisms present. That soil was particularly poor and had never been cultivated. It would have been sparse in microbes and that might have had an effect. Benny's lot will let us know, I'm sure. By the way, what type of gun was it?'

'A 9mm handgun. That was what the forensic guy said when he bagged it up. I wouldn't know.'

'The army's been using those for more than forty years. Bullets are easy to get hold of, so it's often used by the underworld.'

'Well, he reckoned it was quite an old model. But it was only him speculating. He told me they'd have to wait for an expert to check it. They don't like committing themselves, do they?'

Sophie walked across to Pillay. The boat was nowhere to be found.

'It's so frustrating,' the young DC said. 'I thought we were really getting somewhere when I found its name, but there's been nothing since.'

'I'm visiting Weymouth this afternoon to speak to a colleague about street girls. Do you want to come? It'll do you good to get out for a couple of hours, and I might need your help.'

* * *

Pillay was struggling to keep calm. Seated opposite her in a town centre café was Detective Sergeant Alan Metcalfe. He was the most introverted policeman she'd ever come across.

He met each question with a silence that seemed to last for minutes. She supposed he was examining her words from every possible angle before committing himself to a reply. Even then his answer gave the minimum information.

'I really can't be sure,' he was saying. 'I just don't want to commit myself when I'm not certain about the reliability of the information I have.'

'I'm only here to find out what you've picked up about these Romanian girls. The report we got was that you'd got a whisper about some new girls who were about to hit the streets. I was sent down just to check out the details.' She paused, teeth gritted. 'It's the murders, sir. We need every bit of intelligence we can get. We know another small group of girls were brought across about two weeks ago. After what we found on that farm, we need to find them before it's too late.'

She tried desperately not to look across at Sophie, who was sitting at a nearby table reading a magazine. Could she hear all this? Blood from a stone was an understatement.

'How sure can you be about your information?' he asked.

'We know they were smuggled in through Poole Harbour a couple of weeks ago, because we have one of them who managed to escape. So we're in no doubt, sir.'

He frowned and took another sip of coffee.

Pillay was angry now. 'Look, if you've got information that might help us, it's your duty to share it. Sir.'

'Unless it puts my work at risk,' he answered immediately. 'My snouts, my leads, my efforts. Do you think I'm going to risk losing all my contacts? I've put years into them. They trust me.' His voice had become sharper.

'We found two buried bodies, for Christ's sake. Give me something at least,' replied Pillay, pink faced. 'I have to know something. Please?'

'Five new girls is what I'm told,' he replied.

'Romanian? Can you confirm that?'

'It's possible, but I don't know for sure. What I do know is that some of the local girls aren't happy about it.'

'Do you know who might be running them?'

He shook his head.

'Does the name Midwinter Tide mean anything to you, sir?'

Again he shook his head.

'So there's nothing else you can give me?'

'No. It's all rumour. Everything is in my line of work. The key is separating what might be true from the rest of the junk, which is often put there deliberately. What's the expression? Smoke and mirrors? It's a dark world, being undercover. The crooks know I'm around, so much of what I get could just be misinformation.' He stood up. 'That's the best I can do for you.'

She nodded. 'Well, thank you, sir.'

He turned to go. 'Next week. Possibly.'

* * *

'So you knew he was going to be like that?'

'Well, I suspected. It's just his manner. He sees himself as a bit of a maverick. He's been undercover for some time. It's a kind of experiment HQ is trying. He guards his secrets, keeps them close to his chest, so I had to find a way of coaxing the information out of him. And it worked, didn't it? You played your part well, Lydia.'

'He was so frustrating. The way he examined every question I asked, then looked at me as if I was some kind of forensic specimen. It gave me the creeps.'

'The thing is, Lydia, he keeps his ear really close to the ground, so he's always the first to pick up on anything new in this part of the county. Well, that's what Kevin McGreedie told me. It was Kevin who suggested that you take the lead. He said that if I used my rank, we'd get absolutely nothing. Apparently he's totally opposed to any form of hierarchy. He's a kind of lone wolf. We got what we came for, so let's go home.'

157

CHAPTER 19: NEED YOUR LOVE SO BAD

Thursday, Week 2

Neither of the Howards had any religious faith. The loss and emptiness that followed Graham's disappearance had led them both to question any beliefs they might once have had. So they decided to hold the funeral service at Gloucester's crematorium.

Sophie looked around her as she stepped from the black limousine. She'd expected to see a handful of people and was taken aback by the numbers present. Many of them were friends and neighbours of the Howards, but she caught sight of several figures in uniform. Her boss, Dorset's chief constable, with ACC Jim Metcalfe and Matt Silver. Kevin McGreedie had come across from his Bournemouth base. She also spotted Archie Campbell, now ACC for West Midlands. There were several officers standing with DC Peter Spence, presumably from the Gloucester force. Finally, Tom Rose, Barry Marsh and Lydia Pillay from Swanage. Sophie swallowed. The level of support from all her colleagues, past and present, was overwhelming. They were all such busy people. How could they do this? She was about to say something to Martin, but realised that she wouldn't be able to speak. She straightened the jacket of her dress uniform, squeezed Martin's hand tightly, and stepped forward to take her mother's arm. She walked into the building and the inner chapel as if in a dream.

Susan had chosen the first piece of music: Fleetwood Mac's "Need Your Love So Bad". Sophie knew its significance. It had been the song her mother and father had listened to together, on the evening she'd been conceived.

A local representative of the Humanist Society conducted the service, and Martin gave the eulogy:

'I feel privileged to be able to speak about Graham Howard, because, in a way, I've known a part of him throughout my adult life. The part I speak of is, of course, his daughter and my wife, Sophie. He would have been so proud of Sophie, of the person she is and the things she has achieved. Of her calm nature, and yet her love of excitement. Of her brilliant mind, and yet even more importantly, of her wonderful ability to empathise. Many of her qualities were his too. His friends speak of his open-mindedness, and of his willingness to listen to their problems. Of his gentle nature, of his great personal strength of character and of his tenacity.

'Graham was born in Gloucester on the fifteenth of May, 1949. James and Florence were overjoyed at the birth of their son. He proved to be everything they wanted: mild-tempered, contented yet interested in the world around him. He was a cheerful and bright child, who excelled at his local primary school, passing the eleven-plus exam with ease to get into the city's grammar school. He was a good all-rounder, but enjoyed the sciences above all other subjects. Hence his decision to study biochemistry at university. This subject was then in its infancy, but he foresaw how it would expand during the latter part of the century into an area of major scientific importance. Throughout this time, he also kept up his love of literature, particularly poetry. He particularly liked the oriental verse form.

'He decided that he didn't want to travel too far away from his parents, James and Florence, for his university education, so he started at Bristol in the autumn of 1967. He worked hard, enjoyed his studies, and joined in with several sports, notably rowing.

'It was at a dance organised by the rowing club that he met Susan. Anyone who has met Susan will tell you what a striking person she is. Knowing her the way I do as my mother-in-law, I can understand him being completely bowled over by this sparkling and vivacious woman. He thought that she was an eighteen-year-old bank employee, as did everyone else there. In fact she was a sixteen-year-old schoolgirl.

'To say that they fell in love is an understatement. It was as if they were truly meant for each other. Florence and James have kept his diaries and some of his notebooks, and can attest to his single-minded love for Susan. Some of his poems to her are beautiful and will be read in a few minutes by Hannah and Jade, his two granddaughters.

'I would have loved to have met him and to have been able to refer to him as my father-in-law. Tragically, that was not to be. You probably all know the story, that he parted from Susan on a street corner and made his way to the station to return home for Christmas. And you are all aware of the terrible sequence of events that followed. He never knew that Susan had just become pregnant. Indeed, she didn't suspect for several weeks herself. He never got to know his wonderful daughter and his two equally wonderful granddaughters.

'We still live in a sometimes harsh world where terrible things can happen. This was a terrible thing, but for James and Florence, after more than forty years of unimaginable loss and lonely heartache, the recent discovery that they have a granddaughter has brought great comfort. And the fact that they could finally meet Susan, and discover for themselves just what force of nature had captivated their son all those years ago. Because Susan Carswell is an inspiration to everyone who meets her, and through my feelings for Sophie, I can imagine exactly what Graham felt about Susan all those years ago.

'On behalf of the family I would like to thank you all for attending. To those members of the police force here, particularly those investigating the nature of his tragic death more than forty years ago, I'd like to offer our gratitude. To those who have travelled so far to be with us today in order to offer comfort to James, Florence, Susan and Sophie I say a heartfelt thank you. Now Hannah and Jade will read to you.'

Sophie reached across and squeezed Jade's hand as the teenager left her seat and followed her older sister to the front of the congregation.

'My great-grandparents, James and Florence, have kept a little notebook all these years. It's titled, "Poems For Susan" and we've chosen five of them. We think they were written in the autumn of 1969. Our grandmother, Susan Carswell, wants us to read them to you today. We will read them from the notebook, written in our grandfather's hand. Jade will read "Two Haikus for Susan". I will then read "Three Poems for Susan."'

She took a step back, as Jade lifted the small, old notebook. Her clear voice carried across the silent room.

'Two haikus for Susan.'

'The scent of your hair
Like roses in the moonlight
Weeping as you leave'

She waited for a short while. Sophie sat between her mother and her grandmother, and held both their hands.

'We live in a dream
You and I are so perfect
The universe sleeps'

Jade bowed her head and took a step back. Sophie watched tears trickle down her daughter's face. Jade left them there, glistening on her cheek.

Hannah took the notebook and stepped forward.

'Three poems for Susan.'

'Your skin is like soft gold
That I hesitate to touch.
Your breath is like mountain air
That I am unworthy to taste.
Your hair is a silk web
In which I long to be ensnared.
Your arms are pale shadows
In which I find true joy.'

'I came to you in friendship;
You gave me hope.
I spoke to you about life;
You brought me companionship.
I reached out to you in passion;
You taught me patience.
I expected so little;
Yet you brought me love.'

'What can I offer you, my sweet love?
How can I put into words what you have brought to my
life?
The honey touch of your lips thrills my heart,
Washing cascades of emotion through my veins,
Rippling pulses of delight through my body.
I dare not ask for more;
What you bring to my life is more than I could ever hope
for,
Ever dream of.
You are everything to me, and everything I will ever need.
Susan. You have altered my world.'

Hannah, too, was in tears by the time she finished. The
two girls walked back to their seats and Martin reached across
and touched them both.

The rest of the memorial service went by in a blur of which Sophie was barely conscious. The final piece of music, chosen by Florence and James, was Va Pensiero from Verdi's *Nabucco*, the crying out of trapped spirits for freedom. The congregation remained silent for a long time after the music stopped. A cold wind was blowing across the courtyard outside the crematorium. As the family moved across to the reception room, one wreath in particular caught Sophie's eye.

* * *

'I realised I'd be expected to wear uniform, ma'am, but I didn't think you would. But it's exactly right.'

'I'm proud of who I am, Lydia. And what I do. The police force is people's main hope for justice. We have to live up to that expectation. My uniform is part of that. You should be proud of it too.'

They were standing in a corner of the function room that formed part of the crematorium complex. Martin had urged Sophie's grandparents to use it today, realising that if they had the social gathering elsewhere, many people would slip away. Sophie saw Archie Campbell talking to Jim Metcalfe and the chief constable. He beckoned her over, so she slipped her arm through Pillay's and started to walk across.

Pillay held back. 'No, ma'am. They don't want me.'

'I need another woman with me, Lydia. I know what they're like.'

Campbell greeted her. 'I was just telling your present lords and masters how much it broke my heart when you left, Sophie. Professionally, of course.' He winked.

'You haven't changed, Archie. Always the teaser.'

'But seriously, you know I'll do anything I can to help this investigation along. I've already told that to the crew here in Gloucester.'

'Thanks. I wouldn't have expected anything less from you.'

'You might be able to help us, Sophie. Billy Thompson has refused to tell us anything new. He was happy enough to give us the location of your father's body, and how the incident happened, but he clammed up after that. I suppose he's cleared his conscience, and that's that as far as he's concerned. He's only got weeks to live, maybe only days. It's possible he knows more, but he claims not to remember who the killer was, just that he was kicked out of the gang immediately after. We haven't told him that Graham was your father. I just wonder if you want to pay a visit and speak to him. It might shake up his memory a bit more.'

'Yes. Oh, yes. I had a couple of run-ins with him when I was still with you. I wonder if he'll remember me. He sent some flowers, by the way. I was puzzled when I first saw them.' She turned to the chief constable. 'I could stay here with my grandparents overnight and visit him tomorrow. Sir? Matt's down with us at the moment, and I'd be back for the afternoon. Would that be okay?'

'Of course. You must go and speak to him. You and your young DC here seem to be getting good at clearing up crimes in Campbell's kingdom. Maybe we should bill them. And if Archie's mob finds whoever did it, assuming he's still alive, then I want to be involved. I want to be there when he's charged.'

'And I'll be there as well, Sophie. In fact I'd like to read the charge sheet. You need to know how much we value you, and how much we're all behind you on this,' said Campbell.

'Thank you, both of you. It means a lot to me. I was just telling Lydia that we must always be proud of what we do. She reminds me of me when I was younger.'

Campbell looked at the young officer.

'In that case, anytime you want a change of scene, contact me.'

'You're pushing your luck, Archie Campbell. She stays with us,' said the chief constable. He turned to Sophie again. 'This must all have been pretty traumatic for you, Sophie.'

'That's an understatement, sir. I feel as if I've been through a mangle. I feel stretched, squashed and reshaped. And it's not over. I feel it in my bones. But to discover my grandparents after all this time has been wonderful. Just look at them.'

Jade was holding Florence's hand and was introducing her to some of Martin's family who'd attended the funeral. Martin, Hannah and Susan were standing with James at the bar, supping beer.

'I can't imagine what it must be like for them, discovering a family after all this time, one they didn't know they had,' Pillay said. 'It's one of the most moving things I've come across, ever.'

'Do you want some leave, Sophie? You should spend time with them,' said the ACC.

'I know. And yes, I do, but only once the present case is over, or reaches a lull. I can't leave it yet, hanging like it is. It's school half term in a few weeks and I want to take that off with Martin and Jade. And the Easter break, maybe. God, time is just shooting by too quickly for me.' She watched Hannah hold up her beer glass to the light. 'We may have to move on to a proper pub. It's not real ale in here.'

'I've heard of this real ale stuff. What exactly is it?' asked the chief constable.

Archie Campbell nearly choked on his drink. 'Christ, Bill. You never change, do you? I can't believe you've just said that. The chief constable of Dorset, of all places, and you don't know what real ale is? Don't you remember that night out we had, all those years ago in Nottingham? I made you taste every cask beer they had.'

'Well, I remember setting out, but the rest of it's a bit blurred.'

The group erupted in laughter.

Sophie steered Pillay away. 'You see, Lydia? They're human underneath. As mad as hatters.'

She spoke to some of the other guests, then navigated her way across to Florence.

'Gran, can I stay with you tonight? Change of plan.'

'Of course, my dear. And Martin as well? But don't you both have work tomorrow?'

'Just me, Gran. There's someone I need to visit in hospital in Wolverhampton, and I've only just found out. It'll be easier to get there from your place.'

'It will be lovely to have you with us for an evening, Sophie. We're both getting on and we don't have too much time left. We want to make the most we can of every day left to us. And that means seeing you and Martin and the girls as much as possible. It's a blessing that's come totally out of the blue.'

CHAPTER 20: VISIT TO A DYING MAN

Friday, Week 2

Billy Thompson was a pale shadow of the man Sophie remembered. He'd been a thickset, fleshy individual with an intimidating manner. Little of that remained now.

He lay partly propped up in bed, and opened his eyes when she sat down. He looked her up and down. His eyes still have that shrewd, calculating glint, she thought.

'Hello, Billy. Long time no see.'

'Well, I'll be damned.'

'You're certainly not bound for the better place, that's for sure.'

He cackled and reached for the oxygen mask that lay beside him on the bed.

'I hear things aren't so good. Lung cancer, is it?'

He nodded. 'Too many fags for too many years. Bloody death sticks, that's what they are.'

'I also heard that Bobby died last year. I'm sorry about that, Billy.'

'Car crash. He always was a lousy driver. Trying to get away from you lot, apparently.'

'So the old days are over, Billy. It's the end of an era, isn't it?'

'Seems that way. Not that you'll be sorry. It's what you always wanted, isn't it?'

'No, Billy. What I wanted was both of you put in front of a jury and locked up. Not dead.'

'So what are you now? No longer a sergeant, I'll bet.'

'No, I'm a DCI. In Dorset. Down at the seaside.'

'Archie Campbell will be missing you. He's up near the top now. All change, eh?'

He coughed, gasped and continued. 'What brings you all the way up here then?'

'To thank you for the flowers. To see you. To ask you one last favour. I'm calling on your sense of family, Billy. I desperately need some information that only you can provide. And you owe it to me.'

'I don't think I owe you anything, little Miss Prim.'

'Yes you do. Your gang stole my father from me.'

'What the fuck do you mean, stole your father? What kind of crap is that? And what flowers are you talking about? Is this Campbell's doing?'

'Billy, everything I'm going to tell you is God's own truth. I had no father. He disappeared before I was born. And I hated him. I despised the man who was capable of getting a young girl pregnant and then walking out on her. She was only sixteen when I was conceived. As a small girl, when I said my prayers each night, I'd go through a list of people for God to bless. I'd leave him out. I even cursed him. Every single day. Because he'd left my mum and me to fend for ourselves. I could never understand why he did it. My mum was lovely. Everyone said so. I was lovely. I knew that because all my teachers told my mum.' She paused. 'I knew it anyway. I tried so hard to be good. And my mum was a naturally kind person. So why would any man choose to walk out on us? He must have been no good, that's what I thought. He must have been a nasty one, to do something like that. Disappear and never come back. So I hated him with all my being. It became part of what I am.'

By now her tears were welling up. She'd never told anyone this, not even Martin.

'But he hadn't walked out on her, had he, Billy? He'd gone to Gloucester to visit his parents, and late at night one of your gang shot him. You dumped his body down a disused shaft where it's lain for forty long, cold years. And I've spent those forty years hating and cursing a man who didn't deserve it. Do you know how that makes me feel? Have you any idea what this is doing to me? All that hate? I feel sickened at myself. I despise myself, because I let him down. My own father. He got nothing but loathing from me all that time, and now I discover he didn't deserve any of it. He only ever deserved my love and sympathy. And where does that leave me? I want that killer, Billy. I want the man who did it. I want to feel his life in my hands because of what he's put me through.' She breathed deeply for a moment. 'That funeral was my father's, Billy. And I saw the flowers you sent.'

He coughed again. Then he regarded her, silent. It was a long time before he said, 'Charlie. His name was Charlie. He was tall and skinny, a youngster with sandy-coloured hair. I can't remember anything else about him, because he never worked for us again, not after that night. I didn't even know he had a gun with him. I couldn't be doing with crazies like him. He fucked off out of the area once I'd finished with him, and good riddance. Stupid, unreliable bastard.'

'How come he was working for you that night, Billy?'

'I think Andy brought him in. I can't remember why.'

'Who's Andy?'

'My brother.'

'But I thought there were only two of you. You and Bobby. I never came across any Andy, and I was up against you for quite a few years.'

'Andy was the youngest, our step-brother. Our Dad remarried after Mum died, and Andy was the result. But he

169

had no common sense, no savvy. He could be a right fucking nuisance at times.' Thompson wheezed. He took a sip of water. 'He should have stayed up here with us. But he kept saying two was enough and he was just getting in the way. He was chummy with a bloke he met at a young offenders' place he spent time in as a teenager. They headed down to the South Coast area together, and he only came back for Christmas. Then he vanished completely. We could never trace him. Bobby even tried to get his pal Blossom onto it, and he couldn't find him either.'

Sophie felt a tremor run down her spine. 'Blossom? A woman?'

'No. He was a short, thickset, ugly bloke Bobby knew from school. God knows why he was called Blossom. He spent a lot of his time along the South Coast, running rackets, so Bobby asked him to find Andy. But no luck. There was no trace.'

'Do you remember anything else about this Blossom?'

'I've given you what you wanted. You won't get anything else out of me. I've still got my pride, even if the rest of me's rotting away.' He coughed.

Sophie leant forward and squeezed his hand. 'Thanks for telling me, Billy. Maybe you've a slight chance of the better place after all.'

'I suppose you'll tell that bastard Campbell now.'

She looked at him and shook her head.

'You're not going to? You're gonna go after him yourself? Fuck. I'd take my hat off to you if I had one on.'

He dissolved into a fit of weak coughs and took another draught of oxygen. Sophie got up to leave.

'I hope you find him. That's if he isn't already dead. And if you do, will you come back and tell me?'

'Sure.'

'I'll stay alive for that. And I won't tell anyone. Trust me. Maybe you're not little Miss Prim after all.'

'No. I never was.'

Sophie left the ward, passing a well-dressed young woman who was on her way in. The woman sat beside the bed and smoothed her dark ponytail.

'Who was that, Uncle Billy?'

'A copper, Jennie. A very clever copper from down your way. I gave her more information than I meant to. Just be careful, will you? And make sure you find him first.'

* * *

Where should she go from here?

Sophie was sitting at her desk in the small office in Swanage. It was mid-evening and most of the team had gone home, apart from Barry Marsh. He was still logged on to his computer out in the main room, writing up a report on the day's activities. Sophie looked at her own screen, seeing nothing. All she knew was that the killer's name had been Charlie, and that he had been a relatively inexperienced youngster when he'd shot her father. It didn't seem very much to go on. Well, it was more than she'd known before, she supposed. All she had to do was apply some logic, think about the problem rationally.

Billy Thompson had said that Charlie had been a young-ster. So what would his age have been? Eighteen to twen-ty-four? If he were still alive, that would put him at sixty-two to sixty-eight. He'd have been born in the mid to late forties, possibly as late as 1950.

He'd been tall and thin. Would that have changed as he got older? She'd work on the assumption that he would still be leaner than average. He'd had sandy-coloured hair. Would it still be sandy, or would it have gone grey?

If he'd been recruited by the Thompsons, then he would have come from the West Midlands somewhere. She'd have to do a bit of reading to check where the gang had been based in their early years. She seemed to remember that they had lived in Dudley at one time, but that could have been later in their criminal careers.

Finally, she knew that her quarry had been undisciplined and unpredictable. Not in itself uncommon in criminals, but in this case probably worse than most. The Thompsons would have laid down the guidelines for the break-in. But this young man, Charlie, had gone against their instructions. He'd been too wild, so had been ejected from the gang. She guessed that this would also mean he'd been forced to leave their territory. The chances were that he'd have been in some kind of trouble with the police wherever he'd ended up. If he was violent and careless, surely he'd have been arrested at some time? So where would he have gone? London? She couldn't recall anyone who fitted that profile from her brief stint as a DC in the Met, although that had been years ago. What about Bristol and the South West? Or maybe he'd moved to the East Midlands? For some reason she thought there was less chance of him going north, so she'd leave out Manchester or Leeds for the moment.

What was needed now was some work on the database. She had something to go on, at least.

She knew as she logged on that all of her searches would be monitored, but she wasn't doing anything unprofessional — not yet, anyway. She built up her search, step by step. Male, white, tall, thin. Born between 1944 and 1950. Hair colour light brown or sandy, or grey. Area restricted to West Midlands or South West. Name Charles or Charlie or Charley. She clicked the search button and waited.

Marsh popped his head round the door. 'I'll be off, ma'am. I think that's all I can do this evening. We didn't manage to get anything new out of that old chap I saw at the Poole warehouse. What he told me on Wednesday was probably all he knew. But at least we have a formal statement from him.'

'Fine, Barry. I'll be another hour or so, then I'll be following you. I'm doing some tinkering on the database, looking for clues about who killed my father.'

'Well, I wish you luck. It was a long time ago. Shouldn't you be leaving it to the Gloucester crew?'

'I'm an obsessive, Barry. Surely you've realised that?'

'No comment, ma'am. Bye.'

Sophie sipped her mug of tea and watched the short list of names that were appearing on the screen in front of her.

'Oh, my dear God!' she said aloud. There was no one to hear her.

One of the names matched. It matched everything. The name ran through her brain like an electric spark, igniting fuses as it went.

* * *

Sophie was very quiet that evening. When Martin commented on it she gave him a weak smile. She lay awake until three in the morning, her head churning. She was up at six. She took a shower and had laid the breakfast table ready for the family when they rose an hour later. She was sitting outside on the rear veranda, sipping a mug of tea, when the first footsteps sounded on the stairs.

'Mum! What are you doing? It's freezing out here.' Jade popped her head out of the French windows.

'I'm fine, Jade. I'm well wrapped up. I just needed some cold air to clear my head.'

She came into the kitchen wearing a bright smile.

'You're in danger of becoming a nut, Mum. You're starting to show the signs.'

'Oh? And what are they?'

'Calling the cat Greymalkin. Muttering about eye of newt while you're stirring the soup. Hissing "Out damned spot" when you were washing my PE kit last weekend. You know, little things like that.'

'And I really thought I'd escaped undetected, Jade. Can't fool you, can I?'

'No, Mum. I'm just too sharp.'

'And revising Macbeth, I take it?'

'Yup. Test in English on Monday.'

'Well, it looks like you know your stuff. And don't worry. I have a lot on my mind, but I'm not going into mental overload just yet. I just discovered something about the case yesterday evening that has potentially massive implications.'

'But you can't talk about it?'

'Afraid not. Not to a mere mortal, anyway.' She glanced at her watch. 'Well. I'd better have something to eat before I grab my broomstick and fly off into the wide blue yonder. And, Jade, in case you haven't noticed, we don't have a cat.'

CHAPTER 21: SORINA

Friday, Week 2

Sorina lay face down on the bed, her belly on a pile of grubby cushions. Her head had dropped forward and she dribbled onto the soiled cover. She hurt. She ached. She whimpered quietly as her body and mind succumbed to utter exhaustion. She had no strength left. She didn't move — she couldn't. Her brain was in shock, unable to process all the pain, the terror and the horror of what had been done to her. Ricky and Barbu, two strong, heavily built men. She lay, drifting in and out of consciousness. A shaft of sunlight crossed her body, and a pair of sparrows chattered under the eaves above her head.

It was late afternoon when Sorina finally managed to move her limbs. She turned over. There was a small hand basin in the corner of the room. She raised herself, slid to the edge of the bed and tried to stand but her legs would not support her, and she fell to the floor. She lay there for a few minutes, then held onto the edge of the bed, slowly pushing herself upright. This time she managed to make the few short steps to the basin without falling. Waves of nausea shuddered across her body. She held onto the edge of the basin and looked into the mirror above it. She saw a face streaked with tears, snot, semen, dirt. She started to cry, sobbing in anguish as she stared at the face in the mirror. She breathed deeply, tried the taps and found they were both working. She filled the basin with warm water and plunged her face into it. Soap. She must have soap. She found a small bar in a drawer under the basin, and lathered her face and head. She hooked one leg at a time into the water and soaped the top of each thigh. She emptied the basin, and refilled it. She used soapy water as a mouthwash, rinsing out what those men had left.

Gradually Sorina began to recognise herself again. Her small, sharp features re-emerged. She was full of hate. She remembered Nadia's words, following a similar ordeal. 'I will get my revenge on those beasts.' Well, she, Sorina, would do the same. She would find a way to escape. She would find Nadia, and together they would seek vengeance for the evil that had been done to them.

She dried herself with the only towel in the room, and returned to the bed. She lay down and slept.

* * *

Several hours later Smiffy came to collect her. He led her down the stairs to the living room, where the others were eating. They were silent as she entered. They watched her small, shaky steps as she made her way across the room to a chair. They all knew what had happened to her. Catalina came over and put her arms around Sorina. Then she dished up a plate of stew from a large pot in the middle of the table. Smiffy watched them for a moment and then left, locking the door behind him.

The other women watched anxiously as Sorina picked at her food.

'You must keep your strength up, Sorina,' Catalina said.

'We are five. They are three. Why aren't we resisting?' Sorina said bitterly. It was the first time she had spoken like this out loud to the whole group.

'Because they have weapons. And they can call on more people if they need to,' someone said. 'You saw what they did to Stefan. And that pig Barbu has said that they killed others like us who tried to resist.'

Catalina nodded. 'But we can plan. We can talk. We can watch. Most of all, we can agree to stick together. We have all been through it now. They are pigs, beasts, and it will not get better. We must be ready for escape when a chance comes.'

'Like Nadia,' added Sorina. 'If she got free then she will have been found and the police might be looking for us.'

'Yes, and next time someone sees a chance to escape it must be all of us. We must all look for things we can use as weapons, and hide them. But we must not act against them unless we are sure and we are prepared.'

Smiffy came back into the room. He dropped a pile of old magazines onto the table and withdrew to a chair in the corner, picking at his fingernails with a knife. Sorina watched him, peering over the pages of her magazine. How could she have ended up like this? She'd had it all planned before her sixteenth birthday. A job in a hotel where she would meet a handsome young manager and fall in love. A whirlwind romance, and a wedding on a glorious summer's day. A honeymoon somewhere sophisticated and exotic, where they would both be offered jobs. A family, two girls and two boys. It was all going to be so perfect. And now? These monsters had stolen her future. She would not let them see her cry.

* * *

Ricky and Barbu were watching TV and drinking from cans of beer when Charlie arrived.

'I've got a lead on Blossom. He might have a flat near the central gardens in Bournemouth that he never told us about. I'm trying to get my contact to dig a bit more, but it might take a couple of days. I want you and Barbu to be ready for when we do trace him.'

'How will we do it?'

'I'll think of a way. One thing's for sure, I'm not letting you decide after that crazy, fucking do with Stefan. We'll try to make it look like an accident but it'll take some planning. I don't want the cops getting involved before we can clean his place out. If they find this flat of his before we do, then God knows what they'll find there. It might be better just to go for something quick and easy.'

'Any more news about them searching the depot?'

'Yeah. They found the body out back, but are keeping quiet about it.'

'What body? Jesus! Do you mean you buried someone out there? Fuck, Charlie. What were you thinking?'

'It was before your time, Ricky boy. And at least we buried it. We didn't leave it out on some fucking rock. It was twenty years ago or more. Just a head case, someone from the past that Blossom knew. He turned up and tried to blackmail me. Can you imagine that? I just laughed at him and then I shot him in the head. No one else knew he was there, so we buried him that night. We always meant to dig it up and get rid of it at sea, but we never got round to it.'

'So Blossom was involved?'

'I told you he was vicious. God knows why he's gone soft all of a sudden, but I bet it's only skin-deep.'

CHAPTER 22: FRICTION BETWEEN FRIENDS

Friday Evening

Blossom and Jennie were sitting in a café near Bournemouth seafront. As she stirred her coffee, Jennie leaned over, exposing her cleavage. It was early evening on the fifth day of Blossom's new job, and Jennie had phoned him to suggest meeting after work for a light meal.

'So tell me more about this ex-boss of yours. What did you say his name was? Charlie Duff?'

'Why do you want to know about him? He's just some bastard. Let's talk about you. Tell me a bit more about yourself.'

She sighed. 'I was adopted, Blossom. When I talked to you a few days ago about my middle-class childhood, I meant my adoptive parents. They were fantastic. Well, they still are. They were so good to me.'

'How old were you when you first went to live with them?'

'Only a few months. We were in the Midlands until I was about two. Then we moved down here. My dad's a doctor, that's why he wanted me to study medicine.'

'Have you ever thought about tracing your real parents?'

'Yes. I think all adopted people do. But I haven't found them. I think they're both dead. The adoption agency had almost no details. The addresses they gave me were in old Victorian terraced streets. They've been knocked down and no longer exist.'

'Do you know why you were put up for adoption?'

'I think my mother was a young teenager. I expect she just couldn't cope.'

'And your old man?'

She looked down. 'Don't know. Maybe it was just a one-night stand. What about you?'

'I come from Birmingham too. There's not much to tell.'

'How did you get the name Blossom? You can't tell me that's your proper name.'

'It's been my nickname since I was at school. I won a poetry competition — the only time I ever won anything. I had to read it out to the class. It was about blossom in spring and the other lads never let me forget it.'

'How did you end up working for this Duff character?'

'Him again?' Blossom stretched back in his chair, his hands clasped behind his thick neck. 'His wife, Hazel, was my cousin. I always got on well with her. She seemed to think she should look after me so I didn't argue. And it was easy money.'

'What did you do?'

'Oh, you know. Punch a few faces occasionally, collect some money, move people about when they needed a driver, sort out disputes, troublemakers. That kind of thing.'

'So this job you've just started as a security guard isn't anything new for you?'

'Christ, no. It's right up my street. Easy as pie.'

'How come you fell out with him? Especially if his wife was looking out for you?'

'She died a couple of years back. Cancer. And without her there, he started turning nasty. He could be a cruel bastard. Reverting to type I expect.'

'What do you mean?'

'I don't want to talk about it. Don't keep pushing, Jennie. It's starting to bug me.'

They left the café in silence and walked back to the block of flats.

'You were away early this morning,' Blossom said. 'You took the car, too. That's a bit unusual for you.'

'Had a client to visit. They're a long way out of town.'

'Somewhere nice?'

She shrugged.

'I mean, was it local or a bit of a trek?'

'I'm like you, Blossom. I don't want to talk about it. Okay?'

They walked on in silence until they were near their building. Suddenly Jennie stopped and flung her arms around Blossom.

'I'm sorry, Blossom,' she said. 'I don't want to end the day on a bad note. You've become one of the best friends I have. I was up in the Midlands this morning seeing my client. I'd arranged it because an uncle of mine is in hospital with lung cancer and I wanted to visit him. He doesn't have long to live. He's the only blood relative I've managed to find.'

'So you have found someone. You didn't say that before.'

She shrugged her shoulders.

'Can he tell you much about your parents?'

'I only met him for the first time a few weeks ago. He can hardly speak, he just gasps, and he was only my father's step-brother. Much older than him too. They lost contact when my real dad was still a teenager, so he can't help much. All he could do was confirm that my dad's probably been dead for a long time.'

'I thought you said you never knew about your dad. You said it was a one-night stand.'

'That's what I always thought. Maybe it wasn't quite like that.'

'So how did you find this bloke, your uncle?'

'I didn't. He found me. I guess he wants to tie up loose ends before he dies. He told me today that he felt a bit guilty because he knew I existed but had never tried to find me before. But he did confirm that my mother's dead. He knew that for sure. Anyway, that's why I'm a bit tense. I don't know what your excuse is.'

Blossom laughed. 'I ain't got an excuse. It's just me. I clam up when people ask too many questions. I always wonder what they're after. I'm sorry too. Look it's getting wet out here. Why don't you come up to my place and we can have a drink? It's a lot smaller than your flat, but I try to keep it clean and tidy.'

They walked up to the flat. Blossom poured Jennie a glass of wine and opened a beer for himself. Then he excused himself to visit the toilet.

'Another sign that I'm beginning to get past it,' he said. 'Me bladder's not what it was.'

She waited until she heard the bathroom door close. She picked up his mobile phone from the table and scrolled through the numbers. By the time he returned, the phone was back in its place and Jennie was standing at the window, sipping her wine.

'It's nice,' she said, looking around her. 'Small, but it has everything you need. And you're right. You do keep it neat.' She took another sip. 'Didn't you ever get married, Blossom?'

'Not for me. I'm not your tall and handsome type, am I? I always felt out of the running when it came to women. What could I offer them?'

'We're not all as shallow as that, Blossom. You've got qualities that a lot of women would appreciate. I'd imagine you like looking after people, and that you care about them. That's quite important.'

'Well, I always felt that I'd come off second best in any beauty contest, so I never bothered. I've had a few girlfriends, but nothing serious. It's left me free and I ain't regretted it. And I'm fifty now, so there's not much hope, is there?'

He took another swig of his beer.

'I don't think that's true. There are an awful lot of older single people looking for a partner. Most people are scared of having a lonely old age. The personal columns are full of people in their fifties and sixties. And at that age looks matter less than you might think. Most women will be looking for someone with a kind heart and a willingness to share. And I bet you fit that bill really well.'

'Are you trying to butter me up?'

'I wouldn't dream of it,' she laughed. 'You're shrewd enough to see through me right away.' She glanced at her watch. 'I have some work to finish off, so I'd better be leaving. I've got to go into work tomorrow morning. But we could meet for lunch if you wanted.'

He nodded.

* * *

Back in her own flat, Jennie stood at the window with another glass of wine. How should she play this? Blossom was the only link she had with her missing father, the only contact that her uncle Billy could remember. She thought about their conversation.

'Your dad'll be dead, Jennie, I'd bet on it. But I want to know for sure and I expect you do too. This guy Blossom might have the answer, but you'll need to be careful. I heard that he used to be really violent when he was riled. And there's a chance he might have been involved in whatever happened to Andy. According to what your uncle Bobby said, he's a mixed-up character, so don't provoke him. In the end it might just be better to come clean with him and tell him who you are. You'll have to judge that for yourself.'

'This is all a shock to me, Uncle Billy. Meeting people like you, finding out my real dad was probably involved with a criminal gang. Sometimes I ask myself if I want to carry on. My parents would have a fit if they knew. But you're the only hope I have of tracing him, so I'll do the best I can. But I'm not optimistic. I don't know how long I can carry on this act. Getting that flat below his was a stroke of luck in one way, but I can guess how it's going to look to him. It just seemed such a good idea at the time.'

CHAPTER 23: FAMILY SECRETS

Saturday, Week 2

Jennie arrived at the pub before Blossom, so she bought some drinks and took them across to a table in a quiet corner. She still hadn't decided what her next move should be. How to go about finding out what Blossom knew? She saw him enter the bar and waved.

'This one's for you,' she said. 'It's about time you started drinking the proper stuff, instead of that crappy lager.'

'Feeling bossy, are you?' he said.

'Absolutely not. The exact opposite.' She smoothed her ponytail. 'Look Blossom, I've got something to tell you. I don't really know how to say it, so I'm just going to go ahead anyway and sod the consequences. I expect you'll get angry and walk out. It might be the end of our friendship.' She took a gulp of beer.

'I'll save you the bother. You're gonna tell me you're Andy Thompson's daughter.'

She stared at him. 'What? How did you know?'

'Lots of reasons. I knew your mum and you look just like her. She used to pull her hand through her ponytail just like you. And I'm not as stupid as I look. Ever since you moved in I've thought you reminded me of someone. There's lots of other little things that you do as well, just like her. You're obviously a bit of a goer, just like she was. And you kept asking about Charlie. Too often. But I didn't know for sure until yesterday when you told me you were adopted. And that you'd been up to see your uncle in hospital. That'll be Billy, won't it?'

She nodded.

'So he must have told you I knew your dad? You've known for a while?'

She nodded again.

'What a fucking mess. Is he really dying? Your Uncle Billy, I mean.'

'Lung cancer.'

'So he wants to find out what happened to Andy, same as you do?'

'Yes. Blossom, did you really know my mum?' She reached across and gripped his hand. 'Please? I know nothing about her. Uncle Billy said he didn't know much about her either.'

'Her name was Linda Stockwell. She died when you were born. Some kind of complications. Andy never got over it. You got put up for adoption and he just vanished for a long time. God knows what he did or where he went. I was down here by the time he surfaced, so Bobby Thompson put him in touch with me. But he'd frazzled his brain with drugs. There was no sense left in him. It was a fucking disaster.'

'What about my mum?' she held his hand tighter.

'You get your brains from her, as well as your looks. She dropped out of college to live with Andy, but they were both wasted all the time. Never ate properly. She made an effort to get off the drugs when she was pregnant with you, and then it all went wrong.'

Jennie saw that his eyes were damp.

'Were you in love with her yourself? You were, weren't you?'

He clasped her hand, hard. 'That's why I feel the way I do about you, Jennie. It's all too fucking weird. When I look at you, it's like you're her and I get those feelings again. But it's also like I'm a kind of uncle to you. I keep having to tell myself I'm from their generation, not yours. It's all too much and it scares me. And nothing scares Blossom Sourlie. I don't do scared.' He paused. 'I really hated him.'

'Who?'

'Andy. Your father. Because he fucking ruined her with those drugs. It was him started her on them. He was the worst thing that could have happened to her. He was a total waster, and I could never understand what she saw in him.' He sipped his drink. 'I worshipped her, you know. I'd have done anything for her, anything. But I didn't step in when I should have, and I've regretted it ever since.'

He sat silently, looking out of the window. He seemed very alone, and sad. Eventually he said, 'So do you know what's the most important thing in my life right now? Keeping you safe. 'Cause I'm guessing that you know a bit more than you're letting on. I don't want you meddling with the people you're thinking of meddling with. They're nastier than you could ever imagine. I could never forgive myself if something happened to you, not after I failed your mum.'

She reached across and touched his face. 'Bless you, Blossom.'

He put his hand over hers, holding it to his cheek.

She thought for a while and then asked the question he'd been evading for days.

'How does Charlie Duff fit into all this?'

'Where do you think Andy got his drugs from all those years ago? Who do you think he came to for help when he came down here? Who do you think got him hooked again? And who got fed up when Andy mucked up his operations?'

'So what happened to him?'

'What do you think? These people are crazies, Jennie. They don't behave like people do in the nice, neat, normal

186

world. Andy disappeared. You can guess what that means.' Blossom sighed. 'I never saw him again, and I didn't miss him because I hated him after what he did to your mum. Good fucking riddance, is what I thought then. And I don't feel too different now, twenty years later.'

'So Charlie Duff supplied the drugs that ruined my mother's life and wasted my dad. He killed my dad when he wasn't useful any more. And you don't want me to meddle? Why haven't you been to the police with all this?'

Blossom didn't answer.

'Are you implicated somehow? Were you involved?'

'I was a business partner in the company that fronted the operations. Me, Hazel, Charlie and Ricky, their nephew. I'm too involved, Jennie. The cops would hang me out to dry. Especially now. I did all the running about for them for years. I know their secrets, so yes, I'm implicated in it all. My mind keeps going round in circles, looking for a way out. But I can't see one.'

'Look. Let's eat some lunch and get another drink. I need to get to grips with everything you've told me. I feel kind of elated. I'm just so glad to have the truth after all these years.'

Neither of them had much appetite. They picked at their food in silence.

'Blossom, are you in any danger from them?'

'What do you think? They're vicious animals and I've walked out on them. I know too much. I don't know how much longer I'm gonna be safe around here. They'll be looking for me and if they find me, I'm a goner.'

'Wouldn't you be safer away from this area?'

'They don't know about the flat. I kept that to myself. They're all based over in Poole. But you're right, it's too close for comfort. I've got one more week on this job, then when it finishes I'll have to get away. But I don't know where, unless I go back to the Midlands, but I lost all my old contacts years ago. So where can I go? I'm no good at scheming, Jennie. I left that to Hazel and Charlie. I just do what I'm told, and I like it that way.'

'Well, look. Once you've finished this job with Roy, he should be able to give you a reference. That means you've got a foot in the door. He might know of an opening somewhere else, away from here. Why not ask him? If you do move away, will you keep the flat?'

'I suppose so. Haven't really thought about it. It all scares me. I just don't like change. It screws my brain up.'

* * *

'How the fuck am I meant to contact you then?' Ricky was furious, spitting beer as he spoke. 'If you decided to fuck off out of it I could be left carrying the can for everything.'

'Sit down, you pillock. Just use my mobile number, but watch what you say, in case it's being monitored.' Charlie Duff sighed. His erratic nephew was proving to be a real problem. Hazel had always handled him so well. 'I'm just not taking any chances. I haven't been home since they called at your place last Sunday, and I'm not going back there anytime soon. They've got a car watching your house, probably mine as well.'

'How could they be on to you? There's nothing to connect us, is there?'

'If they do enough digging, they might find something. And that blonde bitch worries me. I told her Hazel's name. It was fucking stupid of me, but I can't unsay it now.'

'I still can't see it.'

'God, you're fucking thick. The name of the house, you prick. It's our names. Hazel loved doing anagrams. Anyway, I'm not taking any chances, so I'm staying away from the place and using my flat instead. You need more help here, so it kills two birds. But I have to keep everything else ticking over as well. I can't be here all the time. That fucker Blossom may think he's ruined everything by walking out, but it's not gonna happen.'

'Can you bring someone else in?'

'Yeah. I've got someone lined up, but I'm using him to find Blossom at the moment. Once we've dealt with him we'll be laughing again.' He took a swig of his beer. 'We're getting closer. We know the area he's living in. He's been seen out with a bird. I've just got to figure out a way to do it.'

'When do we move into town and start working the girls?'

'I need a couple more days to get the place ready. I thought I told you that?'

'It's just that they're talking to each other. We don't know what they're saying unless Barbu is in with them.'

'They always talk, Ricky. All the girls we've brought in have done that.'

'No, this is different. Smiffy's worried. He's the one who noticed it. He reckons it's because that one escaped. It's given the others ideas.'

* * *

Catalina was talking to Sorina in the locked living room, trying to keep up her spirits.

'Where do you come from, Sorina?'

'Timisoara. And Nadia. Nadia is older than me. I had only just left school, and I had a job in a café near the hotel where Nadia worked. She came into the café sometimes and we became friends. She found me a job in the hotel and we used to talk about our plans for the future. When they came and told us that we could work and study in England, we were so happy about it. Where were you living?'

'Arad. Each one of us is from a different town or village, but all in the west, near the border with Hungary. Only you and Nadia came from the same town and knew each other. I think they like for us not to know each other. It makes it easier for them when we are not friends. I overheard Barbu saying it to the dead boy.'

'But why did they bring Nadia and me, then? We worked together in the hotel. They knew that.'

'You are both young, and you look alike, both small, slim and blonde. You could be sisters. I think they maybe had a plan for you both. That changed when Nadia escaped. And her escape is why we have moved so much, I'm sure. They have been in a panic.'

'Do you think she is safe? I hope she is, and is trying to find us. She is such a good person. My mother would only let me come because Nadia was going to be with me. She trusted Nadia to look after me.'

'I'm sure she is trying, Sorina. If she has gone to the police, then they will all be looking for us. And she knows how bad they can be. She was the first one that two of them raped. She will not rest until we are safe, I'm sure of it.'

'But how will they understand her? She doesn't speak English. None of us do. That was the thing that puzzled my mother. It is obvious now. They are going to put us onto the streets as whores, and we cannot talk to anyone. So how will Nadia speak about us?'

Catalina did not reply. Sorina stood up and walked to the window.

'Even if we escape, Catalina, where will we go? I haven't seen anyone since we arrived here. We could die out there.'

'I don't think we would. England is a much smaller country than Romania, but it has more people. It is a very crowded land. I learned that in my job. An English lady told me that you are never far from a village or town, wherever you are. At least I think that is what she said.'

'Do you speak a little English, then?' Sorina said.

'Yes, but keep quiet about it. Those men don't know.'

'Do any of the other girls?' Sorina glanced back at the other three, all watching a music video channel on TV.

'No. Sorina, you must have realised. They are all farm girls. I worry about them, because I see them beginning to accept this new life. I heard Elisabeta talking at breakfast. She said that there will be plenty of money for us. And drugs to keep us happy. You see? They are already beginning to accept what that pig Barbu has been telling them. You and I must be careful what we say and what we do. I wonder if they have only brought peasant girls before. So why did they bring you, me and Nadia? What were their plans for us? And have they changed since Nadia went? I think about it at night.'

CHAPTER 24: DEATH IN THE GARDENS

Sunday Afternoon, Week 2

A young man wearing black trousers and a dark hooded jacket sat in his car, his eyes never leaving the building across the road. He saw the short, squat shape of Blossom Sourlie leave the building accompanied by a woman with a ponytail. He took his mobile phone from his pocket and made a call. He waited until the pair were out of sight, then slid out of the car and made his way to the front door. He chose an entry button at random and spoke into the microphone.

'I've got some presents for Mr Sourlie. He's left me a key for his flat but I've forgotten the flat number and the main door's entry code. Have I got the right address?'

He listened to the reply.

'I'm his cousin,' he said. 'I'm just back from six months abroad with the navy. It's some stuff that needs to go straight into his fridge. Could you buzz me in, please?'

He waited, then opened the door and made for the stairs. He took them two at a time, glancing around as he climbed. No one came out of their doors and no one passed him. Blossom's flat was a loft conversion, the only one on the top floor. The

man took a small implement from his pocket and started probing the lock. A couple of minutes later he was inside the small
apartment, and looking around the rooms. This wouldn't take
long. Any address book, diary or notebook, Charlie Duff had
said. Group photos and snapshots. Anything that might point
the finger at Blossom's erstwhile partners.

The man was soon out of the flat. There hadn't been much
to find. Duff had told him Blossom wasn't a big writer. An
address book, a couple of notebooks but no photos. He was
back in his car and away in minutes.

*　*　*

Blossom and Jennie meandered slowly along a footpath
towards the town centre and the seafront. Few other people
had ventured out, despite the occasional patches of blue sky.
They stopped at an ice cream van, then walked a little further
before sitting down on a bench to talk.

'I needed some fresh air,' she said. 'I've been working all
morning on a report. It's left me feeling muzzy-headed.'

She licked her ice cream.

'There's still stuff you haven't told me about Charlie
Duff, Blossom. And I still think you should get the police
involved somehow. He needs to be dealt with, surely?'

'If there was a way, I'd do it. I've been thinking of waiting
till I finish this job at the end of the week. With a bit of luck
I'll be off somewhere else after that, so I'll contact them after
I've gone.'

He sounded despondent.

'What is the problem, Blossom? Surely the police will
do some kind of deal with you? And it's not as though you've
done anything too bad is it, from what you've said? He's the
one who supplied the drugs and killed my father, not you.'

She looked at him, but he refused to meet her eye.

'What haven't you told me, Blossom? I've been thinking
about it since yesterday, when you said they were animals.
How bad are these people?'

'It gets about as bad as it can get. I'd be looking at spending most of the rest of my life in the clink. Don't you think I want to make a clean break? Fuck, of course I do. But that's too high a price.'

She stiffened. 'What do you mean, it gets as bad as it can get? What exactly has he been doing? Drugs? Assault? Murder? Rape? What?'

He spoke quietly. 'All of those. We've been running in girls from Romania and selling them on for work on the streets.'

'You've been trafficking women? Christ, Blossom. What kind of warped people are you? And what do you mean, all of those? What else have you done?' She looked into his face. He continued to look down. She'd seen the TV news about the women who'd been smuggled across to the farm near Poole Harbour. And the horrific discovery made by the police there. 'Oh no. Not those girls' bodies in Studland. Oh, Jesus. Not you, Blossom. No.'

She stood up.

'I didn't know, Jennie,' he whispered. 'I only found out about them a few days ago. That's why I quit.'

But she'd already grabbed her bag and was moving away. Blossom didn't try to stop her.

Jennie walked away, tears blinding her eyes. Her only contact with her parents. A man who'd known and loved her mother, and what had he turned out to be? Evil, evil, evil. Had anything he'd told her even been true? She walked on, thoughts whirling in her mind. She heard a faint popping noise behind her, but it didn't register at first. Then something made her turn and look back. Blossom was lying on the ground, sprawled across the path. She caught sight of some dark figures disappearing up a path behind the bushes.

She ran back. She crouched down by his body and held his hand, but she knew it was too late. It had always been too late.

CHAPTER 25: THE TWO DAUGHTERS MEET

Late Sunday Afternoon

As a child Nadia had been told the story of Pandora's Box. It made so much sense now. Evil, once unleashed, can never be put back, never unlearned, never un-experienced. She was safe. She was in a secure house with her mother, under constant guard. But she couldn't escape her memories. Only one thing made her get out of bed early each morning. Her friend DCI Sophie called in every day on her way into work. She'd tried to get Nadia to call her just Sophie, but the teenager was too much in awe of her. She copied the other police officers, and called her ma'am or chief inspector. This sounded right to her, though she always followed her formal greeting with a hug and a cup of tea for her rescuer and heroine.

Nadia told Sophie about her recurring memories, and how difficult it was to cope with them. Sophie said, 'Nadia, it is life. It's what it means to be human. Your experiences have been worse than most, but you must not let the memories take over. You must master your experiences, not let them master you.'

But Sophie arranged for a counsellor to visit Nadia. She and her mother had regular visits from a young Romanian woman interpreter, but she struggled to put into words the anguish Nadia was feeling. Nadia now understood that she would come through this in time. But she slept fitfully and was troubled by constant flashbacks.

Most of all she worried for Sorina. She had promised Sorina's mother that she would look after her. How was the fragile young girl coping with the ordeal? It was almost too much to bear, sitting in this house and imagining Sorina's pain.

It was a relief to go out and visit Jade for a few hours. She and her mother were now enjoying tea and cakes in the Allens' lounge. Nadia had shown her mother the small guest room where she'd slept the previous weekend. She was now chatting with Jade, in her limited English, about the latest fashion trends.

* * *

Sophie's mobile phone rang and she left the room to answer it.

'Hi, Kevin.'

'Sophie, there's been a fatal shooting in the central gardens. We think it's your man, Blossom.'

Sophie was at the scene within half an hour. She ran across to the group of detectives standing with Kevin McGreedie.

'Blossom Sourlie,' he said. 'Single gunshot wound to the head. The woman witness said all she heard was a popping noise, so they must have used a silencer. She was about a hundred yards away, but didn't see the actual shooting. She says she was walking away from him at the time.'

Sophie looked down at the body. It was the short, powerfully-built man she'd met at Brookway Farm.

'How did you know it was Blossom Sourlie?' she asked.

'The woman knows him. Her name's Jennie Brown. She lives in the flat below his, and was with him until just before the shooting. They had an ice cream, and she left him to walk back to her place. Then it happened. She says that she just caught sight of some figures heading up the path there.' He pointed to some steps leading up behind a shrubbery to the road above. 'It's all taped off. The forensic squad should be here soon.'

'Where is she?'

'In my car with one of the local bobbies. She's a bit hysterical and wants to go home, but I've kept her here. I'll come with you.'

The two detectives walked back across the gardens. The car's windows were misted over, obscuring the features of the woman sitting in the back.

'Thanks, Kevin. I'll take it from here if you don't mind,' Sophie said.

She climbed into the front passenger seat and turned to speak to the woman. She stared at her, aghast. What was going on? She got out of the car and walked across to a fence that surrounded the gardens. Her mind was reeling. She gripped the handrail as if she was about to fall over a precipice.

Get a grip, Sophie, she told herself. McGreedie had turned and was beginning to walk back towards her, and she waved him away. She took a deep breath and returned to the car.

'So we meet again. It's a bit of a cliché, I know, but seeing you here has taken me by surprise. It can't be chance, can it?'

'Sorry? I don't understand,' the young woman said.

'We met briefly last week. I passed you in the ward at Wolverhampton hospital. I was leaving and you were coming in. You were doing what you're doing now, pulling your fingers through your ponytail. You were wearing the same coat.'

'Christ. I can't cope with all this.'

'You need to tell me what's going on. Jennie, isn't it? Look, I'm nearly as shocked as you.' She paused. 'Do you live close by?'

Jennie nodded. 'It's only a couple of hundred yards further on. He lived in the flat above me.'

'Okay, let's walk. The fresh air will do you good, and I certainly need it.'

They got out of the car. Sophie asked one of the uniformed constables to follow them. Then she took Jennie's arm in a firm grip and started walking.

'Jennie, I need to know what's behind this. I know what you've told my colleague, but there's more, isn't there? You were on your way in to visit Billy Thompson at the end of last week. He was in a room by himself, so there was no other reason for you to have been there. I've been wondering about you on and off since then. And you just happen to be here when that man Blossom gets killed. What's the connection?'

'I think he was killed by someone called Charlie Duff. Blossom told me that he'd walked out on Duff's gang a week ago.'

Sophie was still reeling. She forced herself to speak. 'Okay, but that doesn't explain why you were visiting Thompson last week.'

'He's my uncle. And I think Charlie Duff killed my father.'

'Your father?' Sophie stopped walking and gripped Jennie's arm so tightly that the younger woman winced. 'Your father? Andy Thompson?'

'Yes. I never knew him, or my mother. As I told Blossom, I was adopted at birth. I only found out about my birth family six months ago when Uncle Billy contacted me. He'd just been told he had terminal cancer, and he decided to trace me. Last week was only the third time I'd met him.'

'And he wanted to know what had happened to his brother, so he was using you to find out. Was it him that suggested you use Blossom as a lead?'

By now they'd arrived at the apartment block. A police car was parked across the entrance, and a constable was hurrying out of the front entrance. Sophie stopped him and asked what was going on.

'His flat's been broken into, ma'am,' he said. 'We've only just discovered it.'

Sophie checked that the door to Jennie's flat was still secure. She ushered Jennie inside and told her to remain there with the constable until she returned. She ran upstairs to Blossom's apartment. Drawers and cupboards had been left open, and their contents strewn over the floor.

Sophie returned to Jennie's flat. She sent the uniformed officer outside.

Jennie seemed to have calmed down. She offered Sophie a mug of tea, although her hand shook as she pushed it across the table.

'Can we start again please, Jennie? From the beginning? Tell me a little about yourself. Try to relax if you can, although I realise it might be difficult.'

'I'm thirty-four. I'm an accountant with an insurance firm in Ringwood, and I've lived in the area for almost ten years, but not in this flat. I was adopted as a baby in Birmingham. I never knew who my birth parents were, and didn't want to know because my adoptive parents were so good to me.' She wiped her eyes with a tissue and blew her nose. 'We moved to Southampton when I was about five. I never bothered with my past because I was so happy with my parents. I did some checking about ten years ago, but got nowhere, so I left it alone. Then about six months ago I got a message from someone claiming to be my uncle. He said he was my father's half-brother, and had known about me but had never bothered to trace me. Now he was dying he thought we should meet, and that I might want to help find out what had happened to my father. Apparently they'd lost contact many years ago. I thought about it for quite a long time before deciding what to do. In the end I went to visit him and he told me that my birth father's name was Andy Thompson. They hadn't got on at all well, so Andy had left the Midlands and come down to the South Coast area. He'd made one brief trip back for a family Christmas party and then vanished. On that visit he told them he'd met up with Blossom again. Blossom had once been a friend of one of my other uncles.'

She took a sip of tea.

'So we agreed that since I was living here anyway, I'd start looking. Uncle Billy sent me an address that he thought was

Blossom's. He never told me where he'd got the information from. I did a bit of asking around in the other flats and found that he lived on the top floor but was hardly ever here. Then this flat came up for sale, so I decided to buy it and move in. It's a lovely flat in a fantastic location and I thought it might give me a good chance of meeting and talking to him. And that's what happened. Please believe me, I knew nothing about any criminal connections or gangs or anything, until the last day or two.'

'So Billy didn't give you the full picture?'

'What do you mean? Did he know?' She looked genuinely surprised.

'He pulled the wool over your eyes, Jennie. With his younger brother Bobby, he ran one of the biggest criminal gangs in the Birmingham area. I had regular run-ins with him when I was with the West Midlands major crime unit, but we could never pin anything on him. He and I became a bit like chess opponents, circling round each other. But in a strange way I kind of liked him. I never knew they had a younger step-brother until last week when I visited him. Anyway, go on with what you were saying.'

'Last week Blossom started living here full time, so I used the opportunity to get to know him and find out what had happened to my dad.'

'And did you? Find out, I mean?'

'Yes. He implied that my dad had been killed by the boss of the gang down here. Someone called Charlie Duff, as I told you. Years ago. And, you see, it fits with what Billy told me. He said to look for someone called Charlie.'

Sophie wondered if Billy realised what kind of people he'd been sending his niece to seek out. Lethal killers. He certainly knew that Duff had killed her own father.

'And did you find out anything else?'

'Yes. More than I'd ever hoped for. Blossom knew my mother. He told me that she'd died giving birth to me. He told me that my father was a waster, a drug addict. Blossom said he'd always loved my mother. I was trying to convince him to go to the police with what he knew, but he resisted. I only found out why today. That's why we argued, and why I was walking away from him. I'd just realised what he'd been involved with and it horrified me.'

She looked at Sophie. 'Is that why you're so interested in him?'

Sophie nodded. 'But that's only part of it. How long ago did Blossom say your father was killed?'

'He wasn't definite. But I got the impression that it was a long time ago, maybe ten, fifteen years or more.'

'Jennie, a few days ago we found the body of an adult male. It was buried under a patch of waste ground owned, we think, by Charlie Duff. We haven't got anywhere with identifying it yet. Forensic experts have given us a rough age of late twenties or early thirties and they say it's been buried for about fifteen years. Would you agree to a DNA sample? It would help us both. We might get a positive ID, and you'd have that part of Blossom's story confirmed.'

'Yes, of course,' she whispered. 'But it may not be necessary. I've already been DNA profiled. I did it a few months ago privately, soon after Uncle Billy contacted me. I expected that a DNA analysis would be useful if I was meeting people claiming to be from my birth family, so I got it done. I'll get you the results. You may as well take them for checking.' She got up and took a manila folder from a nearby bureau. 'In just a couple of weeks I've had my whole life turned upside down. I may as well see it through.'

Sophie looked at her closely. How much did this woman deserve to know? Sophie gambled. She reached across the low table and took hold of her cold, shaking fingers.

'There's something else you need to know,' she said softly. 'Something that Billy Thompson probably hasn't told you. Something that no one else knows, apart from me. Something that means that you and I are linked by two extraordinary events. Blossom told you that it was probably Charlie Duff who killed your father.' She hesitated, trying to find the right words. 'I've only found out in the last few days that Charlie Duff killed my father as well. Back in 1969, when my mother had only just become pregnant. No one else knows, Jennie. Not a soul. You and I are two daughters who've never known our real fathers. They've been taken from us by the same man.'

CHAPTER 26: FREEZING NIGHT

Monday

'Are you alright, Sophie? It's just that you went as white as a sheet yesterday afternoon at the car.'

They were sipping coffee in McGreedie's office at Bournemouth police headquarters. Sophie and Marsh had just arrived in order to be updated on the details of Blossom Sourlie's murder. Sophie grimaced as she took another sip of the hot, bitter liquid.

'Kevin, this stuff is awful. It's like watered-down tar. Can't you get a decent coffee machine put in here? And thanks for your concern about yesterday, but I'm fine. I probably ducked down into the car too fast and made myself dizzy.'

'If you say so. Are you getting enough sleep?'

'Of course. Can we just get on, please? What have you found out?'

'The gun had a silencer. That's why the neighbour he'd been with only heard a popping sound. Ballistics are still looking at the bullets. Two shots to the head. He died instantly. We've searched the area meticulously but there's nothing. They were pros. Either that or they were very lucky.'

'Do you think the woman, Jennie Brown, was involved?'

'It doesn't look like it. Her version of events tallies with the statements we have from other witnesses who were in the gardens at the time. They confirm that she and Sourlie argued and that she walked away. There were two men involved in the shooting, we think. One stood back and kept a watch while the other walked right up to the victim and shot him at close range. It sounds as though Sourlie didn't recognise his killer, which means it probably wasn't this Duff character that she insists was behind it.'

'But the second man stood well back?'

McGreedie nodded.

'So that could have been someone who didn't want to be recognised. Any further on how they got away?'

'A car just at the top of the steps, hidden from the gardens by the shrubbery. It was waiting with its engine running and moved off fast, but not so fast that it drew much attention. The same with the men. They came across to the car from the top of the steps quickly, but not so fast that the few people around noticed much about them. We found the car late last night, abandoned on waste ground in Poole, burned out. At least we think it was the same one. It had been stolen earlier yesterday.'

'So it looks as though there were three of them. One to carry out the shooting, one to keep watch and maybe identify the victim, and a driver for the getaway. Well, it links in with what she said. Sourlie told her that he'd just walked out on the gang. If that's true, then it gives us the motive.'

'She seems to know a lot, considering that she was just a neighbour who'd only known him for a few weeks,' Marsh added.

'I think she's telling the truth, Barry,' Sophie replied. 'Apparently Sourlie had been opening up to her over the past couple of days. He'd told her about a gang member they'd killed a long time ago, and she'd urged him to talk to us. It could tie in with the body we found buried at the depot. By the way, I'm pushing through the DNA profiling of that one as a priority. I'll let you know when the results come in.'

McGreedie finished his coffee. 'You're right about his walk-out giving them the motive. If he was about to spill the beans it would have been a big nail in the gang's coffin. What turned him? Did she say?'

'Apparently he didn't know about the buried bodies on the farm. Those two with the cuts and slash marks. That's what he told her. And that's why they argued and she walked away. She had no idea what he was involved in until that moment. And, as I said, I don't think she was lying. She was clearly in shock when I interviewed her, but I never felt that she was holding back on anything.' Sophie paused. 'I think you should speak to her too, Kevin. She still needs to make a formal statement and since you're investigating Sourlie's murder, it would be useful for you to interview her. Just in case I've missed something.'

'I'll do it if you think it'll be useful. I'll let you know if anything new crops up. It will all feed into the big picture.'

'I still can't see why he opened up to her,' said Marsh. 'It seems a bit strange, doesn't it? If he's the experienced thug we're assuming he is, it doesn't run true to type, does it? He's only known her for a week or so, but he's already told her that he's been involved in drug trafficking, rape and murder. I don't get it. Why would he tell her all that?'

'She said he'd had enough. He hadn't told her all of it until that final conversation when she walked away. And he claimed he didn't know about the murders. He said that his main job was running the boat and getting supplies. He was away a lot, so was a bit out of touch. He walked out on them when he found out. That would have corresponded with us finding the bodies last week. She said that he seemed genuinely disturbed by it. And depressed,' said Sophie.

'Maybe. It just seems odd, that's all.' Marsh still seemed unconvinced.

'I wonder if the rest of the gang are starting to panic,' McGreedie said.

'It's difficult to say. They've now killed two of their own. The young lad Stefan, when he started making noises after he recognised Nadia — although he wasn't important. But this Blossom character was a lot further up the hierarchy, I'd guess. He was listed as one of the directors of the front company, Midwinter Tide. One of the others, Hazel Duff, died a couple of years ago. Maybe there's a power struggle going on and the others are feeling the pressure. Who knows? But at least we know a bit more about who we're up against. We need to be cautious, Kevin. Any gang that can kill its own members so easily is very dangerous. This man Ricky Frimwell looks to be a psychopathic sadist from what we've discovered so far. And the man at the top, this Charlie Duff character? He could be the same.' She paused. 'And thanks to both of you for your concern. But you've no need to worry about me, really. I'm feeling a lot better about things this morning. I slept well last night for the first time in a fortnight, although I'd have been even better if this coffee was drinkable.'

She peered into the cup at the dregs. Barry Marsh hadn't even finished his.

* * *

In the Swanage incident room, Pillay was on the phone.

'No, I don't think you should search it. Just leave it exactly as it is and withdraw. Get your squad car pulled right back out of sight and we'll get someone over as soon as we can. We'll just leave a plainclothes officer on watch, but we don't want to spook any of the gang if they come for it.'

She put down the phone and turned to Sophie and Marsh.

'That was the Poole control room. They've found the boat. They were about to search it, but you probably heard what I said. I thought it was better to keep a watch on it in case someone pays a visit. It's tied up on a small mooring in Lytchett Bay, a creek off the north end of Poole Harbour. It's almost completely covered by a tarpaulin. The name's hidden, but one of the men took a peek under the covering.'

'Absolutely right, Lydia. We'll get Jimmy across there. He can have a quick look inside, then keep a watch.'

'I could do it, ma'am. I've done all the other boat stuff.'

'No, Lydia. I've got something else planned for you. So brief Jimmy, then get back to me in ten minutes. This is going to take a bit of planning.'

* * *

The night was cold and dank. A bone-chilling breeze was coming in from the west. They were protected by the high ground of the Wyke Regis and Charlestown areas west of Weymouth's town centre, but the cold was numbing. Sophie wondered how long Pillay and Nadia would be able to keep up their watch. At least she and Marsh were sitting in a car, albeit with the engine off. The two young women were walking slowly around the seedy area by the railway station, on the lookout for street girls. Both wore hats and scarves. Sophie judged that it would be impossible for anyone to recognise the young Romanian girl. She was hoping that if the gang had decided to put the women out onto the streets, Nadia would recognise them. So far the two of them had made three wide circuits of the area, but to no avail. The pavements were empty. At one in the morning, Sophie finally called them back to the car.

'We'll give it another try tomorrow,' she said. 'There's just no sign of life at all.'

'I'm not surprised, ma'am. It's Monday and too bloody cold for anyone to even think of being out on the streets looking for a girl. I'm perishing.' Pillay warmed her fingers on a cup of coffee.

Nadia rubbed her hands, but her eyes were bright. 'We'll come every night until they are here. I do not mind cold. We must find Sorina.'

Pillay sighed. 'She's right. If they are going to be put onto the streets, then this is the right place. We did spot one working girl and had a brief chat, but she only hung around for a few minutes. They'll be working by phone tonight. I'll just have to pile on more thermal undies for tomorrow night.'

'That's the spirit, Lydia,' Sophie said. 'Now let's all get home to our warm beds. We'll meet again tomorrow morning at eleven. Try to get a good sleep.'

* * *

Thirty miles away, hidden from view in the porch of a chandler's store, Jimmy Melsom was also chilled to the bone. He was sitting deep in the shadows on a low wall beside the entrance door, with a direct view of Midwinter Tide's mooring. He kept glancing at his watch as the minutes ticked away. During the four hours he had spent on watch, no one had visited the area. If the weather had been more benign he would have considered staying beyond one o'clock. As it was, in these freezing conditions he would need the car heater on full for the thirty minute drive home.

He left the porch and walked along the quayside to his car, trying to keep to the shadows. He got in and drove away.

The gap-toothed man watched from a small jeep parked in a shadowy unloading bay between two tall buildings alongside the approach road. He'd only arrived a few minutes before and had, as usual, kept watch for five minutes before getting out. He'd been about to open the door of the jeep when a man walked by. Why had they been waiting in the shadows? Who was he? He stayed in the vehicle and took up his mobile phone.

'Boss? There could have been someone watching the boat. He's just walked to a car and driven away. Might be a cop. But there's no one else around now. Do you think I should give the boat a miss and come back?'

He listened and then walked towards the boat. He boarded Midwinter Tide but didn't stay for long. In less than half an hour he'd started up the jeep and was heading west.

CHAPTER 27: CONJECTURES CONFIRMED

Tuesday, Week 2

Inspector Constantin Enescu from the Romanian police arrived at Dorset police headquarters late on Tuesday morning. Sophie was there to meet him, along with Chief Superintendent Neil Dunnett. Matt Silver had collected him from Bristol airport and had brought him up to date on the case. He and Sophie were looking for confirmation that the Romanian end of the operation was either under close observation or had been broken up.

Enescu, a tall, dark-haired man in his early fifties, confirmed that the Bucharest authorities had opted to keep watch. They had infiltrated the suspected gang with an undercover operative, but had made little progress in discovering any more detail about the UK side of the operations. The Romanian gang had lost all contact with their British counterparts. They were now attempting to expand into Denmark, Holland, Belgium and France.

'We are gaining plenty of information about the methods they use, and we now have the names of most of the girls who've recently been taken to these other countries. Once we have all the information we need, we will move in on the gang while the police in the other countries arrest the men holding the young women there.'

'Does this mean that the gang have more contact with the men holding the women in the rest of Europe?' asked Sophie. 'I mean compared to here, where we think they lost contact as soon as the girls were handed over?'

'Yes, that is so. In the other countries, it is Romanian criminals who have the girls and run them as prostitutes. This means that some of the profits come back to the gang leaders in my country. They have retained control. We think they learned how to do it from observing the gang here in Britain. It was the first.'

'Do you know when it started?' asked Silver.

'More than ten years, we think. We have just interviewed one woman who has found her way back to my country. She managed to escape from the men who were working her in your country. She then made her way to Amsterdam and worked there for herself for many years. Once she had saved enough money she returned to Timisoara to look after her mother who had become ill. But she is not telling us anything helpful yet about the men in Britain. She says that all the police are sexist pigs. There were lots of times when police could have helped or even rescued her but didn't bother. So she says why should she help us now?'

'But she might be saving the lives of these latest young women,' Sophie said.

'I have said that to her myself. But she is, what you say, hardened? There is no kindness or softness left in her. Her life has been a cruel one, I think, and it has had its effect on her. She wants nothing more to do with any of it.'

'So there is nothing more you can help us with?'

'Not yet. We plan to move in on the gang within a month, once we have all the information we need. After that we will let you know anything we find out as we interrogate the men involved. But we cannot arrest them any earlier. It must be done at the same time as the police in the other countries so that no one escapes. But there is one thing. One of the original gang, a man named Barbu, has stayed here in England. He is probably the one in day-to-day contact with the girls.'

'Do you know anything about him?'

'She said that he is cruel and enjoys violence. A sadist? Is that the right word?'

Sophie nodded. 'Yes. That fits with what we know about the gang over here. We suspect that there is at least one Romanian national still with them. Now, how can we help you?'

'I would like to interview the young woman you have, the one who escaped. Her information will add to what we know about how the gang traps these women, and she can confirm many of the details we are unsure about.'

'Yes. We expected that you would, so we have brought her along. She is waiting in another office. Your English is very good, Inspector. Have you been to Britain before?'

'I spent three months here some years ago. I was nominated to take part in a joint programme run by your Home Office and my country's police department at a time when we were looking to modernise. I had good English before then, which was one of the reasons I was chosen. I was here as an assistant and translator to a *chestor*. That is equivalent to your assistant chief constable, I think.'

'Are you in charge of the investigation into the gang?' asked Dunnett.

'No, sir. A *comisar* is running the investigation because of the links with other countries. But I am involved because of my experience, and because I also speak French as well as English. So I am in charge of the international links with the other police forces.'

'There is something else, Inspector,' Sophie added. 'On Friday night we discovered the bodies of two young women buried on the same farm. They'd both been murdered in the same way, by what seems to be a frenzied knife attack. They've been dead for up to two or three years. They haven't been identified yet, but it's possible they are Romanian. We're still waiting for the results of DNA analysis. We've asked for ethnic characteristics to be included in the check to give us a better idea of their backgrounds. One of us will contact you immediately if we find them to be Romanian. It would speed things up if you already had details of any missing women from the same area as the ones we are currently looking for.'

Enescu nodded.

Sophie sat in on the interview with Nadia. She had told the young woman that she need not answer anything that was too upsetting. But the Romanian officer was professional and very gentle. He translated both his questions and Nadia's responses into English for Sophie's benefit. Enescu made detailed notes of all Nadia's answers. He took time to crosscheck with a document he had brought with him. Clearly he had prepared most of his questions well in advance, or had them prepared for him. Sophie was impressed with his professionalism.

When he'd finished, Sophie asked him to keep her updated on the investigation in Romania, particularly following the planned actions in France and Holland. She bade him goodbye, and took Nadia back to her mother in the safe house. They would be back out on the streets of Weymouth that coming night.

* * *

Sophie returned to the incident room in Swanage where Barry Marsh was talking to Jimmy Melsom about the boat.

'Who's watching it now?' she asked.

'A DC from Poole,' Melsom replied. 'I'll take over again late afternoon if you want me to, but I'm not sure it will be very productive, ma'am. I found something odd when I went back first thing this morning.'

'Explain, please, Jimmy.'

'I know you told me to watch it only until about one last night, and it was perishing cold, so I was glad to come away.

211

But I was a bit unhappy about leaving it completely unwatched, so I left a couple of small oil spills on the gangplank, and a few small smears on the grab handles to the cabin. I did it earlier in the evening, when there were other people about. And someone had been on the boat after I left last night. There's a footprint on the gangplank, and smears on the door handle.'

'Fingerprints?' she asked.

'No. Whoever it was had gloves on. The thing is, ma'am, just before I came away I did hear a vehicle approaching, but it didn't come into the car park. I checked carefully as I left, and there was no vehicle there that wasn't there earlier when I arrived. It must have parked somewhere else. I must have missed him by a matter of minutes. I could kick myself.'

'I feel like kicking myself every single day, Jimmy. Don't worry.' Sophie was looking through a sheaf of papers in her in-tray, marked "Urgent and Confidential".

'Nothing else had changed, you say? I wonder what he was doing.'

'If he went inside, maybe he was removing anything incriminating,' Marsh suggested. 'Now we know that there's been some activity, why don't we just break into the boat and search it? My guess is that they've been and gone. We could have a video surveillance system set up to pick up anyone who does visit, though I don't think it's likely. That gives us the option of using Jimmy with us in Weymouth tonight.'

Sophie seemed to have stopped listening. Finally she lifted her eyes from the papers. For the first time in this investigation they looked cold and calculating.

'Sounds good to me. Can you arrange it, Jimmy? Barry and I have some DNA profiling to discuss.'

Holding the papers, she walked with Marsh through to her office and closed the door behind them.

'The body we found buried at that depot looks to be that of Andy Thompson. He was on the fringes of a gang operating out of the West Midlands twenty years ago.'

'Who did the profile match with?' Marsh asked.

'His half-brother, Billy.'

Marsh looked troubled. 'Isn't he the one in hospital? The one whose gang killed your father?'

'Yes. Which is why I'm telling you, and only you. I don't want this spread around, Barry. I don't want people whispering about me, or my father. We've got to keep our eye on the ball here.'

'But, ma'am, couldn't some kind of conflict arise because of this?'

'No. There will be no conflict.'

'What about the gun?'

'The gun is still under analysis. It's been buried there as long as the body. We'll probably never know whether it was the one that shot Thompson, because he was killed by a bullet in the head that went in and came out.'

Marsh looked at her. 'You know that's not what I meant, Sophie.'

'There will be no conflict.'

She turned and walked out. It was only as she walked down the corridor, her hands shaking and the nausea rising in her throat, that she realised that for the first time, Marsh had called her Sophie. And she knew why. He was wondering if the buried gun was the one that had killed her father. She knew it was. It was confirmed by the emailed forensic report in her hand.

* * *

Melsom and Marsh, with a small forensic squad, broke into the boat that afternoon. It was immediately apparent why the vessel had been visited the previous night. There was a strong smell of bleach in the cabin and the small bridge. The surfaces had all been wiped clean.

'Don't worry,' one of the forensic team said. 'We'll find something, somewhere. From what you've said, it will have been a quick wipe down and they'll have overlooked something.'

The documents cupboard had been left hanging open, emptied of its contents.

'I think we'll get it towed somewhere secure once you've finished your first check,' Marsh said. 'Then you can really get to work on it.'

* * *

That night in Weymouth was as unproductive, and as uncomfortable, as the previous one. A biting wind blew in from the north-west, carrying occasional flurries of sleet. The few people out on the streets hurried from pub to car or taxi as fast as they could, hunched into their coats with their collars drawn up. Nadia and Pillay made two rapid circuits but met no one. No girls were out on the streets on such a vicious night. They finished the evening by making a quick visit to the two late-night clubs that were still open, looking to see if any of the girls were inside, but they were both empty.

Shit, thought Sophie as they drove away. This is all falling apart.

CHAPTER 28: NOT FOR THE FAINT HEARTED

Wednesday

The doorbell rang just before eight. Jennie was sipping a mug of tea and listening to the weather forecast on the radio. She walked to the door, looked through the small spyhole, then opened it.

'Good morning,' Sophie said, trying to sound brighter than she felt. 'Sorry to call so early, but I wanted to be sure of catching you in.'

'Tea or coffee?' asked Jennie, as she ushered the detective into her large, airy kitchen.

Sophie could hear from the weather forecast that the current cold snap was coming to an end. Temperatures would climb during the day as a bank of milder air moved in from the south-west. Thank God, she thought. Yet another visit to Weymouth was planned for tonight, and she really didn't know how her body could stand a repeat of the previous two nights' freezing temperatures. She was worn out, and knew it.

'Coffee, please. Milk and one sugar would be great.'

The two women took their drinks through to the lounge and sat in soft chairs in front of a low coffee table. Sophie leaned back and shut her eyes for a moment. She'd never felt so exhausted in her life. She had been physically tired before, but now she felt as if her mind was under assault. The past few weeks had been a time of complete mental and emotional mayhem. And the only people who knew about it were this young woman sitting opposite her, smoothing her ponytail, and an old man dying of cancer in Birmingham. Sophie took a sip of coffee and began to feel a little better. Jennie watched her expectantly.

'I have the DNA results and they confirm what you suspected. They all match with yours. Under more normal circumstances, I'd be offering you my congratulations, but . . . ? How do you feel? You must have very mixed emotions about all this.'

'Yes. My mind's a bit of a blur. I don't know what to think, coming from such a stable background into all this. What are the details?'

'The official check shows that the person we found buried outside the warehouse in Poole was closely related to Billy Thompson, confirming our belief that he was Andy Thompson. I then asked the analysts to compare each of the results with your profile, and they both showed up positive. You have a close link with Billy, strongly supporting his claim that he is your uncle, and you have an even closer link with the body we found, consistent with him being your father.' A tear ran down Jennie's cheek. 'I'm sorry, Jennie. I said that in such a cold, unemotional way because I really didn't know what it would all mean to you.'

She went across to Jennie's chair and put her arms around her.

'There's something else. I've managed to trace a member of the Stockwell family in Birmingham, and she has agreed to give a DNA sample. She would be your aunt if that part of Blossom's story is true.'

'Oh, God. I can't take it all in. I just don't know how to thank you, and this last bit is so unexpected. How have you found the time with all the other things you're doing?'

216

'It wasn't that difficult. I think I told you I worked in the West Midlands for many years. I phoned up an ex-colleague and put her onto it, and she rang me back late yesterday with the news. By the way, the coroner has signed off your father's body because of the detailed post-mortem results, so you can go ahead and make funeral arrangements. As far as we can tell, the DNA match means that you are the next of kin. There are no other close, known family members other than Billy.' Sophie glanced at her watch and took another mouthful of coffee. 'This is lovely. The stuff they supply us with at police stations is so awful.'

She looked around her at the artwork hanging on the walls.

'They're all quite edgy, aren't they? The prints, I mean. My husband would say they are pushing the boundaries. Particularly that one.' She indicated a print of a woman clad completely in tight, shiny, black clothes and wearing high-heeled boots.

'It's part of a set. The others are not for the faint hearted. Would you like to see them? They're hanging in my bedroom.'

They walked through to the bedroom, mugs in hand. Sophie stopped and gaped.

'When Blossom saw them he said they removed any doubt in his mind that I was my mother's daughter. Apparently she was a bit ahead of her time and had similar "interests," if that's the right word to use.'

* * *

Sophie had just arrived at Swanage police station when her mobile phone rang. It was an unknown caller.

'Hello?'

'Ma'am? It's DC Spence from Gloucester. I have some great news for you.'

'Go ahead,' she replied. 'I need cheering up.'

'We've found another witness to your father's murder. We've been trying to trace the other gang members, and one's turned up. He not only remembers what happened, but he's actively helping us. And he's said that he'll testify in court if we ever trace the killer.'

'How reliable a witness will he be?'

'Good. Apparently he's been a reformed character for many years. He goes around youth groups, giving talks on avoiding crime and staying out of prison.'

Sophie leant against the corridor wall. She shut her eyes and breathed deeply. At last the universe was beginning to right itself, tilting back in her direction.

'Ma'am? Are you still there?'

'Yes,' she whispered, barely audible. 'Thank you. Thank you so much. You can't imagine what this means to me.'

She remained leaning against the wall for some time. Then she slipped the phone back into her bag, stood upright, straightened her clothes and continued to walk towards the incident room. She didn't notice Barry Marsh standing behind her. He followed her into the room.

'Morning, ma'am,' he said.

She looked up. 'Hi, Barry. The forecast says that the weather is going to get milder, thank God. So maybe we'll make better headway tonight.'

Jack Holly came in. He was the uniformed officer who had made the first visit to Brookway Farm.

'Sorry to disturb you, ma'am, but I may have a name for the gap-toothed man I saw at the farm last week. I couldn't find him in any photofits but I've been asking around and I finally got a response yesterday evening. An old buddy of mine who lives in Poole says that it sounds like someone called Smiffy. They had him on their radar a long time ago when he was on the fringes of a gang of hoods. He hasn't been in any trouble for years now.'

'That ties in,' Marsh said. 'The members of this gang seem to be experts at keeping their names out of the spotlight. Even Frimwell's record is from years ago.'

'It reminds me of the Thompson gang in Birmingham,' mused Sophie. 'It was always a nightmare trying to pin anything on them. They were so clever at covering their tracks.'

She was about to say more, but thought better of it. This gang had probably copied their methods, which supported the idea of a link. And that link was probably their boss, Charlie Duff. She couldn't even begin to find a way of talking about him. Not yet, anyway. What was he really like? She thought back to her brief encounter with him through the gap in the hedge at Frimwell's bungalow. Cold, narrow, watchful eyes and slightly curled lips. The erect way he held himself. But that was only the exterior. What was going on in that twisted mind? And what was he thinking now? She chose to keep silent. At some time she would have to come clean on the link to her father's murder, but she wasn't ready for it yet. Her thoughts were still too confused.

She looked up. Marsh was watching her.

'Thanks for that, Jack. Every small piece of the jigsaw helps us to visualise the complete picture. If anything else crops up, let one of us know right away.' As soon as Holly left the office, she turned to her sergeant.

'You're watching me.'

'Are you surprised, ma'am? I'm worried about you. You haven't been yourself for days now. I saw you just now, leaning against the wall out in the corridor. You looked as though you were about to faint.'

'If you must know, Barry, it was good news. The Gloucester crew have found a witness to my father's murder, despite the huge time gap.'

'I'm glad. But there's something else, isn't there? Something you're not telling us.'

'That's just your over-vivid imagination, Barry. My advice is to stick to the facts, and stay with the evidence.'

'Ma'am, you can trust me.'

For a moment, a crack appeared in her carefully maintained veneer.

'Do you think I would tell you when I haven't even told my husband?' she snapped. 'No one knows what this case means to me. Not one fucking person in this whole wide, sorry world. Slimy, disgusting worms wriggling in a cesspit.

That's all it is when it comes down to it. Just get on with your job, Barry, and then maybe we'll get to the end of it.'

She stood up and walked out of the room, leaving Marsh gaping. He stood there for a few minutes and then made his way out of the station. He phoned Matt Silver from his mobile.

* * *

When they met again in the afternoon, Sophie was back to her normal, composed self. Progress was reviewed, plans were made, orders were given.

She and Pillay made arrangements for a third night visit to Weymouth, and possible changes to the route the young women would follow. Jimmy Melsom was given the task of contacting letting agencies in the Weymouth area, looking for farmhouse lets in remote locations, although Sophie wasn't hopeful. The gang's previous bookings had been so complex that it had taken Marsh days to untangle them. He said so now.

'You're right, Barry. But the last couple of moves have been rushed, so this latest one might have been unplanned. It's worth a try.'

'Of course.'

The meeting drew to a close and the others left. She glanced up and saw him watching her.

'Sorry for the outburst, Barry. You didn't deserve it.'

'I do care what happens to you, ma'am.'

'I know. And I appreciate it, really.'

CHAPTER 29: SATIN AND SUSPENDERS

Wednesday Afternoon

Sorina looked at the other women. They were lounging on sofas in the sitting room of a small terraced house in Weymouth, skimming through glossy magazines. They were full of articles and pictures about shallow, stupid people and their shallow, stupid lives. But what else was there to read? This was all that their captors provided, as if none of them had the intelligence to read anything deeper. Or maybe that was the idea, to turn them into brainless simpletons who would just do whatever they were told. She saw Catalina watching her, and gave the older woman a brief smile. At least she had one friend. If only Nadia were still here, then she could talk more freely. They could plan for a different future.

The girls were all dressed in cheap, satin lingerie and high-heeled sandals. She could only think that the men wanted them to look sexy and sophisticated. To her they merely looked tatty and ridiculous, like living toys. She guessed that she looked even worse than the others. At least they had curves. In her case the pink, satin gown hung like a sack from her thin body. And the stupid suspenders they made her wear dug into her thighs.

The door handle turned and one of the women came in, fresh from entertaining her very first client in one of the upstairs rooms. She was smiling nervously and holding up a twenty pound note.

'My share,' she said. 'Barbu took the rest. But it is more than I'd earn in a day back home. And it wasn't too bad. He was gentle — and clean.'

Sorina felt like retching. She took a sip of water and returned to a story about some third rate celebrity. None of the magazines carried articles about nurses, farmers, scientists, teachers or anyone who did a useful job. They were just full of vain people who did nothing but go to parties. And anyway, she'd read them all before. No new magazines had come from Romania for some time now. Would English magazines be any different? She hoped so. She wanted to learn more of the language, so that she could read some of the newspapers and periodicals she'd caught sight of when they'd driven into town. Maybe they'd be more like the magazines her teachers had told her she should read, with articles on history and literature. Her teacher had wanted her to stay on at school and study for entry to university. But her recently widowed mother had desperately needed money to clothe and feed Sorina's younger brothers . . . And now?

A second woman came in. Her mood was very different. She slid silently into her chair, looking at no one. Sorina could see her lip quivering. She'd been chosen by a heavier man, who'd smelled slightly of mildewed clothes. His eyes were hard, and Sorina had rejoiced silently when they had skated across her and settled on the more voluptuous, older woman. Was this what it was going to be like from now on? This anxiety as each visitor inspected them and made a choice?

She'd overheard Barbu and the other men talking. They had spoken in English so she hadn't understood much. But she had picked up that they would be taken out somewhere that night because the weather was to be a little warmer. Whatever happened, surely nothing would be as bad as that afternoon with the two men in the farmhouse. Maybe that had been its purpose. It was a warning to show her the worst that could happen, so she would accept lesser evils more readily. They hadn't touched her since then, but she still had flashbacks of that dreadful hour. Her hatred remained. It burned inside her every time she looked at Barbu or the other man. Even hearing Barbu's voice was enough. She'd never thought it was possible to feel such hatred. She'd like to do to him what they'd done to that young man, Stefan, the day after they'd arrived. She'd like to see him kneeling in front of her with his hands tied. She'd like to hold the knife and slide it across his bare throat, and watch his lifeblood spill out onto the ground in front of him. She would exult in his death. She would dance for joy as his life slipped away.

She looked up and saw Catalina watching her. She realised that her breathing had quickened and her face felt hot. She took another mouthful of water and made herself calm down. Stay calm and in control, that's what Nadia would have said. Stay vigilant.

* * *

No other men appeared that afternoon, so, as dusk set in, the women were told to get some rest. They dozed fitfully until they were woken in the middle of the evening. The two women who had entertained men in the afternoon were left alone. The other three were given new clothes to put on: low-cut tops, short skirts, boots with high heels, tight jackets. Sorina grabbed a scarf from the hallway as they left the terraced house. Barbu bundled them into a waiting car. Outside, it was overcast but the air was much warmer than it had been for the past few days. The gap-toothed man drove while Barbu told them what they were to do.

He gave them cards with the address of the house.

'We will be close by and watching,' he said. 'We will negotiate with any men who stop for you. Get any men who talk to you to bring you back to our house. If they don't, and take you to a hotel or somewhere else, come back as soon as you can with all the money. If you try to escape I will find you wherever you are and I will kill you. I will do it slowly and make you scream in agony before you die. Then I will tell your families back home how you chose to become street girls here in England and how you took to drugs. If you don't want your families to know your shame, you must do just as I say.'

It was a short drive. The car pulled up in a quiet street and the two men pushed them out. The girls followed them a few hundred yards to a spot near a cluster of pubs and take-away premises.

They stood, close to the kerb, with the two men a few yards away, leaning against a wall.

Despite the milder weather, Sorina soon began to feel cold and she began to stamp her feet, walking up and down the pavement to keep her limbs from stiffening. At one point a car slid to a halt in front of her, and the window wound down. She could sense the occupants inspecting her. But before she could speak, the car moved slowly off, drawing to a halt again in front of the other two women. Sorina could see Catalina and the other woman step forward, followed by the gap-toothed man. Then Catalina got into the car, which accelerated away. Sorina stood watching. Tears gathered in her eyes. She heard voices, and turned to see who it was.

CHAPTER 30: REVENGE

Wednesday Night

There were more people out in Weymouth town centre tonight, moving in and out of the pubs, cafés and restaurants. Sober people, drunks, chancers, even a cluster of elderly people leaving a nearby church hall. A folk band was playing in one of the pubs and Pillay and Nadia could hear the music drifting out of the door.

The two young women turned a corner into a side street. Not only were there more townspeople in the area, there were a couple of street girls there too. One was climbing into a car. Pillay stopped and turned aside to use her walkie-talkie unobserved. She held her hand up, indicating to Nadia that she should wait.

Back in her car, Sophie was feeling more confident about this evening's operation. She'd been able to secure the help of several of the town's squad car crews, who were ready to lend a hand if needed. The nearest car was cruising around the town centre, keeping an eye on the pubs as closing time approached.

The walkie-talkie crackled into life. Sophie radioed through to the squad car. She asked Marsh and Melsom, waiting in a car parked behind hers, to follow her. She drove carefully round the corner and pulled in. She watched as the two young women approached a small group of girls.

* * *

Pillay had told Nadia to wait while she radioed, but the young Romanian began to run past the small cluster of people. She was heading towards a solitary, slightly built figure standing some distance beyond the car, which was now moving away. Pillay hurried after Nadia, past the woman still standing at the roadside. She ran past two men, who seemed to be watching her. Then she realised that they had switched their attention from her to Nadia, some yards in front. The young Romanian had ignored everything she'd been told and had flung her arms around the slight figure standing forlornly by the roadside. Pillay heard movement behind her. She glanced back in time to see both men step forward. They were close behind her. She swung around to face them, loosening her coat.

'Police! Stay where you are.'

One of the men stopped, confused. The other moved towards her, reaching inside his jacket. Pillay took several steps back, trying to maintain a distance between them, while pulling her stun-gun from its holster. She shouted as loud as she could.

'Police! Taser. Taser. Stay where you are. I say again, primed taser. Stay where you are.'

The man kept coming, so she triggered the gun. He fell to the ground. A small figure rushed past Pillay towards the man, lying on the ground. It was the girl Nadia had gone to. The girl began to scream and kick at the body. Nadia ran up and tried to hold her back. Sophie, Marsh and Melsom arrived at the scene and were at last able to pull the hysterical girl away.

'This is Sorina,' said Nadia. 'That is Barbu. He has raped her.'

The other man hovered in the background. He stood, his mouth open, watching the scene play out in front of him. The gap between his front teeth was unmistakable. Sophie pulled out her taser and smiled coolly at him.

'Are you going to give us any problems?'

He shook his head.

'Well, it's nice to meet someone who's so cooperative. Let me introduce myself. I'm Chief Inspector Sophie Allen. I'd like you to accompany us to the local police station, where I do believe you might be able to help us with our inquiries into a series of major crimes. And any help you do give us will, of course, be very much appreciated. Mr Smiffy, I believe.' She turned to Marsh. 'Just like that character from the Beano comic strip. Very original, aren't they?'

Two squad cars screeched to a halt beside the small group, followed by a van. The detectives left the two men in charge of the uniformed officers. Sophie watched the two Romanian girls, still hugging each other. Then she turned to her sergeant.

'Barry, let's get the heavy mob ready. I think we've just cracked it. All we need is an address . . . And look what we have here!'

Sorina was holding out a small card printed with an address and several phone numbers. Marsh took it from her, looked at it and nodded.

'Praise be. All my birthdays have come at once,' said his boss.

*　*　*

It took less than twenty minutes to get the snatch squad in place. While they waited, Sophie got on the phone and arranged for a raid on the old cottage that had been the girls' base over the previous few days. Nadia's recent exposure to spoken English proved to be a real boon. She was able to translate Sorina's description and give the local police a clear idea of the cottage's whereabouts.

The raid on the terraced house yielded up one man, a relative youngster. After a few minutes of angry bluster, he said little

227

else. Catalina was in one of the bedrooms with a client. When she finally realised she was safe from her abusers, she burst into tears. Her client was led away for questioning.

'Blast,' Marsh said, as the detectives finally left the house. 'None of the leaders yet. I hope we're not going to be disappointed.'

'Don't panic, Barry,' said Sophie. 'It'll all fall into place, trust me.'

She looked strangely serene, almost distant.

* * *

They raided the cottage an hour later. The police snatch squad split into three small groups. Each approached the isolated building from a different direction, and each team was accompanied by a firearms officer. Sophie knocked on the door but there was no answer and no lights went on. The place looked deserted. Melsom emerged from one of the outhouses.

'There's a car parked beside one of the sheds.'

A tall, burly sergeant pointed at the door. He raised a heavy ram that he had carried from his van. 'Shall I?' he asked.

Sophie reached out and turned the handle. The door opened.

'Sorry, Greg,' she said. 'I'm sure you'll get another opportunity soon.'

The team spread out, working its way slowly through the old building. They found some clothes and other items left by the young women, but the gang leaders had gone. They assembled in the large kitchen.

'The stove has been on, ma'am,' Marsh said, pointing across the room. 'It's still warm, and there are a few logs smouldering inside. Someone's been here tonight.'

'None of the guys we've taken in so far had a chance to use a mobile phone, did they?' asked Sophie. 'Am I right in that?'

Everyone shook their heads.

'So they are unlikely to have been warned.' She turned to Melsom. 'There are a couple of coats hanging up in the lobby. Can you bring them through, Jimmy?'

Melsom returned with three, one of which was an expensive, man's wool coat. Sophie felt through the pockets. She pulled out a mobile phone from a pocket on one side. It was still switched on. She felt the other side, slid her hand in carefully, and pulled out a handgun. She looked at Marsh.

'I think there might be someone still here. The car, the phone, the stove, the mobile, and now this. They all point to it. And they couldn't have done a runner even if we were seen arriving, not the way we came in — from behind the building as well as up the track. I want us to take another look, this time in every conceivable nook, cranny and hidey-hole. But we need to be careful. We mustn't assume that this is the only gun. Check your vests and don't take any chances.'

The team spread out through the building. This time they opened all the cupboards and wardrobes. In the bathroom Pillay spotted a laundry chest, covered with an ornate rug. She tapped Sergeant Greg Buller on the shoulder and pointed at it. He positioned himself at one end, pointing his gun at the middle of the chest. Pillay crouched opposite him and opened the lid. Ricky Frimwell tried to jump out but Buller floored him with his fist. In seconds, Pillay had him handcuffed.

Sophie was sitting at the large kitchen table when they brought him downstairs.

'Well, well, well. Mr Smith. We met before at the old farm. When was that now? Goodness, exactly two weeks ago. Doesn't time fly? And I understand you've changed your name since then. Ricky Frimwell? A much more interesting name. More *history* to it, I would say. History like the events at the Agglestone Rock. But I'd better not jump the gun. I'm sure all of that will come out over the next few days. You know, I just love this stage of a case, Mr Frimwell.'

He scowled.

'Every forward step we make, we seem to find new problems, new obstacles. Even evidence of other crimes. And sometimes real horrors, like in this case. Perpetrated by people like you. Because that's what they are, Mr Frimwell. Horrors.' She paused. 'Then the fog suddenly clears and we find you, and we find witnesses, and we find evidence. And you cannot begin to imagine the joy that brings me. I think I'll just ask this nice sergeant here to make the arrest statement and leave it at that. But I will be speaking to you again, Mr Frimwell.'

CHAPTER 31: S & M

Thursday Evening

Charlie Duff wasn't an avid devotee of bondage. It was Hazel who'd introduced him to S&M. She had always been keen to try out new experiences and she'd been a real enthusiast. S&M had brought out the dominant side of her character. Since her death three years earlier Charlie had occasionally returned to the club they used to frequent. His particular interest was carefully choreographed submissive experiences. Hazel had once suggested that this counterbalanced his normally violent nature. The next special event was due to take place that evening and Charlie had received numerous invitations by text. Several promised a "uniquely enjoyable experience." He decided to go. He'd also received a couple of reassuring text messages from his nephew. Things were going well, so he felt he deserved an evening off to enjoy himself.

He felt a bit foolish leaving his flat dressed in black vinyl trousers, so he took his outfit in a bag and changed at the venue. The setting was a large country house outside Bournemouth. He got a drink from the bar and took a stroll around to see what was going on. He wandered through the various rooms sipping his large glass of wine, finally settling to watch a rather portly middle-aged man bent over a chair and being spanked by two attractive brunettes. He felt the familiar sensation — a mix of fear and excitement.

'You look as though you might enjoy that,' said a soft voice in his ear.

He turned to find himself looking at a slim, shapely woman. She was dressed in a tight, black, lace-up bodysuit covered by a diaphanous, silk caftan decorated with red butterflies and belted around the waist. Her long legs were encased in fishnet tights and knee boots. She wore black satin gloves that extended to her slim elbows. Her face was obscured by an ornate black and red mask, and he caught sight of wisps of dark hair peeping out from behind it. The most extraordinary thing about her was her eyes. Looking out at him from behind the mask were yellowish green slits, like a cat's.

'Not just yet. I need a few more drinks first.'

'Just find me when you're ready. I'll be around.'

She smiled and walked away. Definitely one to follow up. And those eyes. He could still smell her perfume.

After a while, watching was no longer enough. None of the other women he saw came anywhere close to the one who'd whispered in his ear. He started looking for her, but couldn't see her anywhere. He bought another drink and searched all the rooms. He was beginning to get a little desperate, making a nuisance of himself by peering closely at every woman he saw. He headed back to the bar and bought himself a large gin and tonic. Just his luck. He'd got an offer from the most gorgeous creature in the place, and had been stupid enough to turn her down. Now what? He took another large mouthful.

'I'll have one of those.'

There she was, sliding in beside him. Where had she come from?

'Okay,' he said. He suddenly felt tongue-tied.

He went to the bar and bought two gin and tonics.

'Are you feeling a bit more in the mood now?' she asked. He saw that she was holding a riding crop.

'Yeah. Absolutely.'

'Listen, it's all a bit naff in here. Why don't we go somewhere else where we'll be more comfortable? Maybe your place, or mine? Then we can relax and really enjoy ourselves.'

'Fine.'

'Well, which one? I've got decorators in, so my place smells of paint. What about yours? Where do you live?'

'I've got a flat in Poole.'

'Well, that sounds just fine. Let's go in your car, shall we? I'll leave mine here.'

Duff swallowed his drink. He stood up too quickly and staggered slightly.

'How many drinks is that you've had? Maybe I'd better drive. We wouldn't want you getting stopped, would we? I don't want my evening ruined.'

They collected their coats and made their way to the car park. He indicated his car, a large black BMW.

'I'm fine,' said Duff. 'I can drive.'

She stopped dead. 'Are you contradicting me? Do you want me with you tonight or not?'

He didn't know what to say.

'Hand over your keys.' Her voice was sharp.

He did so. She touched his lips with her gloved finger, then gave him a sharp slap across his cheek. Her perfume was making him dizzy. She unlocked the car and climbed into the driver's seat. Duff settled in beside her, feeling confused. She drove expertly out of the parking area and into the main road. It took less than fifteen minutes to reach his flat near the seafront, yet she didn't once exceed the speed limit. She drove the big car like a dream.

'Whereabouts?' she asked.

Duff gave her directions, and she was soon pulling into the residents' parking area.

'Very nice,' she said.

'What do I call you?' he asked.

'How about Madame Butterfly?' she suggested, and giggled.

'What's funny?'

'It doesn't matter.'

They went inside.

'It's even nicer inside. What a lovely flat. It shows a woman's touch . . . But maybe not recently.'

'My wife died three years ago.'

'Oh, I'm sorry to hear that. Now, let's have another drink and you can show me the bedroom. Behave yourself well, and you'll experience something tonight that will stay with you forever.'

* * *

She tied his arms and legs to the bed frame, using soft cords that she took from her bag. She pushed a small gag into his mouth. She brought her face close to his bulging lips, but then slapped his cheeks several times with her open palm.

She knelt beside him on the bed, took hold of the riding crop and brought it down with a crack across his torso. He jerked forward convulsively, but the cords held.

'Good knots,' she said. 'I learned them in the brownies. I worked hard for my badges, just like I did for everything else in my life. I was such a good girl in those days. Not like now.'

She took a small knife out of her bag. Ignoring the panic in Duff's eyes, she slit the front and arms of his shirt.

'Worried, were you? Well, you have every reason to be. I can be really cruel when I want to. I'm not really Madame Butterfly at all. She used the knife on herself, didn't she, rather than the man who deserved it?'

She pulled his shirt away, and then slit his trousers. She wriggled back slightly, picked up the riding crop and lashed him without stopping for several minutes. He cried out through the gag.

'More than you bargained for? Well, just you wait. You see, Mr Charlie Duff, I know who you are and what you've done. You didn't expect that, did you? So you have every right to be scared.'

He looked back at her, his eyes wide in terror.

'Do you think they all felt like you're feeling now? Your victims? But that's enough talk. Actions speak louder than words, don't they?'

She beat his torso until the skin was crisscrossed with bright red weals. Then she sat back on her heels.

'Well, Charlie, that was starters. Now for the main course.'

She moved the knife back and forth in front of his eyes.

'Try to relax. I'm not going to kill you, even if it seems like it. Would you like another drink? It'll help deaden the pain. Nod once for yes.'

He nodded.

'Now this is the deal. I'll take the gag out so you can have a drink. But if you make a sound I'll cut your eye out. Is that clear? Behave yourself and you'll keep your eyes and survive this. Do you understand?'

He nodded. She removed the gag and held the glass of gin to his lips, supporting his head with one arm. He swallowed greedily. She forced the gag back into his mouth. Holding the knife like a pen, she carefully made a number of small incisions on his forearm. He was gasping for breath, snorting through his nose for air. The lower part of his face was coated with tears and snot.

'I'll explain what I'm doing. It reads, "Deut. 32, 35." You have got a bible, haven't you? Well, if you look it up, you'll find that it says: "Vengeance is mine, and recompense, for the time when their foot shall slip; for the day of their calamity is at hand, and their doom comes swiftly." Quite apt, don't you think?'

Duff felt something cold and smooth on his skin. She was applying ointment to the cuts.

'Wouldn't want you to get an infection, Charlie. I just want the scars there, though they'll probably fade in time. I thought about a tattoo but it would take too long. I don't want you to think I'm copying Lisbeth Salander either, even though she is one of my heroines.'

She paused.

'We'll both have a short rest now. We need a few minutes to gather our thoughts, don't we? I need to stretch my legs before dessert. I think I saw a kitchen directly ahead as we came in. Is that right? I'll need some kitchen towels. And I need another gin and tonic, just a small one. I'll take the glass away with me if you don't mind. There'll be not a trace of me left behind, to paraphrase Mr Paxton.'

She left the room for a few minutes. Duff's breathing slowed. He began to wonder if his ordeal was nearly over. He tested the strength of his bonds, but they were well secured. He let his arms relax and tried to calm his racing thoughts.

She returned to the room and clambered back onto the bed. Under each of his wrists she placed some folded towels.

'Now, Mr Duff, you mustn't wriggle during dessert. Not if you want to stay alive. Keep your hands and arms absolutely still, because I'd rather not sever a major blood vessel. Do you understand?'

He nodded. He watched, terrified, as she reached into her bag. She took out what appeared to be a small, slim case for reading glasses. She opened it and extracted a surgical scalpel.

'Just a small nick on each wrist, Charlie. It won't hurt very much, but you must stay very still. I'll be very thoughtful and smother each cut in antiseptic ointment like I did your arm. That's kind of me, isn't it? Then I'll finish off with some surgical tape. Not like you, Charlie. You dumped the bodies of those dead girls out in a field, for the worms and the bugs to work on their cuts and slashes. For the mould and mildew to infect the injuries you gave them. So you're really lucky, aren't you? Are you going to nod for me?'

He nodded as hard as he could.

'I'm sure the police will be doing their job, Charlie. I'm sure they're getting closer and closer to you. But I have to make you suffer. It'll keep me sane, stop me going mad because of what you did to me, my family and friends, and to so many others. But I want to see you brought to justice. I want to see you splashed across the papers, shown up as the monster you are. I want you in prison for the rest of your life, because that's where you belong, locked up in a stinking cell. I'm just sorry it won't be a medieval dungeon, stinking of putrid ooze, where you could rot away to a pile of pus . . . Anyway. On with the job.'

Duff felt a sharp cut to his left wrist, followed by a painful twinge, then nothing. This was repeated on the other side. He turned his head and saw that she was covering his wrists with surgical tape.

'There,' she said. 'All over. But I'd better explain what I've done, hadn't I? You probably don't feel anything? Is that right?' He nodded. 'Well, that gives you the clue, I'm sure. I've severed the nerves in your wrists. Just think, no arthritic pain in your hands or fingers. What a blessing for you in your old age. The downside is, of course, no movement either. Well, we can't have everything, can we, Charlie? At least it will be almost impossible for you to pick up a knife or gun again. Your bullets have altered and shattered more lives than you knew. You never had children, did you, Charlie? That's a good thing. They'd have been like the spawn of the devil.'

He squirmed and grunted into the gag.

'I really don't want to hear you, Charlie. It's too late anyway. I've done it. Now, I'll just take my stuff and get out of your life. I don't expect we'll ever meet again, so can I express my pleasure at such a rewarding evening? Oh, and I'll make sure someone is here to find you in the morning before your cleaner arrives. I don't want to spoil her day. But I'm afraid it won't be anyone you can manipulate or blackmail into helping you. Oh no. I'll choose your rescuer carefully.'

She cleaned his face and lips carefully with an antiseptic wipe.

'I would give you a farewell kiss, but I can't afford to leave any DNA traces.' She walked to the door, and waved a satin-gloved hand. 'No fingerprints, either. Would the police bother, I wonder, when they've got a mass murderer like you all trussed up and waiting for them? So just relax and enjoy the last few hours of your bondage session. I wish you goodnight.'

She closed the door quietly behind her.

CHAPTER 32: YOU'RE THE BOSS

Friday Morning

Barry Marsh sniffed the air inside the entrance hall.

'What do you smell, Barry?' Sophie said in a low voice.

'Money. And plenty of it.'

She nodded and looked around her. 'Yes. Not a place for the plebs, I'd guess.' Her voice was little more than a whisper.

'It's a lot more upmarket than the block I live in. We complain about our maintenance charges, but I hate to think what the costs are here.'

The lift door opened.

'Even the lift doors are quiet. We don't have a lift in my place, just stairs. But I suppose that's good for my fitness,' he went on.

There was no reply. She's still not her normal self, Marsh thought. Hardly a word out of her during the drive over here, and she'd let him make most of the arrangements with the backup squad. They'd decided to leave the armed unit outside in their van, while the two of them carried out an initial check of the apartment block. What was worrying her? He pressed the button for the third floor.

'Has anyone found out who sent us the tipoff?' he asked.

'No. It came in via a 999 call. All the operator could say was that it was a woman's voice, describing where we would find Duff. She said the door would be unlocked.'

So it proved. Marsh rang the bell, but there was no response. He turned the handle and peered in. The interior was in semi-darkness, with just a dim light coming from two doors that were ajar.

'Hello?' Marsh called. 'Police! Is anyone in?'

There was no response so they made their way inside. Marsh checked that his radio was still live. He glanced inside the first set of rooms, a lounge and dining room, tastefully furnished. The curtains were drawn. The next door opened into a kitchen, fitted out with units in a pale lemon colour. The morning sun shone in through the windows. Marsh turned to speak to Sophie, but stopped. She was shaking. She was leaning back against the doorjamb with her eyes closed and a slight tremor running through her body. Should he say something? Just then she opened her eyes and looked at him. She moved back out to the hall.

Three more doors, all closed. The first led into a bathroom, fitted with bath, separate shower, toilet and his-and-hers basins. The second opened into an empty double bedroom decorated in pale green. They stood in front of the last door. Sophie glanced at Marsh as he turned the handle and pushed. Marsh heard a groan. The air smelled tired and used. The curtains were drawn and the room gloomy, but the detectives could see a figure lying on the bed. The arms were pulled tight up to the bedhead, and a thin duvet covered the lower part of the torso.

Did he imagine that his boss shuddered? What was wrong with her?

'Exactly as described. Shall I let some light in, ma'am?'

There was no answer, so he walked over to the window and pulled the curtains apart. He returned to the bedside and stood beside Sophie. She was looking down at the shivering, moaning, barely conscious figure. Marsh couldn't read the expression on her face. She stood in silence. Her lips were moving but no sound came. He waited for an instruction but there was none.

'Ma'am? We need to cut him free. Shall I do it?'

He took a knife from his pocket and moved it towards the ropes securing Duff to the bed. He suddenly felt a grip on his wrist and stopped in surprise. He looked round at her. She turned to look into his eyes, and her face was ghost-pale and shining.

'He killed my father.'

'What?'

'Charlie Duff. He's the man who shot my father in Gloucester.'

'Christ.' Marsh's arm was stretched out, with her hand clamped to his wrist. Neither of them moved.

'Jesus. That's why . . .'

He looked into her eyes and saw desolation there. Her gaze, focused on Duff, was empty of all expression, as if the sight of him had ripped her spirit from her body. An eternity seemed to pass, and finally she blinked, shivered and loosened her grip slightly.

He slit the ropes, and Duff's arms fell onto the pillows. Marsh spoke into his radio. 'Team up here now. No danger.'

'I don't want to touch him, Barry. If I touch him I don't know what I'll end up doing to him.' She spoke in a whispered sob.

Marsh checked again that there were no weapons under the covers and then removed the gag from Duff's mouth.

'He needs some water.'

Sophie made no move.

'I'm not leaving you alone in here with him. Please, get some water for him, ma'am.'

She looked at her sergeant. Her forehead shone with tiny drops of sweat, like miniscule pinpricks of light. Her eyes searched his as if she was lost, and looking for direction.

'Sophie, this is a time for celebration. Don't let it become something else.'

She touched his arm again, this time gently.

'You're right. Yes.'

She went out and returned with a tumbler of water which she handed to Marsh. He poured some of the liquid into Duff's mouth. Duff swallowed greedily as the rest of the police team entered the room. Thank God, thought Marsh. He had the feeling that some dreadful catastrophe had just been averted.

'Is the place secure?' he asked.

The leading uniformed officer nodded.

'Call an ambulance.' Marsh looked at the dried blood-stains that covered Duff's chest and wrists and spattered the bedclothes.

Charlie Duff was beginning to come round.

'She slit nerves in my wrists,' he croaked. 'Fucking bitch cut me up.'

Marsh looked at Sophie. She shook her head slightly.

'Get him to hospital,' she said quietly. 'We'll do the other stuff there on Monday. I want him fully conscious, and there's a queue of people who will want to be there.'

'Whatever you say, ma'am. You're the boss.'

CHAPTER 33: FAMILY LUNCH

Sunday

They were all sitting in the dining area of an old coaching inn in Gloucester. Sophie watched Jade chatting amiably to Florence and James, with her own mother, Susan, occasionally joining in. She felt so tired. It was all she could do to sit upright in her chair. A waitress appeared with the first course.

'Didn't you order a starter, Sophie?' Florence asked.

'No, Gran. It will be all I can do to get through my main course. But don't worry. It's just tiredness. I'll be fine in a day or two. Martin is driving today, so I can relax and enjoy my beer.'

She took another mouthful, and swirled the liquid around in her mouth. Florence looked at her.

'Different times, Gran. I picked up the taste for beer before I went to university, and I've never lost it. Martin and I visited every real ale pub in Oxford. I could say that it's all his fault, but it wouldn't be true. To be honest, I think I was the major culprit. I don't drink loads of the stuff, but I do enjoy a pint or two.'

Jade wore a look of horror on her face. 'And there was me blaming Dad. You just stood there, Mum, and let me ramble on last week about his taste in wine and beer, and then I find out you're just as bad. There's really no hope for me, is there?'

Florence looked worried but Jade said, 'Don't worry, GeeGee. I was only teasing them. They tease me in return. It's the modern way of parenting, I expect.' She turned to face her great-grandmother. 'And do you know that they have spies out secretly watching me? One of the maths teachers at my school gives them monthly reports on what I get up to. Probably with secretly taken photos as well. I have to ask myself, is nothing sacred?'

Martin choked on his final spoonful of soup. 'Don't take her seriously, Florence. I just happened to meet her maths teacher a couple of weeks ago while he was on a quick visit to my school.' He turned to his daughter. 'How did you find out?'

'He's a double agent, and I turned him. It's just fantastic what you can achieve by fluttering your eyelashes. I thought that teachers would be immune to that kind of thing, but apparently not. Really, it should be added to their training programme.'

* * *

Sophie waited until everyone had finished their starter course before she spoke.

'I have something important to say to you all. It's quite difficult, but you deserve to know. You're all aware that we closed the case on Friday, and that's why I was able to visit today, and it's lovely to have a cause for celebration. We're due to make the final arrest tomorrow, in Bournemouth hospital as it happens, because that's where the gang leader currently is, under armed guard.'

She paused and felt Martin squeezing her hand.

'But things are not quite as simple as that. I've been keeping you all completely in the dark since the funeral, though Martin and Jade guessed that something was going on. I told

Martin last night and we decided that it was time to tell all of you. But I'm finding it very hard.' A tear rolled down her cheek. 'I ought to be celebrating, but I'm not. All I feel is a dreadful emptiness. You see, the gang leader, the one we think is behind all the murders in Studland, the man I've been hunting down for the past three weeks, is also the man who shot Graham all those years ago. We're charging him tomorrow.'

Jade finally broke the stunned silence. 'Was that the morning I found you out on the veranda? Is that when you knew?'

'Yes. It all fell into place the evening before. I kept it from everybody until I was sure. Even my investigation team.'

'Are we supposed to know this, Mum?'

'Yes. You are the immediate family of a murder victim and have the right to know when we plan to charge someone with the crime.'

'Is there any doubt?' Susan asked.

'No. The evidence is clear, and the Gloucester team have found a witness.'

'Let me get this clear,' Susan continued. 'As well as investigating the murders in Studland, you've also been tracking down Graham's killer?'

Sophie nodded.

'Without telling anyone? By yourself? Separate to the Gloucester enquiry?'

A nod.

'Is that allowed? I mean . . .'

Martin broke in. 'Susan, there's no point in commenting. I've already said everything that could be said after she told me last night. Anyway, she told the Gloucester and Midlands lot as soon as she was sure. I was on the phone to Archie Campbell this morning before we set out. He's over the moon and just laughed at my concerns. His exact words were, "Sod it, Martin. She got the result."'

James Howard rose to his feet.

'I need to say something. I have to tell you how much this means to me. Because today I have discovered something

245

unexpected. That even at my advanced age, someone can do something very special that completely restores my faith in human nature. And to discover that this someone is my own granddaughter is just beyond all expectation. Sophie, you have just become the very best person I have ever met in my entire life. To have carried all that on your own shoulders is beyond belief. So, ladies and gentlemen, I want to propose a toast. Raise your glasses please and drink a toast to my very own and very special granddaughter, Sophie.'

'Looks like I've arrived just in time. What's going on?'

'Hannah! I thought you said you couldn't make it?' Martin said, rising from his seat.

'I managed to get someone to stand in for me at the last minute. Jade texted me with the name of this place, and I got a taxi as soon as I got off the train. Mum, you're crying. I think you and I need to visit the loo.'

'Yes, Hannah. I do too. And I need one of your special hugs. A big one please. Probably the biggest one you've ever given me.'

CHAPTER 34: THE ARREST

Monday

The morning was bright. Occasional bursts of sunlight glinted down on the hospital grounds. Charlie Duff was propped up on his bed, his bandaged wrists lying on the coverlet. He was looking out of the window. A nurse popped her head inside the door and he turned to look at her. Duff could just make out the shape of the policeman on guard outside his door.

'Just to warn you. You have some important-looking visitors. They've just arrived at reception. Are you okay?'

'You're joking. What do you think?' He held his heavily bandaged wrists up. 'Is this the best you lot could do?'

'Do you need the loo?'

Duff shook his head, and the nurse disappeared. He heard the sound of footsteps in the corridor outside, followed by the sound of quiet voices. He guessed that they were talking to the policeman outside.

The door opened. Four police officers entered, all in full formal uniform, along with a woman in a business suit.

'Mr Duff, you may recall that we have already met. I am Detective Chief Inspector Sophie Allen, of Dorset police.

I'd like to introduce these officers. Here on my right is Sir William Black, the chief constable for Dorset. The officer beyond him is Assistant Chief Constable Archie Campbell from the West Midlands force. He is also representing the Gloucestershire Constabulary. Here on my left is Detective Superintendent Matt Silver, also from Dorset police. I understand that Mrs Julia Bellringer has been acting as your lawyer so we asked her to accompany us here.'

Duff's mouth dropped open. 'What?'

'I'll hand over to Superintendent Silver.'

Matt Silver held up the charge sheet.

'Charles Wilfred Duff. You are hereby charged with the murder of Stefan Bratianu on the morning of Monday the sixteenth of January this year. You are also charged with the assault and rape of Nadia Ripanu on the previous day. You do not have to say anything. But it may harm your defence if you do not mention when questioned something which you later rely on in court. Anything you do say may be given in evidence. In both cases you are being charged along with your nephew, Richard Nelson Frimwell.' He paused. 'We are also continuing our investigation into the deaths of two young Romanian women whose bodies have been found buried at Ridgeway Farm near Studland. We are close to completing those investigations, and expect charges to follow soon. The same applies to the deaths of Andrew Thompson, whose body was found buried at your company warehouse and offices near Poole quayside, and Benjamin Sourlie who was murdered last week in Bournemouth's central gardens.'

The chief constable continued. 'Mr Duff, evidence has come to light of a vicious murder committed some forty-three years ago in Gloucester city centre. A young man was murdered for no reason other than the fact that he chanced to walk by as a gang, of which you were a member, was carrying out a jewellery robbery late at night. That young man was shot dead and his body disposed of down a disused mine shaft. I will now ask ACC Campbell to take over.'

'Charles Wilfred Duff. You are hereby charged with the murder of Graham Thomas Howard in the early hours of the morning of Saturday the twelfth of December 1969 in central Gloucester. You do not have to say anything. But it may harm your defence if you do not mention when questioned something which you later rely on in court. Anything you do say may be given in evidence.'

Duff tried to speak, but he seemed to be finding it difficult to form words.

'What?'

'He was my father,' Sophie said simply. 'You murdered my father.'

'You're mad.'

'No, Mr Duff. You buried the gun in the waste ground at the back of your warehouse in Poole many years later, near the body of Andy Thompson. The bullet was still lodged inside my father's ribcage. Forensic tests have shown that the bullet was fired from that gun.' She took a breath. 'We also have a witness who has identified you. By the way, Billy Thompson and his family send their regards.'

They turned to leave. As they reached the door, Sophie turned back to the bed and leaned over to whisper quietly in Duff's ear.

'I say again, you stole my father from me. You deserve everything that's happened to you. I wish you could rot in hell for what you've done, not only to me but to all the other mothers, fathers, brothers, sisters, partners and children of your victims. You're a sick blot on humanity, and whatever has happened to you, and will happen to you as a result of your trial, can never be enough.'

* * *

'But I'm worried, Barry. Can't you see how it all fits? And it was you that found her searching for him on the database. Someone did that to him. Someone tied him up, scarred his chest and arms and did that to his wrists. And it was a woman, he's adamant about it. Who else would have the motive?'

'Look. I'm as uneasy as you. But if you think I'm going to march in and arrest her on these flimsy suppositions, then you're mad. There's plenty of other women with enough motive to torture Duff. What about the girls he raped over the years? What about the families of those murder victims? What about members of the Thompson family in Birmingham?'

Pillay and Marsh were standing on the pavement of Kings Road, looking over the bridge of the small brook. They had decided that this conversation needed to take place out of earshot of the police station.

'It's the cold-bloodedness of it, Barry. It must have been planned meticulously, that's what makes it so unusual. Family members looking for vengeance don't go to those lengths. They pay a visit and beat someone up, or even kill someone. And how would they know about his visits to that S&M club? Think about it. It was almost unbelievable. He was groomed into that visit, with the text messages reminding him of the upcoming evening, and promising him something special. Yet the club say they didn't send them. So who did? And how come Bob Thompson can't trace them? How did whoever did it know the evening was coming up? How did they get his mobile number? And you know what struck me? It was when Duff said that the woman seemed so totally in control, so assured, so confident in what she was doing. And I thought, there's only one woman I know who fits that description.'

'But the point is, Lydia, there's not one scrap of evidence. Not a trace. Not the slightest little bit of a clue left for forensics to find, except for that hair. And what did it turn out to be? Acrylic. She was wearing a wig. And a facemask. Even contact lenses. All of the glasses used for drinks that night have been through the dishwasher several times, so there's no chance of any DNA from them. CCTV only shows a few shadowy images of the woman. She was careful to stay out of any camera hotspots, almost as if she knew where they were focused. Bob has interviewed the staff on duty on Friday night. They reckon she could only have been there a short while. She must have waited in the ladies loo before she made her second appearance.'

'But isn't it a private members club? Doesn't there have to be a sign-in register or something?'

'Formally, yes. But this is not your average club, Lydia. A lot of the people there want to remain unidentified, and the staff understandably don't push them too hard. Even so, the door staff can't remember her coming in. They think she slipped in quietly at some point without signing in. As for Duff's mobile phone number, he might have given it to any number of women over the past couple of years since his wife died. For all we know she had it quite legitimately. The only neighbour of Duff's who saw anything remembers that she was a middle-aged, dark-haired and heavily made-up woman with a single bag and that she didn't speak as they passed on the stairs. She had no car with her, of course, so Bob doesn't know how she left. None of the local cab companies remember a client that matches her description. She probably had it all planned in advance, and had left her car nearby. But how did she get to the bondage venue? Again, no taxi driver remembers giving a woman a lift there. Look, I know what you're saying, but there really is nothing to go on. And I don't think we'll ever find anything. We just have to leave it. None of it makes sense unless she had help of some kind and that rules the boss out, surely?'

'Shouldn't we at least tell Matt Silver?'

'I already have. We had a quiet chat about it yesterday, and came to no conclusion. The boss's name was mentioned as someone with a motive. But we went no further.'

'How did he take it?'

'He'd already thought of it. I could see it in his eyes. But there is one other problem, Lydia. Whoever did it knew exactly how to sever those nerves in Duff's wrists. How would she have got that knowledge?'

251

'A quick look at the internet will give you pages that show the wrist nerves in fine detail. I know, I've googled it to see. And she's good with her fingers. She does embroidery and fine needlework for a hobby. She gave me a small tapestry for my birthday last month that she'd embroidered herself.'

'That may be the case, but it's very different from carrying out what was a surgical procedure. Look, Lydia, this is mad. We're going nowhere, and we'll continue to go nowhere. In the end, it's not our problem. Bob Thompson over in Bournemouth is in charge of it, so let's just leave it to him.'

'If you say so, but I had to get it off my chest. It's been keeping me awake at night, and few things do that.'

Marsh turned to face her. 'If something else comes to light, then I promise I'll bring it up again. For what it's worth, I don't think it was her. It would go against her whole being, her whole reason for existing. Justice and the law are so central to her character that I find it impossible to match her against what that woman did to Duff, however strong the boss's motives might have been.'

He thought of the two occasions when he'd seen a different side to his boss. On the previous Wednesday, when she'd been so furious that she'd almost hit him. Then he'd had a momentary glimpse into a very different person, someone who was plumbing the depths of a desperate, personal anguish that she was unable to share. And just three days previously when they'd found Duff semiconscious and mutilated, she'd seemed lost in a dream world. He pushed the memories into a dim recess of his mind. Above all else he valued loyalty and Sophie Allen, his complex boss, deserved it.

'No, it wasn't her. Trust me.'

Pillay looked at him and turned back to the police station. Marsh watched her go. He knew that he'd failed to convince her.

CHAPTER 35: THE FINAL VISIT

Wednesday

Billy Thompson had deteriorated badly since Sophie's last visit. His face was like a wax mask. His breath came in short, shallow gasps. His eyes were shut, but Sophie saw a slight flicker as she sat down. She took his hand.

'Hello again, Billy.'

He made a sound, but she couldn't understand it. His other hand pointed weakly towards the water jug on the bedside table. She poured some into a tumbler and held it up to his lips. He swallowed some of it, but most dribbled down his chin onto the coverlet. Nevertheless, he must have taken in enough to refresh him slightly, because one eye opened weakly, then the other.

'Got him then,' he gasped.

'We arrested Charlie Duff last week, yes.'

Thompson laughed, a broken cackle that left him gasping for breath.

'No. Before that.'

'What do you mean?'

He breathed out the words almost one at a time. 'Before you arrested him. Heard he suffered. Serves the fucker right.'

'Nothing to do with me, Billy. We only arrived after. But he's not too bad. He's recovering quite well in hospital. The surgeon thinks he can save a little movement in each hand, enough for him to cope with a spoon or fork. Which is all he'll need, anyway, once he's in prison for the rest of his life.' She looked into his eyes. There was still a slight glimmer there. 'I met your niece, Jennie. I like her. She feels things deeply, Billy, just like me. We may not always show it, but we do.'

'Will you do me a favour?'

'If I can, Billy.'

'Andy's funeral is tomorrow. I don't want Jennie there by herself. I'd go, but . . .' He waved weakly. He tried to raise himself but gave up, falling back onto his pillow with a gasp. 'Will you go? Please?'

'Of course. I'd already planned to. We've become good friends, you know.' She smiled. 'She's coming up this way again next week to visit some of her mother's family. You need to know, though, that the people she'll always love most will be her adoptive parents. She's adamant about that. They gave her the life she has now.'

'That's how it should be. But I'll never forget what you did, finding what happened to Andy,' he wheezed. 'I never told anyone what you said. Never will. Fuck. What an end to it all. Little Miss Prim. Hah.'

He collapsed back onto his pillow, coughing weakly.

'I've got rid of all those feelings I told you about, Billy. I think I'm at peace with myself now. But I came close to losing my sanity over it. You're a good listener.'

'What else can I be, lying here, dying?' He coughed again. 'At peace? You? Hah. Don't believe it.'

'Bye, Billy. Bless you.'

* * *

On her return to Dorset, Sophie called at the safe house where Nadia and her mother were packing their few belongings.

Sorina was there too, along with Catalina. They had both been discharged from hospital.

The four women were due to fly back to Romania early the next morning, although they would be returning later in the month to help prepare evidence for the trial.

Nadia poured her a cup of tea. She presented Sophie with a bouquet of flowers.

'Is not enough,' she said. 'I wish to give you much, much more. But I cannot. I cannot say how I feel. My heart is full for you. The flowers are from all of us.'

'They're lovely. Thank you, all of you. Nadia, there will always be a place in my heart for you. Do you promise to write? Jade is expecting you to.'

'Yes. I send photos from my home. Sorina and I, we come to visit, if you will have us?'

'Of course. Write to Jade and she will let me know. She'd love to see you both.'

'She will take us clubbing? She said so.'

'Why doesn't that surprise me?'

EPILOGUE

Sophie Allen sat on a bench under a tree, looking across to the bedraggled flower beds that surrounded the crematorium. It was late afternoon and the weak February sun was about to slip below the horizon. She pulled the collar of her coat up and snuggled deeper into its warm lining. The woman with the dark ponytail approached, carrying a small package that contained her birth father's ashes. Sophie moved aside to give the younger woman room to sit down. They linked arms and spoke for several minutes. Then they stood up. They hugged briefly and then these two women, the daughters, both deeply scarred by their recent discoveries, went their separate ways.

THE END

ACKNOWLEDGEMENTS

This novel would not exist without the help and support of a number of people. It is dedicated firstly, to my wife, Margaret, for being who she is: the most important person in my life, now as always. Secondly to my daughter-in-law, Kat, who is always willing to offer help with grammar and punctuation. Lastly, to my three sons, their wives and my grandchildren.

If you have never visited the Isle of Purbeck on Dorset's Jurassic Coast then you should really try to do so. The area has beautiful scenery, picturesque beaches and some of the best pubs in the South West of England. The DCI Sophie Allen novels are partly dedicated to this wonderful area.

CHARACTER LIST

Detective Chief Inspector Sophie Allen is Dorset's acknowledged expert on murder and violent crime, newly appointed to run the county's Serious and Violent Crime Unit. She is 42 years old as the series starts, and lives with her family in Wareham. Sophie has a law degree and a master's in criminal psychology. Sophie may appear at first to be somewhat of a 'cold fish,' over-intellectual and too clever by half, but conceals a dark past.

Detective Sergeant Barry Marsh is in his early thirties and in Dark Crimes, the first novel, is based at Swanage police station. He's quiet, methodical and dedicated, the perfect foil for Sophie's hidden fragility.

Detective Constable Jimmy Melsom is also based in Swanage. He has only recently joined the CID, and is a little gung-ho in his attitude to crime investigation.

Detective Constable Lydia Pillay is a talented young officer based with DCI Allen at Dorset County police HQ.

Detective Inspector Kevin McGreedie is attached to the Bournemouth and Poole division of Dorset police. His assistant is DS Bob Thomson.

Detective Superintendent Matt Silver is Sophie's immediate boss. He helped to appoint her to lead the Violent Crime Unit but, to his regret, has a largely administrative role in the county police hierarchy.

Detective Chief Superintendent Neil Dunnett is the overall commander. He clashes with Sophie several times in Dark Crimes. The source of the antagonism is not clear.

Martin Allen is Sophie's husband. He is head of the mathematics department at a large secondary school in Dorchester. Martin has a minor, but very supportive, role in the novels. He and Sophie met while at university. He has a more prominent role in later novels in the series.

Sophie and Martin have two daughters. **Jade** is fifteen in the first novel, and appears in all the subsequent stories. She has a lively and very quirky personality. **Hannah**, the elder daughter, is a drama student in London. She is quieter in her approach to life. She appears as a minor character in the first novel, but has a more important role in later books.

THE JOFFE BOOKS STORY

We began in 2014 when Jasper agreed to publish his mum's much-rejected romance novel and it became a bestseller.

Since then we've grown into the largest independent publisher in the UK. We're extremely proud to publish some of the very best writers in the world, including Joy Ellis, Faith Martin, Caro Ramsay, Helen Forrester, Simon Brett and Robert Goddard. Everyone at Joffe Books loves reading and we never forget that it all begins with the magic of an author telling a story.

We are proud to publish talented first-time authors, as well as established writers whose books we love introducing to a new generation of readers.

We won Trade Publisher of the Year at the Independent Publishing Awards in 2023 and Best Publisher Award in 2024 at the People's Book Prize. We have been shortlisted for Independent Publisher of the Year at the British Book Awards for the last five years, and were shortlisted for the Diversity and Inclusivity Award at the 2022 Independent Publishing Awards. In 2023 we were shortlisted for Publisher of the Year at the RNA Industry Awards, and in 2024 we were shortlisted at the CWA Daggers for the Best Crime and Mystery Publisher.

We built this company with your help, and we love to hear from you, so please email us about absolutely anything bookish at feedback@joffebooks.com.

If you want to receive free books every Friday and hear about all our new releases, join our mailing list: www.joffebooks.com/free-books

And when you tell your friends about us, just remember: it's pronounced Joffe as in coffee or toffee!

www.ingramcontent.com/pod-product-compliance
Lightning Source LLC
Chambersburg PA
CBHW011432170626
46808CB00010B/3124

* 9 7 8 1 8 3 5 2 6 8 5 4 4 *